PENGUIN BOOKS

Mr Wrong Number

Lynn Painter lives in Omaha, Nebraska, with her husband and pack of wild kids. She is a community columnist for the *Omaha World-Herald*, as well as a regular blogger for their parenting section. When she isn't reading or writing, she can be found eating her feelings and shotgunning cans of Red Bull.

Mr Wrong Number

Lynn Painter

PENGUIN BOOKS

PENGUIN BOOKS

UK | USA | Canada | Ireland | Australia
India | New Zealand | South Africa

Penguin Books is part of the Penguin Random House group of companies whose addresses can be found at global.penguinrandomhouse.com

Penguin Random House UK

First published in the United States of America by Berkley, an imprint of Penguin Random House LLC 2022
First Published in Great Britain by Penguin Books 2022

001

Printed and bound in Great Britain by Clays Ltd, Elcograf S.p.A.

The authorized representative in the EEA is Penguin Random House Ireland, Morrison Chambers, 32 Nassau Street, Dublin D02 YH68

A CIP catalogue record for this book is available from the British Library

ISBN: 978–1–405–97285–7

www.greenpenguin.co.uk

MIX
Paper | Supporting responsible forestry
FSC® C018179
FSC www.fsc.org

Penguin Random House is committed to a sustainable future for our business, our readers and our planet. This book is made from Forest Stewardship Council® certified paper.

For Kevin

I love you more today than when you swept me off my feet by photocopying your finger and talking in a stupid voice. More than when you stepped on my feet so I couldn't run away from you. Even more, I think, than that time you said I had Axl Rose hair.

Five kids and hundreds of meatballs later, you still make me cackle and I adore you.

1

Olivia

IT STARTED THE NIGHT AFTER I BURNED DOWN MY BUILDING.

I was sitting on top of the fancy granite island in my brother's kitchen, inhaling a bag of his pretzels while systematically knocking back the bottles of Stella that'd been in his fridge. And no, I didn't have a drinking problem. I had a *life* problem. As in, my life sucked and I needed to fall into a coma variety of sleep if I were going to have any shot at formulating a plan for my future when I woke up.

Jack had agreed (after much begging) to let me stay with him for a month—enough time to get a job and find my own place—as long as I agreed to be on my best behavior and stay out of his roommate's way. *He seemed a little too old to have a roommate, if you asked me, but who was I to judge?*

Big brother had given me a hug and a key and left me for

fifty-cent wing night at Billy's Bar, so I was home alone and bawling to Adele on his Alexa. It was already woe-is-me music, but when she started crooning about a fire starting in her heart, it made me think about the fire that started on my deck, and I totally lost it.

I was full-on ugly crying when my phone buzzed and halted the meltdown. A number I didn't know texted:

So tell me exactly what you're wearing.

A pervy wrong number? I wiped my nose and typed: Your mom's wedding dress and her favorite thong.

No more than five seconds went by before Mr. Wrong Number texted: Um, what?

I texted: Seriously, babe, I thought you'd think it's hot.

Mr. Wrong Number: "Babe"? Wtf?

That actually made me snort out a tiny laugh, the thought of some dude getting cold-showered via text. It was super weird that *babe* was where he was getting tripped up, as opposed to the monstrosity of an oedipal-lingerie suggestion, but he'd also used the tired *what are you wearing* line, so who could really say about a guy like that?

I texted: Would you prefer something less mommish?

Mr. Wrong Number: Oh, no—it sounds totally hot. You cool with me rocking cargo shorts, socks with sandals, and your dad's jockstrap?

That made me smile in the midst of my full-on life collapse and resultant crying binge.

Me: I'm so turned on right now. Please tell me you'll whisper dad jokes in my ear while we bonk.
Mr. Wrong Number: Yeah, baby jokes and weather anecdotes come fully loaded. And bonk is the sexiest word in the English language, btw.
Me: Agreed.
Mr. Wrong Number: I texted the wrong number, didn't I?
Me: Yeah, you did.

I hiccuped—the beer was finally kicking in—and decided to give the guy a break. I texted: But go get after it, bud. Land that bonk. ☺

Mr. Wrong Number: This is the weirdest text exchange I've ever had.
Me: Same. Good luck and good night.
Mr. Wrong Number: Thanks for the support, and good night to you, as well.

ONCE THE STELLA started making me tired, I decided to shower—*bye-bye, smoky hair*—and go to bed. I dug through my duffel for clothes, but then I remembered—duh—the fire. All I had were the clothes that'd been in the bottom of my gym locker and some rando mismatched separates that'd fallen onto the floorboards of my back seat on multiple laundry days. I found a Cookie Monster pajama top, but discovered I didn't actually own a single bottom; no pajama bottoms, no jeans, no shorts—the only pants I owned now were the stinky gym shorts currently covering my ass.

Was not owning pants my rock bottom?

Thank God I had clean underwear. I had one pair of neon-yellow boy shorts that said *Eat the Rich* across the back, and their presence in my life kept me dangling from the balcony that hovered just above Bottom.

I took a thirty-minute shower, tipsily smitten with the pouring-rain showerhead and Jack's roommate's expensive conditioner. I accidentally dropped the slippery plastic bottle, which made the pump top break off and sent the majority of the luxurious crème slathering out all over the slick floor of the shower. I knelt down and scooped as much as I could back into the bottle, setting it carefully on the shower shelf and hoping no one would notice.

Spoiler: They always noticed.

But two hours later I was still wide-awake, lying on the floor of my brother's office on his squeaky old air mattress, staring at the ceiling through puffy eyes and replaying over and over again all of the terrible things that'd happened before I fled Chicago.

The layoff. The cheating. The breakup. The fire.

And then I said, "Screw. This."

I got up, went into that shiny kitchen, cracked the seal on a bottle of tequila that had a smiley mustachioed sun on the bottle, and I made myself the world's biggest night-night toddy.

I might have a headache in the morning, but at least I'd get some sleep.

"LIVVIE, IT'S MOM. I thought you were coming over today."

I opened my eyes—well, only one would open—and looked at the phone my mother was shouting at me from. Eight thirty? She'd expected me to show up at their house at dawn? God, the woman was like some kind of sadistic, dog-torturing serial killer or something.

Why had I answered again?

"I was. I mean, I am. My alarm was just about to go off."

"Well, I thought you were job hunting today."

Adele started blaring through the apartment again—*what the hell*—and I yelled, "Alexa, turn off music."

My mother said, "Who are you talking to?"

"No one." The music still blared. "Alexa, turn off Adele!"

"Do you have friends over?"

"Oh, my God. No." My second eye finally opened and I sat up, my entire forehead clenched in a massive ache as the music came to an abrupt halt. "I was talking to Jack's stereo."

She sighed one of her why-is-my daughter-such-a-nut sighs. "So are you not job hunting, then?"

Someone please kill me. I said through wicked cotton mouth, "I am. The internet makes it okay to start at noon, I swear, Ma."

"I don't even know what you're saying. Are you coming over or not?"

I took a deep breath through my nose and remembered my

wardrobe problems. Until I could wash my bottoms, I was hosed. So I said, "Not. Until later. The job is my number one priority, so I'll swing by after I get some apps put in."

And also after I found a pair of pants.

"Is your brother there?"

"I have no idea."

"How can you not know if he's there?"

"Because I'm still in bed, and the door is closed."

"Why would you sleep with the door closed? That spare room will get really stuffy if you don't open it up."

"Oh. My. God." I sighed and rubbed my temple. "I will get out of bed in a minute, and if I see your other-gendered offspring, I will tell him to call you. Okay?"

"Oh, I don't need him to call me. I was just wondering if he's there."

"I have to go."

"Did you deposit that money yet?"

I pressed my lips together and closed my eyes. Leave it to my mother. The only thing worse, at the age of twenty-five, than having to ask your parents for money because you rolled into town on fumes and literally didn't have a dime to your name, was having a mom who wanted to talk about it. I said, "Yes, I did it online last night."

As if I had any choice but to deposit that mortifying parental contribution as fast as humanly possible. Because after the smoke cleared (literally) and it became apparent that my building was no longer standing, I'd had to spend what little money I had on survival items like an oil change, new tires, and a whole lot of gas to get me home to Omaha.

Thank God I still had one final paycheck coming next week.

My mother said, "You did it on the computer?"

I gritted my teeth. "Yes."

"Evie's husband said you should *never* do that. You might as well just give your money to the hackers."

My head was throbbing. "Who is Evie?"

"My bridge partner, the one who lives in Gretna. Do you never listen to me?"

"Mom," I said, contemplating pulling the old *cutting out, I'm in a tunnel* cell phone trick. "I don't memorize your bridge partners' names."

"Well, I only have one, dear, it's not that hard." My mother sounded deeply offended. "You need to stop with the computer banking—just go see the teller in person."

I sighed. "Should I have driven *back* to Chicago to deposit it in person, Ma?"

"There's no need to get snippy. I'm just trying to help."

I sighed again and clambered to my feet from the low, low air mattress that'd bottomed out every time I'd rolled over in the night. "I know and I'm sorry. It's just been a rough couple of days."

"I know, hon. Just come over later, okay?"

"Okay." I walked over to the door and threw it open. "I love you. Bye."

I tossed the phone on top of the desk and squinted as the living room's natural light assaulted my eyeballs. God, the hangover. I had that equilibrium tilt going on, the one that let your body know you were still too boozed up to drive, and I stumbled in the direction of the Keurig, desperate for coffee.

"Well, good morning, sunshine."

I froze at the sound and instantly felt like I was going to throw up.

Because Colin Beck, Jack's best friend, was watching me toddle toward the kitchen. As if the universe hadn't already beaten the living shit out of me, there he was, standing beside the fancy breakfast bar with his arms crossed, witnessing my walk of shame with an eyebrow raised in amusement. He was wearing his I'm-better-than-you smirk and dickish good looks while I traversed the apartment in underpants and a too-small shirt like some sort of Winnie-the-Pooh variety of dipshit.

I blinked. Had he gotten *more* attractive?

What a prick.

The last time I'd seen him was my freshman year of college, when I'd gotten kicked out of the dorms and had to spend the final month of the semester living at home with my parents. Jack brought him over for spaghetti on a Sunday, and Colin had found the story of my stray-dog rescue turned mauling of multiple dorm tenants turned subsequent fire-sprinkler deployment turned massive dorm-wide flooding dismissal to be the funniest thing he'd ever heard.

Today he looked like he'd just come back from a run. His damp T-shirt hugged his über-defined *everything*, and some kind of tattoo snaked down his right arm.

Who did he think he was with that, The Rock?

Colin had one of those movie-star faces, with the perfect bone structure and a killer jawline, but his blue eyes had a mischievous spark that offset the beauty. Rowdy eyes. I'd fallen in love with that face briefly at the age of fourteen, but after eavesdropping on a conversation where he'd referred to me as the "little weirdo" at age fifteen, I'd taken an extreme right turn into loathing and never looked back.

"What are you doing here?" I walked around him to where the Keurig sat on the smooth counter, and I pressed the power button. The cool air reminded me that my backside was totally exposed in my idiotic vanity plate underpants, but I'd be damned if I let him think that he had the ability to faze me. I forced myself not to tug on the Cookie Monster pajama top as I searched the cabinets for coffee, telling myself that it was only a butt as I said, "I thought you moved to Kansas or Montana."

He cleared his throat. "In the cupboard next to the fridge."

I glanced over at him. "What?"

"The coffee."

He was *such* a know-it-all. He'd always reminded me of an East Coast mobster, the way he knew everything and was always right. So I lied and said, "Well, I wasn't looking for coffee."

He quirked an eyebrow and leaned against the breakfast bar. "You weren't."

"Nope." I bit down on my bottom lip and said, "I was actually looking for, um, for tea."

"Oh. Of course." He gave me a look that told me he somehow knew that I hated tea. "Well, it's in the same cupboard. Next to the fridge."

Holy God, how could this be happening? Am I seriously talking to Colin Beck in my underwear?

"Thank you." I fought the urge to roll my eyes as I walked over to that cupboard, wanting coffee so bad I could cry. There was one kind of tea in there, Earl Grey, and all I knew was that

I'd hate it as I pulled out a K-Cup and took it back over to the machine. "Where's Jack?"

"Um." I felt his eyes on me as he said, "He's at work."

"Oh." *So why are you here?*

"He said you're staying for a month." He leaned his tanned forearms on the counter—how the hell did he have sexy *forearms*, for God's sake—and started messing with his running watch. "Right?"

"Yep." I grabbed a mug from the counter, filled it with water from the sink, and removed the lid of the near-empty reservoir on the Keurig. "Does my brother know you're here, by the way?"

That made him look up from his wrist. "What?"

I leaned closer to the coffee machine and started pouring. "Is he expecting you?"

He made a sound in his throat that was a mixture between a cough and a laugh before saying, "Holy shit—you don't know that I'm his roommate, do you?"

Oh, God. He couldn't be serious, right? I searched his face, desperate for him to be messing with me, even while knowing he wasn't. But before I could get more of a read on his expression, he waved his hands in my direction and barked, "Water. Watch the water, Liv."

"Shit." I'd missed the reservoir completely and poured water all over the counter. I grabbed a towel and tried wiping it up, but the bar towel wasn't absorbent in the least and only served to push the water from the counter to the floor.

While that arrogant jerk watched with an amused grin on his face.

"You don't have anything better to do than watch me mop up my mess?"

He shrugged and leaned into the counter like he didn't have a care in the world. "Not really. I like what you're doing with your hair these days, by the way."

"Is that right? Do you?" I gave him a mocking smile that felt more like the feral baring of teeth. "I call this my moving-in-with-Colin hairstyle. Looks and feels like a dumpster fire."

"Speaking of fires, I'm curious, Marshall. How the hell did you manage to burn down an entire apartment building?" He tilted his head and said, "I mean, you've always been a bit of a train wreck, but burning love letters on a wooden deck like some kind of pyro is next level, even for you."

I tried to swallow but my throat was pinched.

Not because that jackass thought I was an idiot; he'd always thought that. My misadventures were a guilty pleasure for Colin, like a train wreck reality TV show that you didn't want to admit you watched but always binged on when you came across it.

I was his *Sister Wives*.

But the fact that he knew the tiny details of something that'd just happened the day before yesterday, in a city eight hours away, meant that Jack had told him. And my brother had clearly told him more than just a vague my-sister's-been-displaced-by-a-fire sort of disclaimer since he mentioned the love letters.

He'd shared with him the awful details.

The cheating boyfriend, the wine-and-letter-burning ceremony on the deck, the four-alarm fire . . . everything. I wanted to vomit at the thought of the two of them, laughing their asses off as Jack regaled him with the tale of my latest tragedy.

The words *it wasn't my fault* hovered on the tip of my tongue, wanting to be shouted. I wanted to scream that statement to every person who was reading the story in the paper, clicking on the link, or watching the reporter grin and mockingly enunciate the words *love letters*.

Because it wasn't my fault.

Yes, I'd been burning Eli's poems. I'd been perilously close to wine drunk as I chain-smoked on the balcony and torched the letters from that cheating bastard, but I'd burned them in a metal pail. I had a huge cup of water beside the pail, just in case. I wasn't an idiot. I'd been fully prepared for my Cheating Elijah exorcism.

But I hadn't been prepared for the possum.

I'd been quietly gazing into my tiny bonfire, contemplating the fact that being alone might not be so terrible, when that ugly little guy had run across the gutter and jumped onto my deck. My gasp had alerted him to my presence, scaring him. Scaring him enough for him to scatter and bump the table that the pail was sitting on top of, knocking the pail onto the deck.

The deck that was covered in an adorable straw mat.

"Listen," I said, trying to sound unfazed, "I'd love to stand around and discuss what a mess you think I am, but I have things to do. Can you please turn around?"

"Why?"

I sighed and wanted to disappear. "Because the more awake I become, the less happy I am to be talking to you sans pants."

His eyes crinkled around the edges. "I didn't think you ever got embarrassed."

"I'm not embarrassed." If it were anyone else in the world, I would laughingly admit that I got embarrassed super easily and all the time, which was what usually was to blame for my trips, spills, and general awkwardness. But because it was Colin, I said, "I'm just not sure you're worthy of an eyeful of this ass."

I walked past him and left the kitchen with my head held high, even as my face burned and I prayed my butt looked good in those ridiculous underpants. It wasn't until I slammed the door of my makeshift room that I allowed myself to whisper-scream nearly every obscenity I knew.

2

Olivia

THE DAY DIDN'T GET MUCH BETTER.

I barricaded myself in the office and applied for ten jobs I was completely underqualified for. There were a few openings for technical writers, which I was qualified for but not excited about, and a slew of other copywriter jobs that I *almost* fit the profile for (but not quite).

In the process I managed to jam up the printer (that I'd used without permission) and spill toner powder on the white rug (spoiler: Cleaning it with water was a terrible idea and the rug was toast), so I was off to a great start.

After that, I drove over to my parents' house to grab some of the clothes I left behind when I went to college. While I depressingly dug through clothes that hadn't been trendy in a decade, my mother showed me the virtual scrapbook she was keeping of links to stories about the fire. You know, just so I could remember it years from now.

Then she fed me lasagna while my father lectured me on adult behavior and the importance of renter's insurance.

I left their house with heartburn, leftovers, and a chip on my shoulder that was a hell of a lot bigger than the *Kennedy Marching Band* T-shirt that I was going to have to get reacquainted with until I got a job and earned new clothes.

I wondered how far the closest plasma donation facility was.

When I got back to Jack's building, I just didn't feel like going up yet. The day had been so filled with one horrendous thing after another that I wasn't quite ready to deal with Colin. Or my brother, for that matter.

Definitely not their irritation when I told them about the white rug.

So I went up to the roof instead.

I'd noticed the sign in the elevator about the rooftop patio, and it did *not* disappoint. It had a ridiculous view of the city below, framed with overflowing pots of bright petunias and fancy chaise longue chairs.

I sat down, tucked my legs under me, and took in a deep breath of summer air.

Ahhhh. It felt like the first time I'd breathed since Eli had shown up at the coffee shop and told me how much he didn't love me.

Had that really been two days ago?

My phone buzzed, and when I looked down, I saw a text from the same unfamiliar number from the night before.

What are you wearing?

Wrong number dude was at it again? What a loser. I texted: Haha. Did that actually work for you last night, btw?

A couple laughed around the fire pit that was glowing on the other side of the rooftop, and I wondered what the possum population was like in this part of town.

Mr. Wrong Number: After the cold shower your mental image dumped on me, I didn't even try. I went home and went to bed.

Me: Oh, poor baby. So sorry I ruined the world's cheesiest attempt at action.

Mr. Wrong Number: You don't know I wanted action. I might've been taking a survey on female attire.

Me: Sure you were.

Mr. Wrong Number: On that note, I'm taking a survey on female attire. Can you describe your current outfit?

I glanced down at my gym shorts and texted: Valentino gown, Ferragamo pumps, and the kickiest little feathered hat you've ever seen. Might've belonged to the Queen.

Mr. Wrong Number: So you're in pajamas.

Me: Basically.

Mr. Wrong Number: Antisocial by choice or bad luck?

Me: Choice. But my luck is, in fact, the baddest.

Mr. Wrong Number: Can't be that bad.

Me: Oh, you have no idea.

Mr. Wrong Number: Three examples, please.

I smiled. It felt wildly freeing to talk to someone who didn't know me.

Me: In college, I was clipping my toenails and ended up having to wear an eye patch for a month.

Mr. Wrong Number: Disgusting, but impressive. #2?

Me: I once got stuck in a tipped-over porta-potty.

Mr. Wrong Number: Good Lord.

Me: Music festival, strong winds. The thing blew over, door side down. I still have nightmares.

Mr. Wrong Number: I want to move on to #3, but I have to know how long you were trapped.

Me: Twenty minutes but it felt like days. My drunk friends lifted it enough for me to squeeze through the door crack.

Mr. Wrong Number: I'm assuming you were . . .

Me: Absolutely covered in waste.

Mr. Wrong Number: I just threw up a little in my mouth.

Me: As you should. And just to add a cherry to the top of your entertainment sundae, the story ends in me being doused with gallons of high-powered water that were dispensed by a fire hose.

Mr. Wrong Number: Wow. You definitely can't top #2.

Me: Oh, you ignorant little fool. #2 is but a warm-up.

Mr. Wrong Number: Well give me #3, then.

I thought about it for a minute. I mean, there were hundreds of embarrassing bad luck moments I could've shared with him. The time I dropped a bowling ball on my toe on my first date, the time I fell into an empty pool and broke my elbow; such was my life. But since I didn't know him and he didn't know me, I shared the rawest one.

Me: Not only did I introduce my boyfriend—now ex—to my stunningly beautiful coworker, but I encouraged him to collaborate with her on a project that required them to spend countless hours alone together in her apartment.
Mr. Wrong Number: Oof.
Me: Right? Probably doesn't qualify as bad luck when it's pure stupidity.
Mr. Wrong Number: I don't know you, so you could be a raging psycho. BUT. If you're not, I think it makes you unbelievably cool, the fact that you'd trust them both that much.

I hadn't actually told anyone in the world what'd happened with Eli yet, so it felt good, having someone say that.

Me: You say that, but would you ever be that stupid?
Mr. Wrong Number: No comment.

I snorted. See?

Mr. Wrong Number: How about I give you one of my stupid moments to even this out?
Me: I thought you said it wasn't stupid.
Mr. Wrong Number: Hush.

Me: Please continue.

Mr. Wrong Number: In college, I proposed to my girlfriend without a ring.

Me: That's not stupid.

Mr. Wrong Number: She said no because—and I quote—"if you knew me at all, you'd know I want a ring."

Me: Oof.

Mr. Wrong Number: Right?

Me: I can't imagine having my life together enough IN COLLEGE to propose marriage. I was still getting floor-licking drunk every weekend right up until graduation.

Mr. Wrong Number: Maybe I should've tried that, instead.

Me: I'm guessing you're over it?

Mr. Wrong Number: Why are you guessing that?

Me: Because you're sending "what are you wearing" texts to randos.

Mr. Wrong Number: I AM over it, but you were a misdial, not a rando. I was sending that text to someone I knew, remember?

Me: Oh, yes—of course.

I stretched my legs out in front of me and looked up at the stars. It was a gorgeous night, and I was actually having fun.

Talking to a wrong number.

God, I was pathetic.

Me: Listen, Wrong Number, you seem like a damned delight, but I don't have any interest in an internet friend. I've seen Catfish and 90 Day Fiancé, and that is not my jam.

Mr. Wrong Number: Nor mine.

Me: So . . . have a great night, then.

Mr. Wrong Number: So that's it? It's either zero or Catfish?

Me: Afraid so.

Mr. Wrong Number: And this isn't the internet, for the record.

Me: True, but still the same.

Mr. Wrong Number: You don't find this kind of . . . entertaining?

Me: I do, actually.

Mr. Wrong Number: So . . . ?

Me: So . . . sticking with my original answer. These things always get weird.

Mr. Wrong Number: You're probably right. Especially with your bad luck.

Me: Yup.

Mr. Wrong Number: Well, good night, then, Miss Misdial.

Me: Good night to you, Mr. Wrong Number.

I put my phone away and it almost felt like I was waking up from something, like I'd just come outside after a month in a dark basement. I felt more relaxed than I'd been in a really long time as I stretched in the moonlight and stacked my hands behind my head.

It was strange to think, but I kind of felt like it was because

I'd unloaded on Wrong Number. I felt *lighter*. Light enough to go back to the apartment, in fact.

Because really, who cared if Jack and Colin thought I was a loser? Why had I let that bother me in the first place? I loved my brother, but the reality was that theirs was just an apartment for me to sleep in for the next month.

A really nice apartment that I was going to enjoy, dammit. Like an Airbnb without the required payment.

I texted Jack: Are you guys home?

Jack: At the Old Market. Why?

Yes! Alone time.

Me: Just curious. Have fun.

I went down to my car, grabbed the trash bag full of high school clothes, and headed upstairs. I'd been so emotionally shredded the night before that I hadn't had a chance to get comfortable and explore the place. I hummed as I rode the elevator, feeling a little more like a functional, thriving adult than a cheated-on loser for the first time since Eli thanked me for introducing him to his soul mate.

When I got inside, I dropped my keys on the table by the door and dragged my garbage bag into the office. I dumped everything out onto the floor in the corner, digging through the pile until I found what I was looking for: the soft green plaid flannel pants I'd slept in every night in high school and my paint-stained CAT hoodie.

It didn't matter that it was June. The apartment was freezing, so the outfit was like wearing a blanket. I burrowed into its softness, slid my feet into a pair of mismatched socks, and threw my hair up in a ponytail. Two quick flicks in my phone's Bluetooth settings, and I was headed for the kitchen.

"Alexa, play *Hit It Mix*."

"Sex Talk" started and I cranked the volume, bouncing a little across that swanky apartment. I'd made the playlist as a joke for Eli, filling it with nasty songs I knew he'd find offensive, but apparently I was tougher to offend because I fell in love with the potpourri of upbeat, über-sexual songs instead.

And now that he was the biggest bastard in the world, the playlist was my theme music.

I did a few pirouettes on the sleek kitchen floor, getting maximum spin in my socks, before wandering over to the windows that overlooked the city. I was obsessed with that part of the apartment. I could stand there—in front of those huge floor-to-ceiling windows—and watch the world for hours.

"Want a beer?"

"God." I turned around, my hand on my heart, and Colin was standing in the doorway of his bedroom, one side of his mouth slid up in a smirk. He was wearing a black shirt and a pair of jeans, his hair still perfect in its Ivy League style. "I didn't know anyone else was home."

He pointed toward the speaker above him in the ceiling. "I kind of assumed."

"I thought you were with my brother." I felt my cheeks get hot as Megan Thee Stallion started singing exactly how her man liked it. *Super* loudly.

I nearly screamed, "Alexa, turn off music!"

Colin's eyes were smiling and he crossed his arms. "So, beer . . . ?"

Unaccustomed to his congeniality, I asked, "Are you offering, or just taking a poll?"

"Offering." He made a face like he knew he deserved that and said, "We've got a beer fridge in the laundry room."

"Um." I tucked my hair behind my ears and said, "Yeah. Thanks."

He walked over to the door next to the bathroom, and when he went inside, I adjusted my hoodie so my bralessness was less apparent. I assumed he'd bring out a beer, but instead he yelled, "You should probably pick your poison. Your brother likes a lot of weird shit."

"Oh." I walked over to the tiny laundry room, where he was leaning down into the fridge and presenting me with—wow—just the finest ass. I mean, his posterior looked as if he was forever doing squats and lunges; perhaps that was his sole method of mobility. Maybe Colin lunged everywhere he went.

He glanced over his shoulder. "See anything you like?"

Good God. I cleared my throat, pointed, and managed, "Is that a Vanilla Bean Blonde over by the Mich Ultra?"

"Yep." He straightened, gave me the blonde, and grabbed a Boulevard for himself. I exited the laundry room with him following behind me, and I wandered toward the kitchen, where I knew the bottle opener lived. "Thanks for the beer."

"Sure." He went around to the other side of the breakfast bar, opened a drawer, and pulled out the opener. Colin held it out to me and said, "By the way, I owe you an apology."

That captured my attention. I grabbed the opener and asked, "For what?"

His eyes were serious when he said, "For what I said about the fire this morning. I was an asshole about it, and it's really none of my business."

I popped the top and lifted the bottle toward my mouth. "And . . . ?"

A flash of irritation crossed his face before he said, "What does 'and' mean? You don't accept my apology?"

"I just don't get it." I noticed his hands were nice—*Stop it, Liv*—as he opened his beer. I watched his throat move around a swallow, and I said, "You're actually apologizing to me?"

"Isn't that what I just said?"

"Well, yeah, but you've always been a jerk to me and you've never apologized." I finally took a sip of my beer then, looking at his slightly confused expression over the bottle.

He sounded outraged as he said, "I've apologized."

"Nope."

"Well, if I haven't, it's because it's always been in good fun." His eyes moved over my face, like he was trying to reconcile the whole of our lives together. "We've always messed with each other. That's kind of our thing, right?"

Did he actually think that? That his Liv-is-a-moron attitude was just our friendly wordplay? For some reason that irritated me, the fact that he didn't even know that I didn't like him; I mean, shouldn't he *know*?

I decided to let it go, though, because we were roommates for the next month. It would run a lot smoother if I played nice.

And for me, nice meant avoidance. Steering clear of Colin was the only way to ensure a peaceful, rent-free month.

"Sure." I got off the stool and pushed it in. "Thanks again for the beer. I've got a million things to do tomorrow, so I should probably start settling in, even though I'm totally wide-awake. It's weird how when you decimate your life, you get wicked insomnia."

He smirked and his eyes were actually smiling. "I bet."

I shrugged. "I'm sure I'll start sleeping like a baby soon, once the smell of soot finally leaves my body."

He actually coughed out a little laugh. "One can only hope."

I started to walk away when he said, "Hey, can I quickly use the printer before you go to bed? I just need to print a three-page doc—"

"No!" I turned around and cursed myself for sounding so panicked. "I mean, can you maybe just use it tomorrow? I'm really, really tired."

His eyebrows furrowed. "You just said that you have insomnia."

I bit my bottom lip and said, "I just have a lot of stuff in the office, all over the place, and I—"

"What happened?" He sounded like a detective who knew I was guilty as he crossed his arms and narrowed his eyes.

I reached up and pulled my ponytail tighter. "Nothing happened. Um, I just don't want—"

"Spill it, Marshall."

I sighed. "Fine. Your printer broke when I used it this morning. I didn't do anything wrong, it just broke. I'm sure I can fix it."

"Can I see?"

I so didn't want him seeing the heaping mountain of old garbage clothes, but it *was* his apartment. "Sure."

I followed him into the office, and as soon as we walked in, I saw him looking at the trash bag and massive clothing pile. It was embarrassing, but at least the mess was covering the stain on the rug. I said, "I know what you're thinking."

"You couldn't possibly."

"I went to my parents' house, and my mom sent me home with a bag full of clothes. She didn't have any luggage, so I had to put them in a Hefty bag."

"Exactly what I was thinking."

"Bullshit."

He just winked, and my stomach dropped to my ankles.

He leaned down and looked inside the printer, where the cartridge door was ajar. "What the hell happened to it?"

"I had to pry off the door with a flathead screwdriver. Don't worry, I googled it first."

He squinted into the printer. "Oh, well, if you googled it."

"I knew what I was doing."

He looked over at me like I was insane, and pointed at the broken door. "Seriously with that?"

I just shrugged.

He started digging inside the machine, and he pulled out two crumpled-up pieces of paper. After a few minutes, he had the printer up and running and the machine back together. He straightened and said, "Boom."

I rolled my eyes, which made him smile. Those wild eyes twinkled as his deep voice purred out, "Need anything else fixed, Liv?"

I knew he wasn't flirting—I knew it beyond a reasonable doubt—but it still shook me. It made my voice sound kind of breathy when I said, "I think I'm good."

His eyes stayed with mine for a split second, like we were both wordlessly acknowledging the spark of flirtation, before he said, "Well, good night."

I swallowed and dropped down onto the air mattress. "Well, good night."

3

Olivia

"DUDE." JACK WAS SITTING ON A STOOL, EATING WHAT looked to be a breakfast burrito and scrolling through his phone. He said, "Why are you awake?"

"I'm going for a run." I put my foot up on the other stool and tied my shoe. His shock was no surprise; I was shocked, too. I usually slept until twenty minutes after my alarm went off, wherein I would scramble to get ready and ultimately end up putting on makeup while driving. This early-morning thing was brand new for me.

I cringed at the smell of the burrito. "God, that smells disgusting."

"Since when do you run?" He looked at me like I'd just said I was going to run *for president*. "You used to have Mom call you out of gym every time they had the national physical fitness test."

"I was eight at the time." I finished tying and switched feet. "You used to have Mom tell Mr. Graham you had a skin condition so you could wear a T-shirt for swimming. I'm assuming you've grown out of *that*, just like I grew out of my unathleticism."

"I don't think that's a word."

"I don't think your face is a word." One day of living with my brother, and I was reverting to childhood behavior. I straightened and put in my headphones, forcing myself not to roll my eyes. Unbeknownst to him, I was still irritated that he'd told Colin everything, so his Mr. Ha Ha I'm Always Funny face just kind of pissed me off.

But since he was giving me pretty choice accommodations, I had to gut my feelings.

He took a big gulp of orange juice and then said, "You sure you should be running at six thirty in the morning, when it's still a little dark? That seems dangerous."

"I've got pepper spray in my sports bra; I'll be fine."

"Because bad guys definitely give you time to dig around in your Under Armour."

"Whatever, Jack. I *dare* someone to mess with me." Today was the first day of the New and Improved Olivia, the one who would exercise regularly, eat well, use a planner, and land a job. As soon as I had money, I was even going to implement a skincare routine like a bona fide adult.

"Mom told me to look out, by the way." Jack leaned back a little and grinned. "She said you've been 'snippy' since you got back and want to fight about everything."

"I don't have time to discuss all of the ways our mother is

off base." She was like a middle-class, real-life version of Emily Gilmore.

"Is she right about Eli?"

Well, *that* certainly made me stop in my tracks. I acted unaffected when I said, "I don't know—what'd she say about him?"

Meanwhile, the sound of his name still made my heart hurt. *I thought he was the one.*

"Just that she thinks he dumped you or cheated." He scraped together the scrambled eggs on his plate with the underside of his fork and added, "She said those are the only reasons you'd be burning his love letters."

Yeah, my mom nailed it. Eli had done both. I didn't want them to know the details, though. For the two years I'd lived in Chicago—one of which I'd lived *with* Eli—my family had acted like I'd finally outgrown my disastrous ways. I had an apartment in the Windy City, a boyfriend who liked craft beer and running, and a job as a technical writer for a Fortune 500 company.

It seemed that Livvie had finally become an adult.

What they hadn't known was that the job was a boring entry-level position that barely paid the bills, the apartment building that I torched was owned by Eli's uncle, so we were charged minimal rent, and Eli and I rarely saw each other during the week because he traveled for work.

It wasn't until he got promoted and no longer went out of town that he realized (a) he didn't love me anymore and *didn't know if he ever had*, and (b) he loved my work colleague more than life itself.

"Actually, I dumped him because his love letters were positively ghastly. The guy rhymed 'love' with 'glove'—can you believe that shit?" I put in my headphones and shook my head. "Don't tell Mom that, though, because she liked him. I'm out of here."

I left the apartment and stretched for a solid five seconds on the elevator ride down. I'd enrolled in a barre class back in Chicago that I actually went to a few times a month, so I was reasonably in shape and it would surely be fine.

Only . . . it wasn't.

I ran two blocks—two—before I had to stop and put my hands on top of my head. I was gasping and seeing little stars, panting like I'd just finished a marathon, when I noticed it was a Starbucks that I was panting in front of.

Yes.

I pushed back my hair and pushed in the door, almost tasting my deliciously creamy frapp as the rich smell of coffee came at me. I knew it wasn't exactly in the New Olivia plan, but a cup of coffee wasn't going to push me off the rails.

The place was buzzing with the early risers, those business-class, hyper-driven individuals who were already dressed in suits and ready to succeed. They were historically not my kin, but perhaps they would be in the near future. I walked over to the line and waited behind two corporately dressed men, trying to soak up a little of their success mojo while they discussed someone named Teddy.

But it wasn't until I got to the front and placed my order that I remembered—oh, my God. I had less than a hundred bucks to my name. I was sub-hundo for a few more days, which meant I had no business getting coffee.

Or calling myself an adult, but that was another thing entirely.

"Oh, my God—I forgot my wallet." It wasn't a lie. I did not, in fact, have my wallet, but I usually paid with the app so it technically should've been a nonissue. My face was hot as I patted myself down like a moron and said to the smiley barista, "I am *so* sorry. I didn't realize that I hadn't reloaded the—"

"I got it." She winked and said, "What's the name for the cup?"

"Um, Olivia." I felt a little emotional as I said, "Ohmigodthankyousomuch."

I moved over to wait for my drink and felt even more excited about this life redo, because I was actually having good luck for once. That *had* to be a cosmic sign, right? I grabbed my drink when they yelled my name, then I unwrapped the straw and took a huge sip of my cosmically gifted beverage.

So, so good.

My phone buzzed, and when I pulled it out of the waistband of my shorts, I saw a message from my anonymous friend who I thought I'd unfriended the night before.

Mr. Wrong Number: I thought we were done, Misdial.

I was confused until I saw the message above his.

Apparently I'd butt texted him a series of letters and symbols.

Me: Sorry, that was a butt dial.

Mr. Wrong Number: Sure it was.

I giggled and looked up. The guy barista with the ponytail

raised an eyebrow, but no one else seemed to be looking my way. I texted: Swear to God.

Mr. Wrong Number: Well, good. Because we are NOT going to banter, right?
Me: Right.
Mr. Wrong Number: You have a good day, Misdial.
Me: You, too, Wrong Number.
Mr. Wrong Number: kkljfhjdfshghgdhgh

I smiled, shoved my phone back into my shorts, and started humming "Walking on Sunshine" as I headed for the exit, excited to get home and tackle more job applications. The morning was rich with possibilities, and I wasn't going to waste a single second. I was pushing the door to exit when it opened and my sister-in-law, Dana, was on the other side with her boys.

"You guys!" I nearly leapt through the door as I scooped up Kyle and spun him around. "What are you doing here?"

I squeezed that little cutie and sniffed his neck, where he still smelled like baby sweetness even though he'd just turned four and wouldn't be sweet for long. Dana was smiling—no surprise, because my oldest brother's adorable wife was always smiling—and holding Brady, who looked like he belonged on a babyGap billboard with his chubby cheeks and yellow sun hat.

"Our new place is just around the corner," she said, shifting him on her hip. "Will said you were back, but I told him he couldn't bug you yet."

"Shut your mouth, Dana," I said as Kyle giggled and leaned forward to hover over my straw. "I want you bugging me constantly. The only upside to moving back home is getting to hang with my dudes all the time."

She laughed and said, "Well, you don't have to tell me twice. Want to watch the boys today?"

I knew I had to job hunt, but surely two tiny humans wouldn't impair my ability to do that, right? "Yes, please."

She crinkled her perfect eyebrows. "I was kidding, Liv."

"Don't be kidding." I leaned my face forward to grin at Brady, instantly getting that mush-happy vibe that my nephews always inspired. "Please don't be kidding. You're not allowed to be kidding."

"Are you serious?"

I shrugged and growled at Kyle as he took a long sip of my frappuccino, which made him belly laugh while continuing to guzzle my drink. "I was going to job hunt today, but that can wait a few hours. Give me the care and feeding instructions and they can chill with Auntie Liv until lunchtime."

"Oh, my God—that would be incredible." Her whole face lit up as she set down Brady and reached for his hand. "We're getting the rugs cleaned this morning so we had to vacate the apartment, but I just knew they were going to get bored after twenty minutes of running errands."

"See? Win-win." I pointed my chin at her diaper bag. "Does that thing have enough stock for multiple morning poopies?"

"It does."

"Well, then, hand it over."

Dana went inside and got her coffee before we made the exchange. She squeezed me into a ginormous hug, and just like that—we were off. Dana was very nearly skipping as she headed toward her car, and we *were* skipping as we took off in the other direction, where my apartment awaited.

Just being around those little turds made everything better. We played I spy outside for an hour (though Brady pretty much just screamed the words *I spy* but had no idea what we were doing), rode the elevator up and down the building three times, shouting, "See ya!" whenever the doors opened and closed on a floor, and then we spent a solid forty-five minutes blowing bubbles off the balcony while aimlessly hoping to hit selected targets.

It was amazing.

I dragged my air mattress into the living room and we made a fort, using it in conjunction with the sofa and the coffee table turned on its side. We were so into our little hideout activities, which was pretty much just eating popcorn in the fort and singing songs from *Moana*, that I didn't even hear someone come in until I looked out of the fort and saw a pair of sleek dress shoes approximately twelve inches from my face.

"Um, hello?" I poked my head out of the fort like a turtle and raised my eyes.

Sure enough, there was Colin, staring down at me with his head tilted slightly as if he was trying to figure out what he was seeing. I scrambled out, my face hot, and I swallowed when I got to my feet and he was looking down at my *Kennedy Homecoming* T-shirt.

Yes, I'm wearing a tee from senior spirit week; eat it. I blew my bangs out of my eyes and tried to remember how to form words, but I struggled because Colin looked like my roommate . . . only he didn't.

This Colin was wearing an impeccably stylish blue suit with a plaid tie and the kind of gorgeous leather dress shoes that always made me wish my squatty hooves fit into men's footwear. *This* Colin had on a starched white button-down shirt and a pair of tortoiseshell glasses that sat perfectly atop his strong nose.

Roommate Colin was cockily attractive, but Smart-Businessman Colin was downright delicious.

His hands slid into the pockets of his pants. "I can't tell you how relieved I was to discover you weren't alone in your fort."

"Ha ha." Kyle crawled out, and Brady followed. I picked up Brady and said, "What are you doing here?"

An eyebrow went up. "At my house? You're asking what I'm doing at my house?"

I rolled my eyes. "You know what I mean. Shouldn't you be at work?"

Kyle walked right up to Colin and said, "Your watch is really cool. Did it cost a lot of moneys?"

Colin's mouth split into the prettiest smile, a wide, funny thing that made my stomach do a full 360 as he said, "It did. A *lot* of moneys."

"I wish I could have it." Kyle did the pouty thing that he was so good at, looking sad but in a cute, puppy-eye way, and murmured, "That would be dope."

Colin's eyes shot to my face. "Did your aunt Olivia teach you that word?"

"No," I said, the exact second Kyle said, "Auntie Liv said it means good."

Colin laughed and my phone buzzed. It was Dana, letting

me know she was parked in the loading zone. I looked at the boys and said, "Your mom's here. We have to race to get all of your stuff back in the diaper bag before she beats us and wins the game. One, two, three, GO!"

Kyle took off running toward the office, and Brady laughed and cluelessly followed. I started picking up toys while Colin went into the kitchen and pulled a Tupperware container out of the freezer. "Those are Will's kids?"

"Yep. Kyle and Brady." I started jamming things in the bag, 100 percent certain it was never going to zip. "Sorry, by the way. I didn't know you came home for lunch or I would've asked before I brought them here."

Totally a lie, but polite, at least.

"No worries. I'm not staying, I just forgot my lunch and thought the walk home would clear my head."

I looked at his perfect image and wondered what he had on his mind. "Did it work?"

"Um." His jaw clenched and he grabbed his keys from the counter. "Not so much."

My cheeks got even hotter, and my impulse was to scream, *I'm sorry, okay?!* but I controlled myself and said, "Well, I hope your day gets better."

His eyes narrowed. "No, you don't."

Finally, I felt like smiling at Colin, and I said, "I might, Beck. You just never know."

Five minutes later, as if they were all a passing storm, I was home alone in the apartment and it was quiet. I was getting a later start than I should've on the applications, but it was going to be okay. Regardless of how on-brand it was for me to blow off responsibilities for whatever sounded fun, this was different.

I was still standing firmly on New Olivia ground.

THE REST OF the week really tested that theory.

I landed five—*five*—job interviews, which thrilled me. I felt like I was going to have a job before Eli even realized that I'd left the city. I was going to be gainfully employed before my mother even had a chance to interrogate me for hours on end about my progress.

Hell, I'd probably have multiple offers to choose from, right?

Wrong.

Because at each of the interviews, I came down with verbal diarrhea.

At the first one, I accidentally mentioned the fire. When I was asked why I'd moved, my mouth had betrayed me and dispensed the truth instead of the generalities I'd carefully practiced.

Mr. Holtings, my interviewer, looked at me over his readers and said, "Fire?"

And for some reason, trying to explain it made me giggle. I started describing what had happened, and I couldn't stop myself from smiling while I said it.

"There was a, um, a fire, and my apartment building burned down." A stifled snort.

And sadly, with each sentence I spewed, I could hear the ridiculousness of the words and how nuts my laughing made me sound. Which, of course, struck me as more and more hilarious and I lost all control.

"It wasn't my fault. I was being careful." I bit my lip to keep from smiling. "But that possum came out of nowhere and knocked over the bucket."

I had to pause to wipe at my tears of laugher.

I was definitely not getting the job.

At the next interview, I accidentally mentioned the *Tribune* and then tried to backtrack and say I hadn't worked there.

"Wait." The very nice woman narrowed her eyes and said, "You worked at the *Chicago Tribune*? How come you didn't put that on your résumé?"

"Oh, I, um, I didn't really work there." I smiled and my brain short-circuited and I actually said the words "I was just kidding."

Side note: If you ever land an internship at a major newspaper, *never* engage in a conversation with your coworker about their vibrator, even if said coworker was the one to bring it up and you were just being polite. As it turns out, if someone in the lunchroom overhears and goes to HR, they will fire you *both*, regardless of who owns Purple Thunder.

But I digress.

Regardless, I was killing myself with my ability to speak. If I could just get a job, I knew I'd make any employer happy. Because I was a good writer. I could proficiently communicate almost anything on paper.

But I had to somehow get through face-to-face meetings first.

At the next interview, I tripped over a chair and reflexively grunted out a semi-loud *fuck me* as it happened. But the two interviews that followed actually went fairly well. I didn't get a callback, and I didn't become buddies with the interviewers, but the fact that I didn't destroy my own chances was a good sign, right?

The only good thing to occur during that series of unfortunate events was the daily communication I exchanged with the stranger. He'd sent a funny butt-dial text the night after my erroneous Starbucks message, and since then we'd been texting every night. Nothing important, just pointless, idiotic conversations about nothing.

The night before was no exception.

Me: What do you think the first guy to ever milk a cow was thinking?
Mr. Wrong Number: Come again?
Me: Ew, I doubt it was that. But was he just super curious, like I wonder what this thing does? Or did he see a calf nursing and he was all DUDE MY TURN?

I'd pictured him shirtless and leaning back against his headboard, smiling as he texted back, but I knew all the while it was pure fantasy that my anonymous bestie would be ripped.

Mr. Wrong Number: Maybe it was a bro thing, where two guys dared each other to touch the teat and then—boom—out squirts the milk.
Me: Touch the Teat. Band name—called it.
Mr. Wrong Number: It's all yours.

Me: Am I interrupting something, btw, with my cow-teat inquiry?

Mr. Wrong Number: Nope. Just lying in bed, wide-awake.

Me: Please don't go creeper on me now.

Mr. Wrong Number: What? I'm not a creep. I'm just lying in bed, naked, practicing my rope-tying skills while listening to Robin Thicke.

I shook my head and rolled over on the air mattress.

Me: Nausea-inducing level of creep right there.

Mr. Wrong Number: Which was the problem? The rope or the nudity? Or the Thicke?

Me: The combination. Brings to mind all the distasteful options of what one could be tying. While Thicke-ing it up.

Mr. Wrong Number: I shall *restrain* myself.

Me: I see what you did there.

Mr. Wrong Number: Is there a reason why the teat question is in play, btw?

Me: I can't sleep, so sometimes instead of counting sheep I start considering the bizarre questions that my brain is constantly churning up.

Mr. Wrong Number: The things you wonder about are batshit crazy.

Me: Like I don't already know that.

But today, on the last interview, the clouds parted and things went really well. Glenda, the editor at the *Times*, was super friendly and we actually connected. I was behaving like a normal human adult and she was really funny, and it couldn't have gone better.

Until.

She said, "What we're looking for with this parenting columnist is someone who can add a real voice to the section. A writer who can tackle parenting topics but still makes readers laugh—or cry—with their very distinct point of view."

I smiled and nodded, but my brain was scrambling. Parenting? What in the literal hell? I'd applied to be an entertainment blogger, not a parenting columnist. I'd seen the post for the parenting position, but I didn't apply for it because—news flash—I wasn't a parent. Like, the idea of squeezing out an entire human and being the person solely responsible for their survival had literally given me nightmares.

Could you even imagine?

Surely I'd lose my grip and drop the kid in the alligator swamp during a leisurely trip to the zoo, or maybe I'd just trip and fall on top of them because tripping was kind of my thing. If there was any way to klutzily, accidentally destroy my tiny human, I would most assuredly do it.

Glenda said, "I read some of your work at ohbabybaby.com, and it's exactly what we're looking for. The tongue-in-cheek comedic angle while still addressing legitimate parental topics is pretty much the vibe we're interested in."

"Great."

"Your article about that Kardashian kid's wardrobe made me cackle."

I smiled. That piece had been one of my favorites.

I'd taken the job writing articles for OhBabyBaby as a side hustle to my boring technical writing job because living in Chicago was expensive. The site's target audience was parents, but it actually wasn't a parenting site. I'd done articles on which celebrities looked best pregnant, whose kids had the best wardrobes, the funniest Pinterest fails, and, of course, gender reveal nightmares.

Was that why she thought I was applying for the parenting job? Had my résumé been read and then promptly misrouted to Glenda because of OhBabyBaby? I opened my mouth to address it, when she asked, "How old are your kids, by the way?"

I swallowed. Blinked. Scratched my right eyebrow. "Two. Um, two and four," I heard myself say, and I immediately wanted to slap myself in the face.

Her face lit up. "Mine are two and five! Boys or girls?"

I felt my armpits get instantly sweaty, and I pictured my nephews. "Both boys."

"Mine are both girls." She beamed at me and I hated myself. I was a lying, child-faking loser, and I didn't deserve the kindness of this woman. She said, "Everyone tells me to buckle up for the high school years."

I shrugged, and pictured the boys again. It was less severe a lie if I pictured actual people as I lied, right? I conjured up Kyle and Brady again. "Mine are killing me now—I don't know if I'll ever make it to those years. Because if I have to watch one more episode of *Paw Patrol* . . ."

"Right?" She shook her head. "I mean, what kind of town leans on a teenage boy to solve all of their problems?"

"An idiotic town whose mayor has a pet chicken. I mean, that fact alone should have sent up all the red flags."

We small-talked about our kids—*please kill me*—for a few more minutes before the interview ended. She shook my hand and said she'd be in touch, and I honestly wanted to cry as I rode the elevator down to the lobby.

Because I wanted that job.

I wasn't a mom and knew nothing about being a mom, but I wanted that job so bad. And not just because I desperately needed employment. I *wanted* to work with Glenda. I *wanted* to write tongue-in-cheek, sarcastic-yet-sweet parenting articles. My creative side was tingling because I knew I could totally kick ass at that job.

If only I had kids.

I walked back to the apartment slowly, teetering in the cheap black pumps I'd worn to homecoming my junior year. I tried talking myself into a little positivity as I headed home; there were still exciting things happening in my life, right?

I was living downtown, which was my absolute favorite thing, so that was cool. In a great apartment, no less, even if it *was* with my brother and I had to sleep on a bed that was made of a raft.

Things really *could* be a lot worse.

Hell, I could be living with my parents.

And I was still getting up early and running every day; for me, that was huge. Even though I panted like a dog and had to stop to walk every three blocks or so, I was a week into my new life and still trying to make it stick.

It helped that Colin was gone. He'd been away in Boston on business, and if he were home, I probably would've blown off running because no way could I ever have him as a running buddy. But with him out of the picture, I'd been able to jog without stress.

I'd also been sneaking into his room and napping on top of his fancy pillow-soft bed every day, so I was more well-rested than I'd been in a really long time. I knew it was a little scrubby of me to use his bed without asking, but that air mattress was killing my back and I was incredibly careful to sleep above the covers.

What he didn't know and all that, right?

My phone buzzed and I pulled it out of the pocket of the skirt I'd worn to the DECA convention my sophomore year.

Mr. Wrong Number: I have time to kill and I'm bored. Give me something to ponder.

I glanced up and moved over to the right, stopping beside a closed storefront so I could text without walking into traffic or getting trampled by my fellow on-foot commuters. I texted: I'm busy. You think I can just come up with these gems on the fly?

Mr. Wrong Number: That is exactly what I think.

That made me smile because it was bizarre the way I kind of felt like he *got* me, even though we were total strangers.

I pushed up my sunglasses before typing: Okay. Do you think an intelligent person who has never done a CERTAIN THING is capable of giving good advice about a CERTAIN THING if they're studious and do the research?

Mr. Wrong Number: First of all, this one's boring. Second, you're asking for a friend, right?
Me: Right.
Mr. Wrong Number: Okay. Well. I think it depends. If you're talking about surgery—please God no. But if you're talking about something a little abstract, like dating advice, then yes, I think it's possible for the right person to pull it off.

Parenting was kind of abstract, right?

Me: Thank you. Okay, I'll give you what you really want now.
Mr. Wrong Number: Oh, baby.
Me: Eww.
Mr. Wrong Number: Waiting.
Me: How many 5th grade boys could you beat in a fight at one time? And no weapons allowed.
Mr. Wrong Number: What if my hands are registered weapons?
Me: Spare me the machismo.
Mr. Wrong Number: Hmm. I'd say . . . twelve.
Me: You have GOT to be kidding.
Mr. Wrong Number: You think more?
Me: Your answer makes me think you've never been around little boys. I'd say no more than six, because you only have two hands. That's three kids per hand.
Mr. Wrong Number: But you're forgetting about the legs.

Me: The legs can hold them off, but not win. The win will be in the hands.

Mr. Wrong Number: You clearly skip leg day.

Me: Listen, I have to go. I'm literally standing on the sidewalk and texting like I'm a teenager.

Mr. Wrong Number: Holy shit—did I ever ask? You're not a teenager, are you???

Me: Relax, I'm 25. You're . . . not a baby either, right?

Mr. Wrong Number: 29 so you're safe.

Me: Although really, it's not like we're sexting or anything. It technically wouldn't even matter if we weren't of age.

Mr. Wrong Number: . . . sending dick pic . . .

Me: I will block you so fast. Unless you've got some sort of . . . special gift. Then I will block you, but slowly.

Mr. Wrong Number: I'll be good.

Me: Thank God. Because I would actually hate to have to block you. Weird, right?

Mr. Wrong Number: Same. And totally weird.

Me: Okay, well, later, Mr. Wrong Number.

Mr. Wrong Number: Goodbye, Miss Misdial. And btw, I would totally get the slow block.

"YOU HAVE TO hold on or you'll fall off."

"Okay." Kyle wrapped his arms around my neck, squeezed, and yelled, "Go, donkey!"

I started crawling across the hardwood floor of the apartment while he rode me like I was an actual donkey. Brady, on the other hand, was staring mindlessly at the TV while my oldest brother, Will, knelt before him, struggling to put on his little shoes.

"Why do you let him do that?" Jack asked from his spot on the couch, a grimace on his face as he watched me. "He's too big."

I crawled faster as Kyle giggled. "Because of *this.* Auntie Liv is his favorite and I'm going to do everything in my power to ensure that never changes."

"Once he's old enough to know what cool is, Uncle Jack will pull in the lead."

"You have *never* watched the boys." Will picked up Brady and threw him over his shoulder while giving Jack a look. "Not even once. Liv, on the other hand, babysat for us even when she didn't live here."

Jack rolled his eyes and said to Will, "Like you would've ever babysat a couple of toddlers when you were single."

I collapsed onto the floor, bucking Kyle off and making him giggle hysterically.

Will shot him a grin of commiseration. "True. I don't even love it now, and they're my own kids."

I sat up, sticking out a hand to deflect Kyle's reboarding attempt. "You guys are crazy; I'd borrow the boys for months at a time if I could."

"Not while you're staying here." Jack pointed at me with his Lone Star bottle. "This is a special exception because Colin's out of town. Just a one-off."

Will and I exchanged a look, because I'd already agreed to watch the boys for Will and Dana's upcoming date night.

"Speaking of Colin," I said, watching as Kyle got herded

toward the door by Will, "what does he do for a living? When I saw him last week he looked . . . I don't know, important. Businessy. I thought he was, like, a salesman."

"You're so clueless," Will laughed, and I flipped him off.

He gestured at his kids, feigning outrage. "The children, Livvie."

"Well, knock off your crap so I don't teach them my bad habits." I rolled my eyes and climbed to my feet. "So what does Colin actually do, then?"

"Oh. Yeah." Jack said, "I think his title is something like senior financial analyst."

I tried to picture it. "For real?"

"For real." He started peeling the label off his beer as he said, "It gives him an unfair advantage in fantasy football that pisses me off."

I walked over to the door to give the boys kisses before they left, but I looked over my shoulder at Jack and said, "I can't believe he works in *finance*."

I kind of assumed he'd be good at his job, whatever it was, but I'd imagined Colin working in real estate or something equally slick, like a sports car salesman.

"You're surprised?" Jack stood and set down his beer. "He has a master's in math and got a perfect score on his ACT."

"Shut *up*." I mean, Colin didn't come across as stupid, but he also didn't bring to mind equations and studiousness, either. His bone structure was too good for that kind of solidity. "I had no idea."

"That's because you always assumed the worst about him."

"No, I didn't."

"Oh, come on. He always gave you shit, and you couldn't take it so you decided he was Satan."

"You have to admit, he has the slick overconfidence of Lucifer."

"Nah." Will put the diaper bag over his shoulder and said, "That's just rich-boy overconfidence. The arrogance that comes from growing up wealthy."

"Probably." My mother had always treated him like he was an actual prince when he came around because according to her, everyone in his family was a fancy lawyer. Grandparents, parents, aunts, uncles; they all worked at Beck & Beck, the city's oldest and most prestigious law firm.

"That's bullshit." Jack brought Kyle's stuffed *Paw Patrol* dog over to where we were in the entryway. "His family is loaded, but Colin and his sister aren't snooty like the rest of them."

"Wait, Colin has a sister?"

How had I not known that? I remembered Jack telling me a whole dramatic story when we were in high school about Colin's dad having an affair with his paralegal and then getting pissed at Colin's mother for being upset about it. Jack had said the guy was so entitled that he lost his shit whenever someone dared to not agree with him.

I'd been fascinated by that story, because it sounded way more like my mother's beloved *General Hospital* than anything I knew to be real life. Jack used to say Colin's dad was a jerk who constantly rode Colin's ass, but I didn't recall anything about a sister. I'd pictured him all alone in the drama. "He's got 'Entitled Only Child' written all over him."

“See? Assuming the worst.”

“Whatever. Come here, Kyle.” I knelt, burrowed my face into the nape of his neck, and blew, which made him erupt into giggles. He hugged me tightly and wouldn’t let go, so it led to me carrying him down to Will’s car because I wasn’t ready to let him go yet, either.

Suddenly I was glad to no longer live five hundred miles away.

After they drove off, I felt my phone vibrate in my pocket. I ignored it as I went inside and rode the elevator up, because I wasn’t allowing myself to engage with Mr. Wrong Number until I was finished with my projects. I still needed to shower (not really a project but definitely necessary), send thank-you emails for the interviews I’d botched, and create a list of ten more positions to apply for tomorrow.

After that, I’d allow myself to play with my anonymous friend.

Who, apparently, would require the *slow* block.

Lawd. I really need to stop thinking about him.

I’D RACED THROUGH my chores and was finally done with my assignments, so I was going to have a little fun and converse with Mr. Wrong Number for a bit. I dropped down to the raft-bed, feeling pathetically excited as I grabbed my phone and opened my messages.

And—*yes*—there was one from him, sent thirty minutes ago.

Mr. Wrong Number: Come out and play.

Butterflies flitted through my stomach as I lay back on the bed and smiled down at the phone. What do you want to play?

Mr. Wrong Number: Such a loaded question from the lady.

I knew the dude was a troll, but I still felt flirty.

Me: How about twenty questions?
Mr. Wrong Number: I thought we wanted to stay anonymous.
Me: We do. Maybe . . . twenty questions about things we like.
Mr. Wrong Number: Sexually?

"Wow." I looked at the phone and wasn't sure how to respond.

Me: That seems like it's crossing a line, doesn't it?
Mr. Wrong Number: It does, but it sounds fun, too.
Me: Okay, well, let's keep it clinical.
Mr. Wrong Number: What does that even mean?
Me: I don't know. Like, discussing sex without being intimate.
Mr. Wrong Number: So we're like an old married couple?
Me: No, we're like scientists discussing data.
Mr. Wrong Number: Permission to request an example.
Me: Granted.

I stared into space, smiling and trying to think of something. I typed, Sample question: What is your favorite position? Sample answer: Missionary.

Mr. Wrong Number: Please tell me the sample answer isn't your actual boring-ass answer.
Me: I cannot answer until the game officially begins.
Mr. Wrong Number: Let's go.
Me: Wait. If you're a really freaky dude, like into stuff that requires chat rooms to meet others like you or if you have a special sex room, I would like to respectfully bow out of this game. No judgment, but we're just on different levels.
Mr. Wrong Number: What if it's just a tiny sex closet?
Me: Tiny Sex Closet. Band name—called it.
Mr. Wrong Number: Question One—What's your favorite position?
Me: I like being on top.
Mr. Wrong Number: Question Two—Traditional on top, or reverse cowgirl?

That made me literally laugh out loud, and I rolled onto my stomach.

Me: Okay, what is with that? First of all, who names sexual positions? Is it high schoolers? It has to be because the names are so idiotic. Unless a Stetson is a requirement for the position. Then it is perfectly appropriate. Secondly, if any female says reverse cowgirl is her favorite, she's lying. The angle is all wrong and who wants to use knobby knees for leverage?

Mr. Wrong Number: Wow. Tell me how you really feel.

Me: Okay, your turn. Question One: What's your favorite position?

Mr. Wrong Number: I like the missionary/from-behind combo.

Me: I didn't know we could do a combo. And I thought you said missionary was boring.

Mr. Wrong Number: No, I said it's boring for you. I'm really good at it, though.

I rolled my eyes and set down the phone. What was wrong with me? Why was I feeling so giddy, talking to a stranger? I'd seen every episode of MTV's *Catfish*; I knew the facts.

But still, I was smitten with my anonymous friend.

The only thing that made my affinity for this weird texting connection okay was that I wanted this guy to be anonymous forever. I didn't ever want to meet him or get to know him in real life; that would ruin whatever made this so great.

So I was fine to play a little.

I opened the door and went into the kitchen for some water. I needed to cool down a bit or I'd end up sending boob pics to a stranger like some sort of irresponsible college girl. I walked over to the fridge, and just as I was opening it, Colin came out of his room.

Oh, sweet Lord.

He was shirtless and shredded, wearing only a pair of black boxer briefs that showed off the corded muscles in his thighs, and I felt the heat rush up my chest and burn my cheeks as I quickly trained my eyes on his face.

Don't look down, don't look down, don't look down.

"Hey." I struggled to make my suddenly dry mouth form words. "I didn't know you were back."

"Well, I am." He walked over, completely confident in his underwear. He looked a little less sarcastic than usual, somehow a little softer as he gave me a half grin. "Looks like it's a thirsty night for everyone."

Wow. Thirsty.

And so much naked.

I cleared my throat and grabbed two bottles of water. "Definitely."

I extended one to him and he took it, his voice a little scratchy when he said, "Thanks."

I think I managed to say *blerg-g'night* or something equally eloquent.

When I got back to my phone, I read Wrong Number's message and felt a little giggly.

Mr. Wrong Number: Last question for the night. Long and slow, or fast and furious?

I imagined there was a sexy eloquence I should invoke, but I couldn't stop myself from my knee-jerk answer.

Me: Fast and furious. Every time.

Mr. Wrong Number: You're not into hot oil, Enya-on-a-loop, tantric kind of bedding?

Wow. I bit down on my lip, wondered yet again what the hell I was doing with this whole exchanging-sex-talk-with-a-stranger thing, and then I responded.

Me: I'll take back-scratching, shoulder-biting, frantic-sex-against-a-wall for five hundred, Alex.
Mr. Wrong Number: I knew you were smart, Misdial. Sweet dreams, okay?

I lay back on the mattress and wondered when it'd gotten so hot.

Me: Like I'm sleeping now, jackass. G'night.

4

Olivia

I REREAD THE END OF THE COLUMN OUT LOUD.

Because the magical thing about having boys is that you somehow manage to adore them in spite of the whiplash-inducing swings they take between beloved and belligerent. One minute they're charming you, waxing poetic about how your hair looks like actual princess hair, and the next, they're wrinkling their noses and informing you that your breath smells like feet. One second they're snuggling, and the next they're leading you to the bathroom to show you how big their poop is.

I suppose that explains the phenomenon of men pulling a "Dutch oven" on their partners. The adorable little boys have grown into men, and they've managed to find spouses who, like their mothers, love them enough to not murder them for their precociousness.

I do not believe my partner would be so lucky.

I saved the article and attached it to the email, nervous but also excited. I'd woken that morning to discover a message from Glenda, asking me to write a quick sample draft of a parenting column. Apparently the job was narrowed down to me and one other candidate, and she was hoping I might nail my audition piece and make the thing a tiebreaker.

Talk about pressure.

"Here goes nothing," I muttered, hitting send and looking around my office bedroom like I didn't even know where I was. The minute I'd seen the email on my phone that morning, I climbed out of bed and went straight to work at the desk. It was now 12:25 p.m., and I felt like I'd just woken up.

I opened the door and all was quiet, so I wandered into the living room, doing a few sock spins across the wood floor.

Man, those boys had *such* an incredible apartment.

I had no idea how Jack could afford it, even with a roommate. Colin, on the other hand . . . the apartment actually screamed his name, with his fancy job and annoyingly suave looks. When I'd seen *Crazy, Stupid, Love* on rerun in high school, I'd been convinced that Colin was Jacob Palmer's separated-at-birth twin or something. Same attitude, same impeccable style, same cockiness.

My stomach growled and I went over to the kitchen. I still hadn't made it to the grocery store, so I was going to have to replace whatever I ate. It only took a few peeks in the cupboards to remember there was nothing good for me to steal. Everything in the pantry was either canned vegetables super healthy (clearly Colin's) or pickles and bologna, both of which were already expired (obviously my brother's).

I was about to give up and run down to the gas station for a pack of Top Ramen when I opened the freezer. *Bingo.* Not only was there a pound of ground beef, but I knew I'd seen some canned tomatoes in the pantry that would go with it perfectly.

I started opening and closing cupboards, desperately searching because I only needed a few staples to make a killer batch of my grandma's spaghetti and meatballs for dinner. If I could find the right ingredients, or something remotely close, I could do a nice thing and have dinner waiting for my roommates when they got home. Also, I could scarf down meatballs throughout the course of the day so I wouldn't die of starvation.

Win-win.

"Yes." I found crackers and there was one egg in the fridge, so I was golden. Minced garlic, onion powder—yep, it'd work. I'd have to go to the store for pasta, but I needed to get a couple other things, anyway. I didn't have much money, but I also couldn't keep going to the mall before every job interview to use the "try-me" makeup, either.

The Estée Lauder lady was going to call the cops if I didn't buy my own mascara soon.

I found a baking sheet and started rolling out the meatballs, but as I starting shaping them between my palms, thoughts started creeping in. Unwelcome, responsible thoughts that made me realize that if Glenda called and offered me the job, I had to say no.

I *had* to.

Because as badly as I wanted it and as desperately as I needed it, I couldn't start that job knowing I'd have to lie to her every single day. I'd been lying like a criminal since I'd pulled into town, God only knows why, but that wasn't usually my thing and it needed to stop.

Also, Omaha was one of those small-town-in-a-city places where everyone knew everyone else's cousin, so there was no way I'd be able to write that column without *someone* latching on to the fact that a single, childless mess of a human was covering parenting.

No, it wouldn't take long *at all* for the truth to get back to Glenda.

I shoved the meatballs into the oven while I worked on the sauce, forcing myself to focus on food instead of negativity. I opened the cans and started pouring everything into the shiny silver pot that had clearly cost a fortune; I mean, it had a French name I couldn't pronounce, so it had to be top dollar, right?

I used a whisk to cut through the tomato paste before turning the gourmet burner (thank God it was electric because I'd recently come to fear the open flame) up to high and looking through the cupboards for a colander. There was one in a deep drawer, a perfectly spotless silver colander that either had never been used or had been cleaned by a robot. I held it up and I could literally see my reflection in it.

I could also see the sauce behind me bubbling over in the reflection.

Shit.

It took a quick run-slide combo to get the pot off the burner as red sauce bubbled out and all over the stovetop. I fumbled through the drawers and found a big metal spoon and started stirring, which made the colander slip out from where I'd tucked it under my arm and fall onto the floor.

And *of course* it was dented on one side. I rolled my eyes and moved it with my foot. That was why I'd always used a cheap plastic colander; you couldn't hurt those. But one tiny bounce for the shiny strainer left it looking like it'd been tossed from a moving car.

I ran into the bedroom while the meatballs finished baking, and changed into the black jeggings I'd worn almost every day my senior year and a Pink hooded T-shirt. I hadn't remembered visiting Victoria's Secret very often in my youth, but I also seemed to have shirts from the lingerie store in every color.

I slid my feet into my old gray Chucks and ran back into the kitchen. I stirred the sauce and took out the meatballs, which smelled so wonderful, before dumping them into the pot. The sauce was good to bubble all day, so I just needed to run to the store and be back in time to clean everything up before the boys got home.

Of course, in light of my recent history, I double-checked five times that the stove was entirely clear of flammable items before I grabbed my purse and keys. It wasn't even one yet, and they didn't get home until after five o'clock.

I had plenty of time.

"OHMIGOD—LIVVIE?"

I turned around in the checkout line and there was Sara Mills, one of my friends from high school. She was still just as pretty, but now she had an Afro that elevated her to runway model *gorgeous*. "Ohmigod, Sara? How are you?"

Sara was one of those three-people-removed-from-the-best-friend kind of friends, where you hung out a lot in high school but always within the confines of the group. We'd shared a lot of good times but completely lost touch after graduation.

She smiled. "I'm good. Living out in West Omaha. I married Trae Billings and we've got a baby—she's six months old."

"No way!" I reached over to hug her and knocked over a box of end-cap cookies with my purse. "Congratulations!"

She laughed and hugged me back. "Same old Liv."

I nodded and picked up the box from the floor. "Unfortunately."

She bit down on her bottom lip and said, "Yeah, I heard about the fire."

"You did?" I adjusted my purse strap and said, "For the love of God, it was only a few days ago. That was fast."

She made a face. "Well, you kind of went viral."

"That senior superlative actually came true, didn't it?"

Yes, I was voted Most Likely to End Up in a Viral Video.

She laughed and I realized that I really missed having friends. In Chicago I had Eli and I had coworkers, but I hadn't had any true "girlfriends" since college. Which was probably why I squealed when she said, "Do you have time to grab a coffee next door? I'd love to catch up."

"Totally."

We chatted while the clerk rang up her groceries—responsible adult things like milk, bread, and vegetables—and then he rang up mine: a case of Top Ramen, a bag of Gardetto's, off-brand tampons, spaghetti, and a twelve-pack of Diet Coke.

My phone buzzed, and I was disappointed to see it was my mom and not my anonymous pal. Your dad needs help with some yard work if you want to make some extra money.

I glanced up, horrified and embarrassed even though no one in the checkout lane could see the text. Was she serious with that—yard work? As in, I could mow the lawn and trim the bushes for an extra thirty-spot from Daddy? Clearly, in my parents' eyes, I had reverted to a fourteen-year-old.

And I knew it shouldn't bother me, but it did.

Because—shit—were they right? I wondered this as I paid for my groceries with the cash my parents had given me, which was both terribly ironic and incredibly pathetic.

I need to get a damned job.

I followed Sara next door and we grabbed a table outside. While ankle-deep in grocery bags, with the late-afternoon sun beating down on our faces, she and I laughed until we were crying as I told her about my Chicago implosion and the resultant fire.

"You found out he was cheating the day you got laid off? And your apartment burned down *that night*? Holy shit!" She was laughing, but it was nice. I could tell she was horrified by my consistent bad luck, as opposed to being entertained by it. "We should be at a bar, for God's sake, not a coffee shop."

Somehow that transitioned into my current living arrangements, and she freaked out when I told her who Jack's roommate was.

"Girl. Are you telling me that you're living with Colin Beck?"

I nodded.

"Colin Beck. Holy hell. Is he still hot?"

"Hotter, actually."

"What a prick."

"Right?"

"I always thought he looked like Ryan Gos—"

"Still does."

She grinned and settled back in her chair. "So your luck just might be changing."

"Oh, God, no." I took a sip of my latte and let the foam float around in my mouth before swallowing. "He's still an asshole. He looks at me like he knows he's better than me."

"Really? Is that how he is?" She pushed her sunglasses up her nose. "I just always thought he seemed intense. Like he had a lot going on in his head. Didn't he get a perfect ACT?"

"Did everyone know he was smart except me?"

"Looks like." She pushed back her chair and stood as my phone buzzed on the table. "I'm running to the restroom. Be right back."

I waited to check my messages until she went inside.

Mr. Wrong Number: I've been in a meeting with a woman for 35 minutes, and she has no idea that there is pear on her chin.

Me: How do you know it's pear?

Mr. Wrong Number: Because it looks like those slippery canned pears.

Me: It could be something gross. Maybe she puked up her lunch just before your meeting and that's a chunk.

Mr. Wrong Number: Ignoring that. What do I do, though? Do I say something?

I coughed out a laugh and typed: You can NOT say anything. It's too late now.

Mr. Wrong Number: But it's driving me insane. I can't concentrate on anything but the pear.
Me: You mean the chunk.
Mr. Wrong Number: You're killing me, Misdial.

"Who is making you smile like that?"

My cheeks got hot and I grinned at Sara, who sat back down and looked at me expectantly.

"Oh, my God, finally someone I can tell."

I told her all about Mr. Wrong Number: how it happened, our pact of anonymity, and the frequency of our chats.

"This is the funniest thing I've ever heard!" She gave me an openmouthed smile. "I wonder what he looks like."

"Right? Like, I have no interest in ever knowing who he is, but it's a fascinating thing to ponder."

"Ponder my ass. You mean fantasize about."

I shrugged. "Potato, po-tah-toe."

"You be careful, though, Miss Unlucky. Combine your bad mojo with the dark corners of the internet, and all of a sudden you've got a creepy stalker breaking into your house to steal your panties."

My phone rang and I recognized the number; it was Glenda.

"Oh, my God—I have to take this. It's about a job I interviewed for—"

"Say no more." She stood and said, "I have to get home anyway. Call me and we'll do lunch soon, okay?"

I waved while she grabbed her stuff, and then answered with a nervous "Hello?"

"Olivia, it's Glenda. How are you?"

Man, just hearing her voice made my stomach hurt. "Great, how are you?"

"I'm good. This is kind of a weird call, because I've been in meetings for hours and everything about the job you interviewed for has changed."

That couldn't be good. "Okay . . . ?"

I heard a door close. "They want the position to be anonymous, and for the column to be written as the 402 Mom. We'll use a cartoon avatar of, you know, a trendy and adorable mom; they're working on the logo mock-up as we speak. But everyone loves the idea of this branded unknown. They want to promote the hell out of this thing, our super cool 402 Mom; so are you okay with the area code pseudonym thing? I'm offering you the job, by the way—did I say that yet?"

"What?" Anonymous? "Wow. No, Glen—"

"Oh, good Lord, I'm a real mess, aren't I?" She laughed at herself and then just sort of launched a slew of information at me. She wanted to run my sample column as the launch piece, and the job would now be writing half the time for the 402 Mom, and half the time providing assorted content—entertainment, lifestyle, local—under my actual name like the rest of the paper's bloggers.

Which would be chef's-kiss perfect, because I'd have a by-line for my parents to see as proof of legitimate employment.

"Wow." My head was spinning. I was being offered the job, and that job was going to be anonymous? So no one who knew me would know non-mom Liv was the mom bomb? I was glad I had on sunglasses because no matter how fast and hard I blinked, the tears wouldn't go away. It was just *such* a perfect position and it sucked so hard that I had to turn it down.

"And did I mention it's a remote position? We'll set you up with a phone, a laptop, a printer, and all that so you won't have to commute to the office every day."

"That sounds incredible, Glenda. But the thing is . . ."

I stopped. Everything stopped. I looked at the downtown all around me, with people bustling and horns honking and the smell of old garbage intermingling with the smell of fried food, and I just couldn't do it. I couldn't bring myself to say no.

Instead I heard myself say, "That sounds incredible. Thank you so much, Glenda."

"Welcome aboard, Olivia. I'll have HR email over our new-hire packet with benefit info, online orientation, job duties, and so on, and we'll set up a Zoom meeting your first day to get everything rolling. Sound good?"

I grinned and wanted to jump up and down, even as I was 100 percent certain that this was a terrible mistake. "Sounds great."

I hung up the phone and squealed, loud enough for everyone in the outside seating area to stop talking and stare at me. I shrugged and said to the blond influencer at the next table, "I got the job—sorry."

I walked back to the apartment with loaded arms and it didn't even faze me; that's how happy I was. I mean, who cared that the Diet Coke was making my biceps burn when I had a dream job that I was going to be starting in mere days?

There was a marketing department working on my promos that very minute, for the love of God.

My luck was looking pretty damned good all of a sudden.

I made a quick stop at the liquor store for a bottle of shiraz before humming all the way home, and I didn't even drop anything when I struggled to punch in the code for the security gate. I wished that dick Eli knew I was landing on my feet. The last time I'd seen him I cried—and then punched him in the stomach—before running out the door like a bawling child.

Not exactly a strong exit.

Part of me really wanted to text him, but I couldn't risk him killing my buzz.

I was still humming as I opened the front door. But the second I closed it behind me Jack appeared, glaring at me with his hands on his hips. "What the hell did you do to the kitchen?"

"What?" I glanced over at the spotless kitchen—my sauce smelled amazing, by the way—and said, "It looks perfect. Why are we whispering?"

He just raised an eyebrow like he was waiting for me to get it.

And then I did.

The kitchen hadn't been spotless when I left. The kitchen had been a disaster when I left. I said, "Did you clean it up?"

He just shook his head and pointed toward Colin's room. "*He* did, and he was already pissed at me for springing a month-long roomie on him last minute. I told him you wouldn't trash the place when he agreed to let you stay. Why couldn't you just pick up after yourself?"

I stepped out of my Chucks and whisper-yelled, "Why is he home already?"

"I don't know."

"Aren't you best friends?"

"We're grown-ass men, moron. We don't tell each other our schedules."

"Seriously?"

"Seriously."

I rolled my eyes. "So, what—did he bitch to you about the mess like he's the house mother here? It *is* half your apartment, you wuss. Get a backbone."

"First of all, it's *his* condo and I pay him rent, which he gives me a big-ass break on, so as always, you're wrong."

"Oh, well, that makes—"

"Second of all, he didn't have to bitch to me because we got home and witnessed your war zone at the same time, numb nuts. I called you a dipshit and took a shower, and by the time I got out it looked like this."

"Geez, Jack, how long was your shower?"

"Shh." He looked over his shoulder, then looked back at me with his face contorted like I was full-out screaming. "And don't do that. Don't turn this on me when you're the one who keeps screwing up and it's only been a week."

"I know, I know." I went around him and set my grocery bags on the counter. "You're right and I'm sorry."

His face screwed up again. "What?"

"Listen, I can fix this." I felt a little bad for putting Jack in a bad position with Colin, especially now that I knew he was doing my brother a major favor by letting him live there for a cheaper rent. "Tell Colin that dinner will be ready at seven, there's good wine, and I have news that will make him happy enough to forgive my little kitchen transgression."

He narrowed his eyes. "Did you make Grandma's meatballs just to butter us up?"

"Yep."

"You tricky little shit, that might actually work." He breathed in deeply and said, "I'll tell him. But just quit being a screwup, okay?"

"Okay." That actually stung a little. "But keep your asses in your rooms until seven."

AT EXACTLY SEVEN o'clock, as I was standing in front of the island, trying my damnedest to open a bottle of wine, Colin came out of his room. He'd clearly dressed for dinner, wearing a button-down shirt and a really nice pair of pants, and I felt like a moron in the black-and-white polka-dot sundress that I'd worn to the "beach party" dance my junior year.

He looked hot and sophisticated as hell, and I was wearing the same thing I'd sported when I was first-based by Alex Brown in the front seat of his dad's Camaro. I'd paired the dress with a black hair scarf and red lipstick, but I still felt like I was wearing the Ghost of Fashions Past.

Colin walked over, his eyes laughing, and he cleared his throat. "Need some help, Liv?"

"What kind of stupid corkscrew is this?" My entire face and neck were hot as I held up the sleek device that looked a little pornographic to me. "It's like rich people want to make things difficult so the rest of us feel dumb."

"Which rich people are you referring to?" He took the wine bottle from my hands, and two motions later it was open.

I rolled my eyes and turned my back to him, walking over to the stove. "The people who make idiotic corkscrews like that. And the pretentious boobs who buy them."

That made him laugh and he followed me into the kitchen. "Did you just call me a pretentious boob?"

I gave him a *duh* look over my shoulder. "Look around you, oh pretentious one. I mean, don't get me wrong, I'm sure the chicks dig it. This is a nice-ass bachelor pad; I'd lose my shit if I came home with you and got to hop around on your pillow-soft million-dollar bed. But I just can't imagine spending so much money on *stuff*."

Shit, shit, shit. Yes, I'd really just mentioned hopping around on his bed.

His face didn't change, thank God, and he stuck his hands in his pockets and said, "You don't know how much I've spent. Maybe I got it all for free."

I ignored that and said, "Your colander is sterling silver."

"So I like nice things—sue me." He tilted his head, and his eyes dropped to my back as he mused, "If I can afford quality, why would I buy garbage?"

"A plastic colander isn't necessarily garbage. Who says silver is better?"

"Is that why you dented it?" He walked over to the cupboard on my right and took out three wineglasses. "Because it's too pretentious for you?"

My head rolled back on my shoulders of its own accord and I stirred the sauce with a big spoon. "Of course you noticed the dent."

But when I looked over at him, his eyes were on my back again. What the hell—did I have back-fat jiggle action going on or something? They stayed there as he said, "Of course I noticed, because I fucking have eyes, Liv. The dented colander was on the floor of the entryway when I got home."

"I'll buy you a new plastic one, which I guarantee will last longer than this thing." I turned to face him, strangely desperate to hide my back as I said, "But forget the colander, because I have amazing news that will actually make *you* happier than everyone else in the world. I mean, other than me."

His eyes were now focused on my face as he waited for the news, and I got stuck in a pause. He must've sensed my Colin-is-so-hot-I'm-rendered-mute condition, because one side of his mouth went up and he asked, quietly, "First tell me what your tattoo says."

Oh. The tattoo. It was silly, but I was unbelievably relieved there wasn't some unsightly and disgusting blob on my back that'd attracted his attention. The tattoo was a quote from *Pride and Prejudice* that stretched down my spine in loose cursive, so Colin would never get close enough to read the whole thing.

"What are you, a cop?" I said it just as quietly, and I wondered if it was my dinner pregaming that made the air suddenly crackle. I said around a smile, "I don't have to tell you anything."

"Don't make me—"

"Wine me, bro." Jack ran across the living room floor in socks and slid into the kitchen, stopping right between us and releasing all of the air's electricity. He was holding out his hand, waiting for a glass, and I had to laugh because he was such a moron.

Still smirking at me, Colin poured him a glass and put it in Jack's extended hand as my brother said, "What is this amazing news, Livvie? You've been found not guilty on all counts of arson?"

"Nope. They still think I burned down the building on purpose."

Jack's eyes darted over like he thought I was serious, which made me shake my head and mutter, "You're such a gullible idiot."

I'd actually gotten an email from the fire marshal that morning with great news on the investigation. As it turned out, my apartment had been the only occupied unit in the building because renovations were underway; mine had been next in line. Apparently the construction company had left some hazardous materials in the stairwell that hadn't been stored properly, which was why the whole building went up into a fast blaze instead of my love letters being pretty much the sole cause of the fire.

Bottom line: I no longer had to worry about being liable for the entire building burning down, thank the sweet heavens.

I turned back to the stove, shut off the burner, and grabbed the handles on the huge pot of boiling pasta.

Colin said, "Hold up, Liv."

I gave him side-eye as he shouldered in and took the handles from me. "Let me guess, sexist, you don't think I'm strong enough to drain a pot of noodles."

Jack groaned and walked over to the beer fridge. "Here we go with the ballbusting."

But Colin lifted the pot, carried it to the sink, and started pouring the water into the colander. "Wrong. You're strong enough, but I'm afraid your Liv luck will kick in and you'll do something like sneeze and throw a pot of scalding water at my face."

"That's fair, actually." I followed him and grabbed the bottle of olive oil from the counter. "Do you think that after you drain the spaghetti, Mr. Saving the World from My Wrath, you can pour me some wine so I don't spill it all over your fancy wood floors?"

"Consider it done." He took the oil from my hand and started drizzling it on the pasta while watching me. "As soon as you tell me your news."

"I could tell you now," I said, turning away from him and walking toward the table, "but where's the fun in that?"

I pulled a lighter from my pocket and lit the candles I'd placed at the center of the table. The whole tableau looked gorgeous, from the pretty white plates to the flickering pillars to the ivory cloth napkins, but it was the dusky lowlights of the city just outside those ginormous windows that made the scene stunning.

When I turned back around, they were both staring at me in shock. Specifically, they were staring at the lighter in my hand, two frozen dudes who appeared to be holding their collective breaths.

"Oh, my God, would you two relax? My one fire was more than enough."

"TO ME, AND to my fantastical new job."

"Holy balls, Liv, you've toasted yourself like ten times." Jack leaned back in his chair and said, "Why don't you save a little for when the job actually starts?"

I didn't care what Jack thought, because Colin was giving me a smirk and I was tipsy-happy at that moment. I said, "First of all, my debut article is in the process of being edited, so technically I've already started. Second, I've got to take celebration where I can get it, bro."

"Yeah, good point." Jack raised his glass, as did Colin, and we clinked yet again.

I let the wine warm the back of my throat and I said, "Let me ask you something, Beck."

"Oh, so we're doing the last-name thing. Okay."

I rolled my eyes and giggled. I was a giggler when I drank. "Were you shocked that I got a job so fast?"

"What?"

"You're just so . . . um . . . I'm-perfect-at-everything-and-you're-a-screwup Colin Beck that I'm guessing you were terrified I'd be living here for a year or longer."

He swallowed—damn, he had a sexy throat—and said, "I never doubted that you'd be gone in a month."

Jack snorted. "You didn't? Man, you had way more confidence in her than I did."

Colin's mouth twitched and he stared into his glass. It seemed like he wasn't going to answer, but then he said, "It had nothing to do with Olivia. We had a thirty-day agreement, and as such, the agreed-upon exit date was thirty days from her arrival."

I could tell by his face that Colin wasn't talking about me. This was business Colin, the guy who wore thousand-dollar suits and had no patience for breach of contract.

Jack started laughing. "You would've kicked her out?"

I said, "I would've shanked you both before I stayed longer than a month, so it doesn't matter."

They laughed, and I was glad I'd cooked them dinner. Colin had visibly loosened up when I told him I'd be moving out soon, and it was the first time I'd really hung out with Jack since moving back.

It'd been—dare I say it—a fun evening.

My phone buzzed and I glanced down at it.

Sara: So did you get the job?

"A good hostess never texts at the table," my brother teased.

"Your phone vibrates so loudly." Colin pointed and said, "You might as well turn the sound on, the way it buzzes. Is it broken?"

"That's why mine is always on silent," Jack said.

Colin said, "Same."

"No, it's not broken." At least I didn't think it was. I responded to Sara, and every time she sent a text back, Jack and Colin made fun of it. They soon lost interest and started talking about sports, so I tuned them out.

Gulping down the last bit of wine in my glass, I picked up my phone and texted: What's up, Wrong Number?

As if knowing I'd just mentally disengaged, the timer on the smart TV kicked on for the Cubs game, so the boys drifted into the living room. I set my napkin on my plate as my phone buzzed.

Mr. Wrong Number: Just finished eating.
Me: Exciting night?

I glanced over at Jack and Colin, who were already sitting and staring at their phones in front of the TV.

Mr. Wrong Number: Not at all, which is why I'm happy you're texting.
Me: I'm not exciting.
Mr. Wrong Number: I believe we ended last night with you telling me that you prefer a good up-against-the-wall bang. Call me crazy, but that's hella exciting.

I snorted a giggle and glanced up. Jack and Colin were both looking at me, Colin with an eyebrow raised, and I couldn't help it; I beamed and giggled again. I thought about trying to explain it away, but instead just waved a hand.

Me: Wow—right back at it, are we?

Mr. Wrong Number: I'd be lying if I said I hadn't spent a fair amount of time today thinking about your response.

Me: And therein lies the joy of anonymity—I don't have to be embarrassed.

Mr. Wrong Number: Hell, no, you don't. Own that shit.

Me: Wouldn't it be great if you could be straight-up honest about these things with an actual partner? I mean, some people say they are, or claim that it's healthy to speak 100% truth, but that's total bullshit. Because if you care about someone, you're not going to look them in the face when they're gently kissing you and say "can you knock it off and just bend me over the counter, babe?"

Mr. Wrong Number: Not a fan of kissing?

I thought about that before responding. I liked kissing, but I liked hot, wild, I-might-accidentally-draw-blood kissing. Gentle kisses made you love-drunk. They made you think and feel and get lulled into believing you were in love, that both of you were, when in reality it was just two mouths mating with each other.

I wasn't interested in ever getting drunk on that shit again.

Me: Imagine if you could just order what you wanted like you were at a restaurant.

Mr. Wrong Number: Example, please.

Me: Good evening, Garçon. For starters, I would like the one orgasm oral—fast and intense, please. And for the entrée, I think I'd like to get flipped over and pounded from behind.

Mr. Wrong Number: Would you like dessert with that, sunshine?

I made another noise, apparently, because Jack was shaking his head when I looked up from my phone.

"Are we a middle schooler now, texting boys at the dinner table? What's with all the giggles?"

I felt the red streak across my hot cheeks. "I have funny friends, that's all. More entertaining than baseball."

"Says you."

I rolled my eyes and went back to the titillating conversation I was having with Mr. Wrong Number.

Me: Yes. I would like the chef's special—the deep sleep on my side of the bed with absolutely no spooning. (Hands back menu, takes sip of water)

"Any wine left in that bottle, Liv?"

I looked over at Colin, feeling totally busted. "Um, what?"

He gave me a funny look. "Did you kill the shiraz?"

"Oh. No." I wrapped my fingers around the bottle and held it up, peering through the dark green glass. "Looks like there are at least two glasses left."

"Nice." Colin stood and stretched his back while I set the phone next to my plate and went to the kitchen for a Dr Pepper. I didn't give it a thought as I went in search of a sobering beverage, but as soon as I heard my phone buzz—it *was* really loud—

my head whipped in that direction. Much to my horror, he was looking down at the table, staring at my phone as the screen lit up from an incoming text.

Shit, shit, shit. I was an adult, but I didn't want that jackhammer to see my sexual dinner menu. I casually speed-walked to the table, grabbed my phone, and looked at him, but he was filling his glass while appearing to watch the Cubs game on the TV.

Whew, he hadn't seen anything. I unlocked the screen.

Mr. Wrong Number: Well I promise, if we were together irl, I would happily serve up that order. Hell, it's what I would fantasize about you ordering, tbh.

It wasn't logical, but his response sent a shiver through me. My fingers slid over the touch screen.

Me: Well it's a shame we can't . . . share a meal. Eat together. Ugh, gross. No way to make it sound like I'm not being creepy. I'm just saying that it's nice to share a common interest, alright?!

I hit send, then added: Did that sound horndog creepy?

I hit send on that, but then felt the need to add: You know what I mean, right?

I looked up as I hit send, and Colin wasn't looking at the TV anymore. No, he was staring down at the phone in his hand as if he'd never seen a phone before.

5

Colin

HOLY SHIT.

Miss Misdial is Olivia?

She couldn't be.

What in the actual fuck?

It couldn't be possible, but I'd seen my text on her screen under the contact name of Mr. Wrong Number.

"You okay, Beck?"

I stared at my phone as it went dark and the messages disappeared. I didn't want to look at her, didn't want to see her face at that moment, but still I raised my eyes from the phone. Olivia was eyeing me from her spot at the table with an amused smirk, the smart-ass grin she always wore for me tilting up one side of her mouth.

"Fine." I cleared my throat and slid my phone into my pocket. "Goddamned wonderful."

I carried my glass over to the sink, needing to get out of there and clear my head. Because I wasn't fine or goddamned wonderful. I set it on the counter, turned on the faucet, and clenched my teeth so hard they hurt. Apparently God had a sense of humor, and Olivia the Hottest Mess Marshall was my fantasy texter.

Hell.

I liked Liv just fine—she was easy on the eyes and fun to mess with—but Misdial was on another level. *Or so I thought.* I'd thought she was funny, charming, sexy, smart, unorthodox, and even kind of sweet.

Not like Olivia.

Could it really be her?

I started scrubbing one of the plates in the sink and felt gutted, like I'd just lost something by losing Misdial. Honestly, I was so damned disappointed I wanted to hit something. I wanted to tee off on something so badly because just like that, without warning, I no longer had a relationship with a stranger on the phone.

And not only was it over for me, but I was going to have to ghost her.

There was no other option.

I couldn't tell Olivia the truth; I'd shared too much and couldn't deal with her having that kind of information. And I definitely couldn't keep texting anonymously now that I knew Jack's baby sister was the recipient.

Oh, hell no.

So . . . I was done. I was done, it was finished, and I was going to have to nut up about the entire debacle and get over it. I'd known better anyway, right?

"So since I cooked, are you doing the dishes?" Olivia appeared at my side, but her perfume had reached me before she did. "I think that's the rule."

She was holding out her dirty plate, her eyes asking permission to dump the dirty dish on me, and I immediately regretted my decision to look at her. Because she looked the same. Long, dark hair, green eyes, pink cheeks—the same Liv I'd always known.

But now she was cross-contaminated with little bits of Misdial. Instead of just seeing the face of Jack's sister, my brain kept loading up things I knew about her, like the fact that she preferred shoulder-biting, frenetic sex against the wall to a sweet romance.

Shit.

I looked back at the sink; I needed time to absorb this jarring turn of events before I laid eyes on her again. "That is the rule."

"Seriously?" I saw in my periphery that she tilted her head, and I could feel her eyes on me.

"Seriously. You had a big day; I'll get the dishes."

She said, "Wow," but stayed put beside me.

God, I just need her to go away. "Better go before I change my mind."

"Colin." She was telling me to look at her with her tone of voice.

"Olivia." I did look at her then, and she was giving me a tiny smile. I shifted my weight to one foot and hoped I looked as exasperated as I felt, because I needed her gone. I raised an eyebrow. “What?”

She nudged me with her elbow, a playful touch of her funny bone to my side, and said, “Thanks for being cool tonight. It was kind of fun until you weirded out at the end.”

She was too close, too earnest, too playful, and I was careful to keep my voice level as I said, “Sure. Now go to bed, Olivia.”

She slow blinked another grin. “Sweet dreams, Colin.”

6

Olivia

MY ALARM WENT OFF, AND EVERYTHING INSIDE ME WANTED to ignore it and sleep in.

But I couldn't risk it. I couldn't risk jeopardizing all of the big-girl, adult things that were finally happening in my life by going back to my undisciplined ways. I had to keep the New Olivia thing going.

Besides, I could always nap on Colin's bed after he went to work.

I put on cutoff sweat shorts and a *Just Do It* T-shirt with a swoosh that had worn completely away, brushed my teeth, and pulled my hair back in a ponytail. Five minutes later I was riding the elevator down to the lobby, adjusting my earbuds while clicking on my favorite running playlist.

And then I was off.

The morning sun was just starting to come up and the city

streets were quiet; it was a perfect morning to run. And the running itself actually felt good for once. I was killing the game, jogging four whole blocks without stopping, when I nearly ran over a dude who was tying his shoe. I came around the corner like a shot, really feeling my stride, when all of a sudden—boom—there he was in the middle of the sidewalk. I tried to sidestep with a graceful, deer-like leap, but ended up tripping over my own feet, sprawling out over the sidewalk, and landing on my knees.

Hard.

"*Shiiiiit*," I hissed through my teeth.

I looked down at my knees and they were both skinned and starting to bleed like I was a fallen kindergartener at recess. And they hurt so screamingly bad that I wanted to bawl. I rolled over so I was sitting up, and tried not to moan.

"Oh, my God—are you okay?"

I looked up and blinked fast as a handsome face and a backward hat looked down at me. I muttered to myself, "Seriously? Are you freaking kidding me?"

Apparently he heard me, because he smiled. "It's no big deal; people fall all the time."

How wonderful to fall like a clumsy oaf in front of a guy who looked cute *and* nice. I climbed to my feet, jumping up and smiling like my kneecaps didn't feel broken and my palms weren't scraped. "I'm fine."

"You're bleeding." He had on sunglasses, but I knew he was looking down at my knees, one of which had a stream of blood running from it.

"Nah." I waved a hand in the air and made a ridiculously

perky face. "I bleed easily. Like all the time. It's seriously no big deal. Um, have a good day, I guess."

I turned away from him and just started running, throwing my hand up in a wave as I did my best to disappear from his sight. I sprinted down the block, desperate to put as much space between him and me as possible, but after about twenty seconds he caught up to me.

Dammit, he started running alongside me.

I didn't even look at him. "What are you doing?"

"Running." There was a smile in his voice as he said, "Do you always run this fast?"

Keeping with the whole compulsive-liar thing, I said, "Yep. It's okay if you can't keep up."

"Oh, I can keep up." I did glance at him then, and he was grinning when he said, "Last one to Starbucks buys?"

I didn't have any money on me, but I wanted a coffee more than I wanted to breathe. I could see Starbucks, so I decided to go for it and said, "You're on."

I took off, running as fast as my legs would carry me. Thank God there were no people around at that early hour, because I was hard-charging down the sidewalk. I could hear the guy's footsteps beside me, so I knew he was keeping up, but I couldn't afford to look over at him or I'd fall down again.

I flew down the block, and when we finally got to Starbucks, I slammed my hands into the door like I was safe on base in a neighborhood game of hide-and-seek. "First!"

I touched the door only a millisecond before the dude, but winning tasted good. He smiled like he didn't mind losing and said, "A deal's a deal. Guess I'm buying you a coffee."

I smiled back at him, panting and feeling like my lungs might explode. "I guess you are."

We went inside together and ordered, both of us breathing heavy, and he went to the restroom while I waited for our drinks. I slyly watched him walk away, and the view was pretty good. Nice stride—confident steps, prominent calf muscles, rounded derriere; so far, so good.

Side note: This was the *weirdest* way to meet a guy. I mean, we hadn't even exchanged names yet officially—even though I heard him tell the barista that his name was Paul—but we were together at a coffee shop. I pulled out my phone and texted Mr. Wrong Number, who must've crashed hard the night before because he'd gone radio silent on me after dinner.

Me: Get this. I went for a jog, tripped over a dude tying his shoe and I ate it, complete with bloody knees. But now hot runner dude and I are getting coffee together, which begs the question. Soul mate or serial killer?

"Here." He came back with a wet, soapy paper towel in his hand that he extended to me and said, "Clean up your knees before they get infected."

I raised an eyebrow. "Really with that, Mom?"

He smiled again and got bonus points for good teeth, grabbed both of our drinks, and gestured with his head for me to follow him to the outdoor seating area. "Really."

He had my coffee so of course I followed him, exiting the cool air-conditioning and grabbing a table out in the hot, humid summer morning. I wasn't sure I cared for his bossiness, but I was definitely going to drink his coffee while I pondered that decision.

He picked a spot, and as soon as I plopped down in a chair, I kicked my right leg up onto the empty seat beside me and started wiping my knee.

"I'm Paul, by the way." He gave me a nice smile, and I noticed that a fairly thick gold chain rested somewhere under his T-shirt.

"I heard." I returned the grin and pointed to myself. "Olivia."

"I heard," he said, his smile growing a little bigger.

I cleared my throat and said, "By the way, did I apologize for almost trampling you?"

He gave his head a slow shake. "You did not."

"Well, I'm sorry. Although the coffee is delish, so perhaps it all worked out just right."

He smiled at that, a nice big grin, and said, "You might just be spot-on about that."

I WAS NO less taken with Colin and Jack's showerhead that day than I'd been the very first night I arrived. It was glorious, like hot summer rain, and it made me never want to get out. So much so, in fact, that I tended to take luxuriously long showers and completely lose track of time.

That morning was no exception.

I'd run home—nearly collapsing from oxygen deprivation, of course—and the apartment was quiet when I went in. Either the boys were both still asleep or they'd both already left the house, but neither mattered because that delightful shower was available.

As I washed my hair and carefully shaved around the enormous wounds on my knees, I felt pretty good about the whole run-in with Paul. I mean, the dude turned out to be a total nonstarter. I was meeting him for brunch tomorrow, but only because I'd agreed to it *before* learning that, one, he'd never heard of Ruth Bader Ginsburg, and two, he and his buddies loved the wings at Hooters.

Combine those factors with his ridiculous necklace, and it was like the trifecta of meninist bullshit.

But it still felt like a win. I'd managed to charm a handsome guy after eating pavement in front of him, and I must've been marginally interesting that morning because he'd asked me to brunch.

I still had some kind of mojo, right?

After I got out and wrapped myself in a towel, I opened the bathroom door and nearly ran over Colin.

"Ohmigod!" I put my hand over my wet, towel-wrapped chest and looked up at him. Man, he was tall. "How do you keep scaring me?"

And how do I keep running over boys?

He grabbed my upper arms to stop me from tackling him, but his tense jaw and burning blue eyes made my body hyperaware of exactly where each of his fingers were on my skin. I'd barely dried off, so there was water all over my arms and my hair was dripping, but I managed to feel hot in spite of the goose bumps that covered me from head to toe.

Because Colin's tanned, sweaty, über-defined naked chest

was also *right there*. And just below those beautiful pecs were the sinful abs that could only be described as perfection. I knew I needed to force my eyes back up to his face, but it was hard because there we were, inches apart, both slick and baring a *lot* of skin.

"My apologies for interrupting you at *my* house." He let go of my arms and I saw him flex his fingers before his hands dropped to his sides. Seriously? He was flexing his hand like he was Mr. Darcy at freaking Netherfield? He gave me a dickish smile and said, "How dare I?"

I clutched at my towel and matched his dickish tone. "You know what I mean. That's twice that I didn't even know you were here."

He made an intentionally assholish confused face. "But you . . . know I live here, so . . . ? Next time should I schedule my day with you, just so you know where I am?"

"Yeah." I tilted my head and made my own intentionally assholish face. "That'd be great."

"What happened to your knees?" His eyes were still on my face, but apparently he'd already noticed the matching strawberries on both legs.

"I was helping an old lady cross the street."

"Liar." His eyebrows went down. "How would that cut open your knees?"

"Um," I started, not even sure why I was lying about this, "I had to save her and it required a diving maneuver."

"Really." He looked like he knew I was making up stories, but he also looked like he should be on a Nike poster with the words *Just Do It* painted across his sweaty body.

"Yes, really." I narrowed my eyes. "You wouldn't know because you'd never risk your fancy clothes by helping an old lady."

"You don't know that."

I just shrugged.

"So . . . you're not going to tell me what happened, then?" He seemed like he really wanted to know.

So I said, "I don't think I will, actually."

I turned away from him, gripping the front of my towel as I walked to my room, and right as I reached the door he said, "Tell me what it says, Marshall."

I glanced over my shoulder and he still looked serious, but one side of his mouth had hitched up into a half smile as he pointed at the tattoo on my back. I shook my head and said, "Not a chance, Beck."

I shut the door and scrambled into clothes, and a few minutes later I heard him turn on the shower. I wasn't sure what'd happened between us in those few crackling moments, but it'd clearly irritated him and had most likely been a product of my imagination.

After all, I *had* been spending way too much time fantasizing about my anonymous pal. My flirtations with Mr. Wrong Number had most likely boosted my libido to an unhealthy level, resulting in me feeling electricity where there surely was none.

It was Colin, after all; you couldn't have electricity without warmth, right?

And on a random side note: Where the hell had Mr. Wrong Number gone?

Colin

Miss Misdial: Dude, where'd you go? I'd be offended if I wasn't 100% confident that I'm too entertaining for you to ghost.

Dammit.

I dropped the phone on the table, leaned back in the uncomfortable kitchen chair, and stacked my hands on top of my head. Now that I'd had some time to think about it, I was a little surprised I'd never noticed the similarities between Misdial and Olivia before. Every word that "Misdial" had texted—the language and attitude—sounded exactly like Olivia, though Misdial had sent a lot of unexpected content.

I'd lain in bed for hours the night before, scrolling through Misdial's texts and picturing Olivia saying all of those things. I'd felt confused, mashing the two together, and I'd ultimately decided to delete the entire conversation and forget it ever happened. Olivia Marshall was Jack's little sister, and the rest was irrelevant.

Which was fine theoretically, but after seeing her wear my towel like a little black dress, I found myself distracted by whatever the hell she was doing in the office. When the blow-dryer turned on, I was preoccupied with the idea of what she was wearing. Still the towel? And after it shut off, as hard as I tried, I couldn't focus on anything other than the question of *what the hell is she doing in there.*

Because she banged, she thumped, and she made sounds as

if she were literally climbing the walls of my office, all while I tried to do my work at the kitchen table.

As if she heard my thoughts, the office door opened and there she was. Today she was wearing a white sundress with a pair of Chuck Taylors, which was a ridiculous combination but so incredibly Olivia that it looked good on her. The dress hit her in all the good spots, and she did the bun-in-hair, glasses-on-nose combo that I pretty much always appreciated.

Yeah, I definitely had perverted librarian issues.

"I'm going to go work at the coffee shop in the Old Market, so you can have your office for the day." She hitched a bag over her shoulder and gave me *that* look. "Just don't mess it up."

"I'll do my best, oh generous one." I tried to keep my eyes on the Excel spreadsheet in front of me, but I couldn't stop myself from looking at her as she walked by on her way to the door. I'd always known she was attractive, but all of a sudden it was as if the universe was shoving her in my face. Great legs, perfect ass, eyes that squinted when she smiled, and the most adorable tattoo of a tiny typewriter on the back of her neck where it would usually be covered by her hair.

And that perfume. It was one of those scents that punched you in the gut and filled your head with dirty thoughts.

"I can't find my key, so if you go somewhere, will you leave the door unlocked?" She opened the fridge and looked inside, making her skirt rise by an eighth of an inch. *Shit—what the hell is wrong with me?* I watched her grab one of my organic apples as she said, "I'm sure it's hiding in my purse."

"Um, no, I will definitely not be leaving my house unlocked." Such an Olivia thing to say. "Maybe you should stick around until you find the key."

She rolled her eyes. "No, I don't want to do that. I'm going to go."

"Well, okay, then; hope you don't get locked out."

She let out a breath. "You seriously won't leave it open for me?"

"No, I seriously won't leave my house unlocked when no one is home."

"Oh, for God's sake, Beck, can't you—"

"Liv." I held up a hand to get her to stop talking. "I doubt I'm going anywhere, so I'm sure you'll be fine, okay? Just go."

She took a bite of the apple, chewing and looking at me as if she expected me to say more. When I didn't, she just said, "'kay, bye," turned around, and walked right out the door.

Shit.

I had to pull myself together; it wasn't natural for Olivia to get the best of me. The only thing I'd ever had a handle on, when it came to her, was that I had the upper hand. She was a mess; I was in control. She did stupid things, and I mocked her for them. There was no room for this sudden Misdial entanglement to redraw the lines of our acquaintance and have her on top. No way.

Although now that I was thinking about it, she'd once told me that she liked being on top.

Thoughts like that were going to kill me.

I tried working in the office, but it was different now. Even though she'd cleaned up (by dragging all of her stuff into the closet and closing the door as far as it would go), the room no longer felt like my workspace. It felt like the room where Olivia slept. It smelled like her perfume, and God help me, a lacy black bra was hanging on the back of the doorknob.

Once I finally refocused and started actually being productive, my phone buzzed.

Miss Misdial: Okay, clearly you are dead or in a coma. I should probably respect that, especially if your mother is holding your phone and wondering wtf this is all about, but I'm selfish. I need a texting buddy, and I'm going to just continue texting into this void regardless of whether you ever respond.

"Holy hell." I sat back in the chair and stared at the phone; so much for productivity.

Miss Misdial: I'm at a coffee shop, and Mr. Earbuds next to me keeps singing along to that old Marvin Gaye song "Sexual Healing." It's on repeat, apparently, because we're on the fifth go-round, and I'm not sure how to proceed.

I wanted to respond, *So heal him already*, so badly.

Miss Misdial: I feel like you'd say something ridiculous right now, like "dude, why haven't you healed him yet," but that's a negatory; he's giving off strong I-will-scream-at-you vibes. I think I shall get out my pepper spray and fiddle with it while I work, just so he knows I've got it.

Holy shit, if Olivia played with her pepper spray, she'd blind herself in minutes.

Miss Misdial: On second thought, we both know I cannot be trusted with the care and handling of pepper spray. I shall move along to another coffee shop, where men who mutter "get up—let's make love tonight" are not afoot. I bid you adieu, Mr. Wrong Number. Oh, and you too, Mother of Wrong Number, should you be canoodling with his phone while he remains comatose. Ciao.

I got up and walked over to the windows, my favorite part of the apartment, and stared down at the city. I needed to get my head right. If I couldn't get my brain to dump Misdial in a heartbeat, perhaps I could get Harper to help my brain.

I scrolled to her contact information and sent her a text.

Me: Remember that time we said it might be fun to go to dinner?

I didn't expect her to respond quickly, but my phone buzzed almost immediately.

Harper: You're seriously asking me out six months later? I'm pretty sure that was New Year's Eve, Colin.

Me: Maybe it took me this long to get the nerve to ask.

Harper: Or maybe it took you this long to remember my name.

It was almost funny how spot-on she was. I'd meant to text her the night I'd accidentally texted Misdial—fuck, Olivia—and I actually hadn't been able to remember if Harper was her first or last name. We'd met at Billy's Bar on New Year's Eve, and she was a knockout but registered as really high maintenance, which was why it'd taken so long for me to consider reaching out.

Desperate times and all that. I texted: Let me take you to M's tonight, HARPER O'RILEY (see?), and I guarantee you'll have a good time.

The phone buzzed.

Miss Misdial: Update. Sexual Healing followed me for three blocks, and when I whipped around and confronted him with my pepper spray, he told me I wasn't that pretty and I should blow myself with my pepper spray.

Holy hell.

Miss Misdial: So now I'm obsessed with his meaning; what could he have possibly meant by that? A. He thinks I have a penis and should fellate myself while somehow utilizing the pepper spray in the self-inflicted oral sex act. B. He forgot the word "up" and wants me to explode. C. He got the word "blow" confused with "bang" and is suggesting I insert a canister of pepper spray into my vagina.

I started laughing; I couldn't help it. Seriously, how could I not? She was beyond ridiculous. It took everything in my power not to add *D. He was using the word "blow" in place of the word "spray," and simply wanted you to blind yourself.*

But just as I was considering it, Harper responded.

Harper: I'll meet you at M's. My uncle is the bartender, so I'll call and get us a table. Seven o'clock work?

Wow. Maybe not so high maintenance at all.

Me: Seven is perfect. See you then.

Olivia

In spite of my shaking hands, I finished an article about the upcoming opening of a new bistro in the Capitol District and I started drafting another 402 column. I hated how shaken up that creep had made me. *Hated* it. I considered myself a relatively strong person, but as soon as I'd noticed him following me, I'd been terrified.

Thank God for pepper spray.

Men would never understand the utter bullshit unfairness

of the fact that they're just built stronger. Small men, tall men, lazy men, soft men; the reality was that most of them—if they wanted to—could overpower me. They'd never know what it was like to not be able to walk alone without being on watch, and knowing that always pissed me off.

Pricks, the lot of them.

I'd been counting on Mr. Wrong Number to read my story, jump in, and make me feel better, but he was still AWOL. Which was starting to make me more stressed than I cared to admit. Because the issue was twofold; first, why was he AWOL—had I done something? And second, why did the thought of him ghosting totally devastate me? I didn't even know him, for the love of God, so how could his silence cause me such indigestion?

But the writing today—oh, how amazing the writing felt.

I experienced what could only be called a buzz whenever I was creating a new piece. Whether it was an article on diapers (done that) or a words-of-my-heart short story, I was alive and thrumming and filled with an indescribable electric verve as I worked to put it all together. I assumed when I was creating that my brain pumped out the same juices as a runner's high, and it made me a word junkie who pressed the feeder bar with the voracious appetite of a freshly trained lab rat.

I spent the entire day lost in that blissful escape, not stopping except to eat a bagel at lunchtime and to get very necessary coffee refills. I quit just in time to squeak into my late-day appointment at the plasma donation center, so I was able to walk home $400 richer, which made me feel better about everything. Will and Dana would be dropping off the boys at seven so they could have their anniversary dinner, so as long as both my roommates had Saturday night plans, I could have some auntie-nephew bonding time with those kid haters being none the wiser.

But because of my luck, Colin was home. He walked out of his room the moment I came in, and gave me a nice smile—a genuinely kind smile—and said, "Marshall. How was the writing today?"

I didn't really know how to respond to his question, and then there was also the issue of his looks. He was clearly getting ready to go out, and he looked crazy hot. Sexy. Like a billionaire playboy who was about to wine and dine a supermodel.

"Great, actually." I took a sip of the blended coffee I'd brought home and said, "I got a lot accomplished."

He looked like he was waiting for more, for something bigger. His eyes flicked to my drink as he started tying his tie, and he said, "Do you have any idea how much sugar is in one of those?"

"I do. I also know that I will never have abs like yours if I keep drinking these, so you can spare me the lecture."

He gave me one of those half smiles he doled out on the regular and said, "I knew you'd noticed my abs."

"For the love of God, Colin, I imagine they can see those things from space." I shook the cup to loosen the bits frozen together in the bottom. "Not noticing them would be like not noticing trees are green."

"Thank you."

"No, no, don't get a big head because I was just stating a fact. I don't actually like them, if I'm being honest. Abs like yours aren't really my thing."

He gave a little chin nod, but his arrogant grin told me he didn't believe me. "Noted."

I dropped my bag on the floor and leaned my elbows on the counter. "I actually think they're a little gross, but everyone else seems to dig them, so what do I know?"

"Gross?"

"I mean, no offense. They're just really . . . um . . . *overdeveloped*, I guess you could say."

He frowned at his tie. "You're calling my abs gross."

"I mean, not *gross* gross—it's just me." I smiled and loved the fact that I was irritating him so much. "I'm sure those things bring all the girls to the yard."

"They do."

"I know, sweetie." I pouted and clucked my tongue at him, and he flipped me off. "Combine them with all of your rich-boy accoutrements, and I bet you're positively buried in females."

Both of his eyebrows went down. "Not that I want to have this conversation with Jack's little sister, who is clearly trying to piss me off, but even without the rich-boy accoutrements—what the fuck even is that—I do just fine."

"What kind of car do you drive, Beck?"

"Don't do that."

"Tesla? Benz? Beemer?"

"Nope."

"Audi?"

His jaw clenched.

"I knew it!" I grinned at him, all lit up inside from the knowledge that I'd been able to get the best of him for once. "That car is a *major* rich-boy accoutrement, and you know it."

"Sounds like someone is jealous."

"Big-time." I lifted my drink and said, "So what are you doing tonight? Board meeting? Philanthropic kegger? Political fundraiser?"

"I'm having dinner with a friend, not that it's any of your business."

"A friend," I asked, my eyes glued to his throat as he worked the knot of his tie up to the collar, "or an I'd-like-to-hit-this friend?"

He coughed out a small laugh and shook his head. "Yet to be determined. She's an I-think-she's-attractive-but-who-knows-if-she's-batshit-crazy kind of friend."

"Oof." I crossed my arms and noticed the wall clock behind him. I was down to five minutes before Will showed up with the boys. "Well, you better get going so you're not late."

"I've got plenty of ti—"

"No, you don't, because you need to buy her a bouquet of flowers on the way." I grabbed his keys from the hook on the wall and held them out. "Get going."

He cocked an eyebrow. "Why? What are you doing?"

I gave him an exaggerated eye roll. "Oh, my God, nothing, you paranoid freak. You need to get to dinner, and I'm looking forward to having a little peace and quiet. Sue me for trying to make it all happen."

His eyes moved over my face, hot blue and commanding of my attention, before he relented. "I'm going to go now, but only because I feel like you really need some time alone. Enjoy the quiet, okay?"

And just like that, he left. *Whew.* That was close.

Will showed up three minutes later and dropped off the boys.

Which was exactly what I needed. We played with trains for a little bit, and then we lay on the floor and watched *Paw Patrol*.

I texted Mr. Wrong Number small bursts of conversation with the goal of lighting up his phone enough to finally get him to respond, but also didn't really expect a response at this point, which I hated to admit I was disappointed about.

Me: I'm assuming you're dead now, Wrong Number, but I'm going to need some confirmation.

Me: Paw Patrol is making me wish I was dead.

Me: What kind of a town relies on a teenage boy and his animals to save them?

Me: Rubble is my favorite Paw Patrol dog, FYI.

I literally gasped when my phone buzzed and I could see that it was from him. I think a tiny part of me actually expected a text from his mother informing me of his coma. I clicked on the message and held my breath.

Mr. Wrong Number: Sorry, can't talk. On a date.

On a different day, I probably would've let him off the hook. Virtually any other time would've ensured my dutiful obedience. But after the pepper spray run-in with the creeper, I was done with men and their shenanigans.

He was going to engage in some conversation, dammit.

Me: On a scale of 1-10, is she a brilliant conversationalist?

He didn't respond until twenty minutes later.

Mr. Wrong Number: I only have a sec because she had to go fix her contact in the bathroom. The answer to your question is that she's a very aggressive conversationalist, if that makes sense.
Me: It does.
Me: How well do you know Miss Date?
Mr. Wrong Number: Talked to her for 10 mins at a drunk party.
Me: Well. You could always give her the Ultimate Dating Filter Screen. Cut your losses if she fails.
Mr. Wrong Number: Please explain.
Me: Okay. For example. I like to suggest doing something really bonkers that would require my date's effort. Like, "We should drive to the airport, park just outside the end of the runway, and watch the planes from the hood of the car."
Mr. Wrong Number: How the hell would that help me right now?
Me: Because in my opinion, there are two types of people. Those who are so happy to be spending time with you that they're down for anything, and those who are not. If she says she can't because of her hair or her shoes or because she has to be up early in the morning, she isn't a girl who will ever just roll with it.

Mr. Wrong Number: That makes a weird kind of sense.

Me: Do it. I dare you.

Mr. Wrong Number: I'll be back.

I set down the phone and watched about thirty seconds of *Paw Patrol* before the boys wanted me to turn on *Frozen II* and get them snacks. I popped some of the popcorn Dana had stuck in their diaper bag, and then the three of us shared it on Colin's fancy leather couch.

Thank God he wasn't home to see *that*.

Colin

"I can't believe our buildings are so close!"

I couldn't, either. I just couldn't believe it. I said, "Small world, right?"

"Ohmigod, we could totally walk to work together when it's nice out."

"I don't think you'd like my hours." We stopped in front of my door and I got out my key. "But who knows?"

I had no idea why I was bringing her home. I'd never really been the kind of guy to bring a girl home on the first date, definitely not since college, so it was a mystery why I was introducing Harper to my residence at this point. In the back of my brain alarm bells were going off, drawing arrows to the fact that Olivia was going to be in the condo, but my brain had been misfiring a lot lately, so what the hell did it know?

I unlocked the door, pushed it open, and immediately saw Olivia standing on the couch.

"Into the unkownnnnnnn!" She was scream-singing along to the animated movie on the TV while her two nephews ran around the living room, shrieking out the lyrics, as well. "Into the unknowwwwwnnnnn!"

The little one saw us and stopped running. Olivia, however, kept bouncing on top of my couch in her stupid Cookie Monster pajama top and green plaid flannel pants.

"Shit." I hadn't meant to mutter it out loud, but the damned top brought to mind Olivia's ass in her *Eat the Rich* underwear.

"Who is this?" Harper asked, smiling down at the kid.

"My unwanted houseguest's nephew."

Olivia heard that. Her head whipped around and she dropped to a sit before scrambling to her feet. I shut the front door and she gave us an embarrassed smile. "Um . . . don't you just love *Frozen*?"

Colin said, "More than life itself."

She pushed her wild hair out of her face. "I thought you were out for the night."

Harper, ignoring our exchange, walked into the living room and went straight for Olivia. "I love it. I used to listen to the soundtrack in my car all the time."

"Shut up—me too!" Olivia gave my date a full-on grin before saying, "I'm Olivia, by the way. Colin's unwanted houseguest."

Harper gave me a bitchy glare before saying to Liv, "I don't know, I think you seem like a delightful houseguest."

I dropped my keys onto the counter and couldn't believe it.

Uptight, judgy Harper was smiling and chatting away with Olivia as if they were best friends. Shouldn't she be jealous or have questions or just be generally irritated by Olivia's presence?

"Anyone want a drink?" I asked as I walked over to the liquor cabinet, not really interested in their answers. I was done.

"I'd love a vodka cranberry," Harper said, barely pausing her conversation with Olivia.

"Ooh, can I have a little bit of the smiley mustachioed-man tequila?" Olivia didn't even look over but said to Harper, "I had it my first night here and it is surprisingly smooth."

"Really?" Harper turned back to me and said, "Can I change my order?"

As they performed a damned infomercial script about the smooth tequila, my ears started roaring. Because—holy shit—was Olivia talking about—

"Are you talking about the Rey Sol?"

She looked over, clearly irritated that I'd interrupted. "I don't remember what it was called."

I reached for the bottle and sure enough, it was half-gone.

I turned around and said to her, "You opened a sealed bottle of someone else's liquor?"

She blinked. "So?"

"So who does that?"

Her eyebrows went down and she looked defensive. She put her hands on her hips and said, "I didn't think it was a big deal, I can just get you another one."

"You're going to replace my four-hundred-dollar tequila?"

Her mouth dropped open in shock. I thought she was going

to apologize, but instead she said, "Oh, my God, who is stupid enough to spend four hundred dollars on a bottle of booze?"

I felt my neck getting warm. "Regardless of the price, you should—"

"And that bottle is so cheesy. Who would think it's a good idea to put a face on a bottle of expensive tequila?" She looked at Harper before pointing at the bottle and telling her, "It's the opposite of luxury. A bottle of Mad Dog has more elegance. I mean, seriously."

I took a deep breath, pinched the bridge of my nose, and said, "Let me get this straight. You drank half a bottle of tequila by yourself on your first night here?"

"Oh." She dropped her arms to her sides and did something with her mouth, like she was biting the inside of her cheek, before she mumbled, "Well. No. I spilled some in the sink when I was trying to get it open. I actually only had one glass."

So Olivia had poured half the bottle down the drain. And not just any bottle, but the ceremonial bottle my sister bought for me the day I graduated from college. The bottle we'd agreed not to open until I went a solid ten years without caving and going to work for the family business.

"How the hell do you dump out half the bottle when you're *opening* it? Explain that magic to me."

"Um, I think I'm going to go." Harper hitched her handbag higher on her forearm and said to Olivia, "It was nice meeting you."

I tried not to grit my teeth as I asked, "Are you sure—"

"Thanks for dinner, Colin," she said while not even looking

back at me. She was all forward motion as she hit the entryway and exited the apartment, the door slamming hard behind her.

"I have to go potty," the older kid said, and Olivia replied while glaring at me, "Okay, make sure you wash your hands."

She picked up the little one and continued looking at me like I smelled bad.

"What?"

She tilted her head. "Aren't you going to go after her?"

"Why would I?"

"Why would you?" She said it like I was a moron. "Um, because she was your date and you kind of acted like an A-hole . . . ?"

"First of all, no I didn't. I was an A-hole to you, not her."

She snorted. "Over an ugly bottle of booze."

"Over a ceremonial bottle you had no business opening."

She gestured for me to hurry to the point. "And second of all?"

"Second of all, it wasn't going to work out with her anyway."

"How do you know that? Harper seemed great."

"I just know."

"Oh, that's right. Colin with the robot brain knows all."

"I might have a robot brain, but that's a hell of a lot better than being an irresponsible, free-spirited freeloader." I wanted to add *who talks to strange men*, but I wasn't supposed to know that. It'd been driving me crazy all day, though, thinking about some creep following her around town.

Her nostrils flared and she tucked her hair behind her ears with a violent jerk. "Free-spirited freeloader. That's . . . really nice, Colin."

Just then there was a knock at the door, and the moment was swallowed up by Will and his wife, thank God. The boys ran to the entryway and seemed thrilled to see their parents, though three minutes later they were crying and hugging Olivia and begging their parents to not take them home.

I talked to Will for a second, but then I did the smart thing and disappeared into my room.

Olivia

"Olivia?"

I heard him through the door—that ass weasel—and his voice was quiet like he didn't want to wake me if I'd already fallen asleep. I kind of wanted to ignore him, but the masochist in me was curious as to what else he could possibly have to say.

"You may enter."

The door slowly opened and he looked down at me. His face was still serious, but I imagined every fiber of his being wanted to mock me.

Because I knew I looked ridiculous.

I was sitting on the air mattress, my back against the wall with my legs stretched out in front of me, cradling the enormous vat of pretzels that I'd stolen from Jack like someone was going to steal them from me.

"Listen, Liv—"

"Nope." I shook my head and pointed at him, gesturing toward his torso. "Can't do this. It feels like some kind of a patriarchal joke, you standing above me with your abs and pecs out like a Greek god while I subserviently gaze upon you from my spot on the floor raft like a peasant. Either sit down at my level, or we'll talk in the morning."

One eyebrow shot up. "Okay."

He came over, disgustingly hot in his bare-chested state, and dropped down beside me on the air mattress with a force that nearly catapulted me across the room.

I hadn't wanted to stare up at his Calvin Klein–clad package while he spoke to me, but I'd imagined him taking a seat on the chair by the desk, or perhaps on the floor directly across from me.

Taking the spot *right* next to me hadn't entered my imaginings.

"Now." I cleared my throat and didn't look down at his leg that was touching my leg. I had no interest in chatting with the guy who'd managed to say out loud what I'd always known he thought, so I turned my face to him and gave him my own eyebrow raise. "Did you need something?"

"Yeah," he said, "I want to apologize."

"Spare me."

"Just listen." His jaw had the slightest hint of a shadow on it, and I hated that it looked good. He swallowed and said, "We always do our whole snarky banter thing, but I was a jerk and I'm sorry."

"You're sorry, but we both know you meant it." I looked down at the pretzels resting between my thighs and traced the lid with my finger.

He sighed and leaned his head back against the wall. "Part of it."

I looked at him then, waiting to see if he was going to explain, and he looked at me. The way his head was leaned back made me notice his throat again—*how could a throat be hot?*—and that wildly distracting Adam's apple. His blue eyes were all I could see when he said, "You tend to be a little . . . free-spirited sometimes, but I don't think you're a freeloader. And I'm totally impressed by this thing you're doing with your life. You landed a great job already. You're working out. Hell, you and your boyfriend *just* broke up and you're—"

"What do *you* know about the breakup?" God, did everyone somehow know what'd happened? Not about the fire—the whole country knew about that—but about Eli cheating and discovering his soul mate, who happened to not be me.

"Just that he didn't help you move and you were burning his love letters." He straightened and turned toward me a little, making the air mattress squeak. "But my point is that you're actually getting your shit together and it's kind of impressive to watch."

"Oh, joy, I've impressed Colin Beck."

That made him slide into a smirk. "Feel good about it, sunshine."

I rolled my eyes but I couldn't help but smile. "I've never known anyone as arrogant as you."

That made him full-out smile like I'd just complimented him. "Now say you forgive me."

"Fine. I'll give you a pass on this one."

"You just couldn't use my words, could you?"

"Nope."

"Fine." He moved his hips back and forth, shaking the air mattress as he said, "I have no idea how you sleep on this thing."

"It's fine. Not all of us are used to fancy Purple mattresses, so we can deal better than you."

"Wait a minute." He crossed his arms, which totally made his biceps pop, and he caught me in his blue-eyed stare. "How do you know my bed is a Purple?"

"You just seem the type." I rolled my eyes, hoping to be convincing.

"And my blanket smelled like perfume the other day."

"So? That's better than it smelling like sewage, right?" I stared at his narrowed, accusing eyes, my chin up, but something in my face must've given me away.

"Holy shit, you slept in my bed when I was out of town, didn't you?" He looked horrified but also a smidge entertained as he sat up straighter and waited for my answer.

"Oh, my God, no, I would never do that." I tucked my hair behind my ears and muttered, "I've just taken a couple naps on it, above the covers."

"A couple naps." He nodded his head and pursed his lips. "Above the covers."

"Get over it—it's not like I wore shoes on it or anything. This thing just sucks," I said, bouncing a little on the raft, "and your perfectly made bed called to me."

He just looked at me with a sarcastic half smile on his face, not saying a word, like he knew everything about me and was both amused and irritated by his knowledge.

"Oh, come on—you never would've known if I hadn't told you, so just forget about it." It must've been because I was tired, but I had to bite the inside of my cheek to stop a giggle from escaping. "It never happened. I was just kidding, actually."

He gave me a slow head shake and a begrudging smile. "I've never known anyone as bratty as you."

"Look in a mirror, Beck." I crossed my arms, matching his stance.

He made a noise—in either agreement or frustration—and climbed to his feet. It was odd; somehow Colin was able to pop right up, sticking the landing of air mattress disembarkment, whereas I usually stumbled and bounced a little before gaining my footing.

He gave me a weird look as he hovered by the door, like there was a lot going on in his head. He glanced at the wall above me before lowering his eyes and saying, "So I guess I'll see you in the morning."

"I guess you will." I set the pretzel vat on the floor next to my bed and leaned down to take off my shoes. I unlaced the first sandal and said, "I've got a nine a.m. brunch date, actually."

His eyes seemed to focus more intently on me when I said that. "Oh, yeah? How'd you meet Mr. Brunch?"

"Running." I pictured Paul's face and wished I would've canceled. "He was there when I rescued the old lady."

"Is that right?" He crossed his arms and said, "So why didn't he rescue her instead of you?"

"Because I was entirely capable, sexist."

"I saw your knees." His eyes dropped down to my legs, and my stomach dropped down to the floor. "Didn't look like you were that capable to me."

"Whatever." I dropped my shoe onto the floor. "Are you going anywhere tomorrow afternoon, by the way?"

"Why?"

I shrugged and said quietly, "I might need a nap."

He shook his head but I could tell he wanted to smile. "Come on, Marshall. What if *I* want to nap on my bed?"

"I won't stop you."

He immediately smirked and his eyes got that rowdy spark. "Really."

Oh, damn. I'd meant it to mean *suit yourself* or *do what you want I don't care*, but it totally came out as a feel-free-to-nap-with-me purr. I tried to sound unaffected as I took off my second shoe and said, "Really. As long as I'm on your pillow-soft bed, I don't care what you do."

His eyes raked over me, from the top of my head to my little bare toes, and I felt it like a physical touch. He let out a big exhale, shook his head like he didn't know what was happening, and turned and left, closing the door behind him.

7

Olivia

"FOLLOW ME."

I walked behind the hostess as she led us to a table, trying not to grit my teeth as I felt Paul do the whole guiding-me-by-my-lower-back thing. Like I didn't know how to get there without his assistance. When my alarm had gone off, I'd seriously considered canceling, but then I remembered we were going to Upstream, and my stomach talked my brain out of it.

Once we sat down, the waitress appeared, and before I had a chance to even think about the menu, Paul said, "Can we get a couple coffees? And we're both having the buffet."

He wasn't wrong, but he'd ordered for me without asking first.

Which made him absolutely wrong, right?

"Should we go get some food?" Paul smiled and gestured to

the brunch buffet on the other side of the restaurant. "I'm starving."

"Me too." I stood and told myself to relax. Just because he probably wasn't Mr. Right didn't mean he couldn't be fun to hang out with. "Let's do it."

We hit the buffet hard, filling our plates until they were heaping. He visited the crepe bar, the omelet bar, and the chef-carved roast beef bar, whereas I just dished up a grip of bacon, two donuts, and a mountain of country potatoes. When we finally got seated, I glanced at my phone—which I'd left on the table next to my water—and there was a message from Mr. Wrong Number.

Mr. Wrong Number: What are you doing?

Me: Can't talk; on a brunch date.

Mr. Wrong Number: On a scale of 1-10?

Me: Too early to tell. At a buffet, so our mouths are too full to actually converse.

"Ahem."

I glanced up and Paul was looking at me. He had on a backward ball cap again, this time with his Oakleys parked on top, and I wondered if he was balding. Not that I cared, but two times in a row made me wonder if he was hiding something. I tried for my best contrite look and said, "Sorry."

I set down the phone and picked up my fork. "So, um, Paul. Tell me all your stuff. Where'd you grow up, what do you do, have you ever murdered, are you in a cult, that sort of thing."

He took a bite of a croissant and said while chewing, "Grew

up here, work in sales, like I'd really tell you, and only the cult of Husker football."

I nodded and scooped up a pile of potatoes. "So you're basically my brother."

My phone buzzed again. I could see who it was, and it was killing me not to pick it up.

"If he's awesome, then yes." Paul dipped his crepe into some ketchup—what the hell?—and said, "Your turn."

"Grew up here, writer for the *Times*, I've only murdered people who deserved it, and no cult action to date."

We drifted into small talk, and Paul seemed like a good guy. He started talking about his job, and I couldn't stop myself from checking my phone really quickly while smiling and nodding.

Mr. Wrong Number: You alive?

Mr. Wrong Number: Did your brunch date murder you?

I glanced up, and Paul had barely noticed my mental absence. "—so it's kind of a temporary thing."

I nodded. "Yeah, totally get that. Um, I'm going to run to the restroom. I'll be right back."

I stuck my phone in the pocket of my dress and scurried to the bathroom. The minute the door shut behind me, my phone was in my hand.

Me: Still alive. He gave me the YOU DARE TO TEXT look so I put my phone away.

Mr. Wrong Number: He's not your dad. Text if you want to text.

Me: How do you know he's not my dad?

Mr. Wrong Number: Ew. How is the date going?

Me: Meh. Like, he's attractive and hasn't pissed me off, but he reminds me of my brother so . . .

Mr. Wrong Number: Oof.

Me: Oof indeed.

Mr. Wrong Number: I have a great idea.

I rolled my eyes but giggled. Proceed.

Mr. Wrong Number: Go back to the date, but keep texting me. See how many texts it takes for him to say something. I'm betting on ten.

Me: I don't like confrontation.

Mr. Wrong Number: Chicken.

Me: I'm not a chicken. I'll do it, but only because I want to.

Mr. Wrong Number: Atta girl.

When I sat back down, I was full-on grinning. Paul smiled back but looked at me like he was waiting for the punch line, for which I had none, of course. We fell back into small talk, and he was entertaining like a comedian when it came to pop culture. I was cackling as he talked about *The Bachelor*, and it was going so well that I actually decided to ditch the texting challenge.

Until . . .

"—so I mean yeah, the dude was a creep, but the hashtag

Me Too stuff has gotten way out of hand. Like, a guy with money can't even be alone with a woman anymore."

I slowly gnawed on a chewy piece of bacon. "What do you mean?"

"These women—not all women, you know—but a lot of women will just make shit up to bring a guy down."

My hands immediately went to my phone, because the date was done.

Me: Game starts now.

Mr. Wrong Number: Excellent. Give me one of your golden questions.

Me: If you had to choose between showering and brushing your teeth—and you could only choose one—which would you pick?

Mr. Wrong Number: Forever?

Me: Yup.

I glanced up and Paul was eating and looking at the table next to us.

Mr. Wrong Number: I guess I'd go with showering . . . ?

Me: You do realize that no one will ever kiss you again if you stop brushing your teeth.

Mr. Wrong Number: Well I don't think I'll be getting a lot of action with B.O., either.

"Do you want to go get more food?" Paul's eyebrows were up and he was staring at me as if waiting for me to participate.

"No, thanks. I'm good." I set my napkin on my plate. "But you go ahead."

He looked perplexed, but went back to the buffet.

Me: I think if I had to choose between tongue-kissing someone who hadn't brushed their teeth or knocking boots with someone who smelled a little rank, I'd pick the latter.

Mr. Wrong Number: The hell you say.

Me: I know but listen. It's gross, but if it's only straight-up sex without foreplay, maybe in a non-facing position, it would be better than licking someone's furry teeth.

Paul sat back down and sighed. I smiled and rolled my eyes as if the person texting me was just *so* annoying.

Mr. Wrong Number: I cannot believe I'm saying this, but you might be right.

"So what are you doing the rest of the day?" Paul wasn't smiling as he scooped up a forkful of eggs, but he was attempting conversation. "Besides texting, that is."

I stifled a laugh and wondered how many texts had been exchanged. Was Mr. Wrong Number close to being right? "I have to work most of the day, actually."

Me: He just brought it up. How many are we at?

"That sucks." Paul cleared his throat and gestured to my phone. "Are you in the middle of something important? Because we can do this another time if you are."

Aw, hell. Even though I knew he wasn't the guy for me, I realized he didn't deserve this, either.

Me: I can't do this. I can't be an asshole. I'm just going to finish up the date.

"No." I set my phone down and took a sip of my *very* cold coffee. "I apologize. I'm all yours now."

"Is that right?" He slid into a grin. "Well, then, check, please."

"Oh, my God." I was pretty sure he thought he was funny, but I couldn't even manage an awkward fake laugh. "Are you kidding with that?"

His smile slipped and he blinked fast as he said, "Yeah. Of course I was."

"Oh. Good." I cleared my throat and pasted on a polite, closed-mouth smile. "I thought so."

AS IT TURNS out, the number of texts doesn't matter when you and your date end up getting into a heated argument. One minute things were okay and we were talking about restaurants, and the next I was loudly explaining to him how every guy who eats at places like Hooters and Twin Peaks are pigs.

"I'm not talking about the girls who work there, Paul." I

knew I should let it go since the date was clearly the end for us, but this was a hot-button thing for me. Especially when he'd just said that the waitresses *liked the attention.* "If a girl wants to use her femininity to profit off the douchebags who are willing to pay to ogle her body, more power to her. But the men who specifically choose to go to a restaurant so they can get a quick peek at some young girl's breasts while shoving food into their sexist faces are just pathetic."

"Okay, I just told you I like the wings at Hooters, so what are you saying?"

I just gave him a look, because I didn't want to say it.

"No, I want to know." He was pissed now and done with pretending otherwise. "Do you think *I'm* pathetic?"

I looked at him, and it was clear that he thought I was going to say no. And since I'd already had one guy tell me to blow myself with pepper spray that week, I wasn't going to poke the tiger by being honest. So I reached for my purse under the table and said, "Y'know, I should probably get going. Thank you so much for brun—"

"You're not going to answer the question?"

I pushed back my chair and stood, ready to run. "It's probably not a good idea."

"Are you kidding me?" He shook his head and screwed up his face. "I don't think you're a very good feminist if you can't even—"

"Oh, my God. Yes, okay?" I pushed my chair under the table and yanked my purse against my body. "I absolutely think you're pathetic. Thank you for breakfast and goodbye."

I walked out of the restaurant as quickly as I possibly could and didn't slow until I had a solid three blocks behind me. I texted Mr. Wrong Number as I walked home: Date ended with me calling him pathetic and him calling me a bad feminist. #winning.

Colin

"Hey."

I glanced up from my laptop as Olivia stepped out onto the balcony, squinting into the sun and wearing a weird little print dress that looked like a series of bandannas tied together. The red, white, and blue print made her dark hair shine and her skin glow. I had the luxury of wearing sunglasses, so it was a rare moment where I could size her up without getting caught.

"Hey yourself. How was the brunch date?"

I'd laughed my ass off when I'd read her last text. It was so on-brand for Olivia that it was almost cliché. And, for the record, it was the last text we would ever share because I *was* ghosting her now. I didn't know why the hell I'd interrupted her date that morning, other than the fact that turnabout was fair play and she'd interrupted mine the night before, but we were phone buddies no more—starting *now*.

"It was good." The sun brought out a few golden streaks in her hair as she stared at the city. "I ate too much."

She was lying. Well, intentionally leaving out details at the very least. "And the guy?"

She shrugged and crossed her arms. "Nice but not really my type."

I set the computer down on the table next to my patio chair. "What *is* your type?"

That made her grin a tiny little grin and shake her head. "Nope. Not sharing. If anyone were capable of ruining my Prince Charming dreams, it'd be Colin Beck."

"Oh, come on, Liv." Why in the hell did I want to hear it in her words so badly? "I promise not to comment."

"Fine." She let loose with an eye roll and said, "Tall, handsome, and not a sexist pig; how about that?"

She took a step to go inside, but then she jerked to a stop and her mouth fell wide open as she stared off into the distance. I followed her gaze, or tried to, but there was an entire city in front of her so it was impossible to pinpoint.

"Oh, my God!" She squealed, and I swear she had tears in her eyes as she smiled the biggest, happiest smile and pulled her phone out of her pocket. "Oh, my God—it's just so beautiful."

"What?"

"See that billboard?" She held out her phone and started taking pictures, but the only billboard I could see was for the *Times* and had a cartoon on it.

"Where?"

"Over there." She pointed toward that billboard, but then her face changed. She blinked and said, "Um, it's a new promo for the *Times*. Cool, huh?"

"I guess . . . ?" I looked over at it and it just looked like an ad. "I mean, what am I missing here?"

Her mouth turned up into a proud smile and she said, "It's our new parenting columnist. She's totally anonymous, but her columns are funny and sarcastic, not the usual boring parental stuff. The first one runs tomorrow and I can't wait to read it."

"Holy shit." I leaned back in the chair and crossed my arms, looking back and forth between her and the billboard. *Of course.* "It's you, isn't it?"

"What?" Her eyes got really wide and she was quiet for a second before she said, "No. Of course it's not—I don't have kids. I'm just excited—"

"Admit it, Livvie. You have the *worst* poker face." She'd always been a terrible liar, and clearly nothing had changed. "You're the 402 Mom, aren't you?"

She gnawed on the corner of her bottom lip, obviously trying to decide whether or not to come clean.

"Spill it, Marshall."

"Fine." Her face went from nervous indecision to that wide smile of excitement. "It's me! But you cannot tell a soul."

She plopped down on the patio chair next to me and made a little squealing noise while wringing her hands. "My boss assumed since I used to write content for a parent-ish gossip site that I had kids. I didn't correct her in the interview, but then my sample column was apparently good enough and I got the job."

Sounded like a recipe for disaster to me. "No shit?"

"No shit." She beamed and said, "I'm serious, though—mum is the big old word. Like, no one can know."

"I get it." I cleared my throat. "But are you sure you want to go this route? People always find out the truth. I'm sure if you confess now—"

"I can't do that—are you kidding me?" She looked at me

like I was out of my mind. "It's too late. They will one hundred percent can my ass if anyone finds out."

"You really think in a town like Omaha it's not going to come out eventually?"

She crossed her arms over her chest, and the corners of her mouth turned down, making her look worried. "We both know my luck, so sure—it'll probably blow up in my face at some point. But until that happens, I might as well ride out this dream job, don't you think?"

I didn't like seeing her look insecure. Brash, unadulterated boldness was usually her game. I said, "You are a phenomenal writer, Liv. I'm sure if you told the truth, they'd find a way to keep you on."

She tucked her hair behind her ears and gave me a tiny smile. "How on earth would you know that? The only thing you've read of mine was the note I left on the counter the other day about my run-in with your grouchy next-door neighbor."

"Your mom used to send links to all your 'Who wore the baby bump better?' stories to Jack and me." It wasn't my thing, reading celebrity gossip, but I'd always been impressed by the way she'd been able to be tongue-in-cheek funny about famous people.

She looked shocked, but then she laughed and said, "Oh, my God—my mother has your email address?"

"When Nancy asks, you answer."

"Don't I know it." She rolled her eyes. "And we shall see about the writing."

I pointed to my MacBook. "I have no idea how you do it.

I've been out here for an hour trying to write a letter decent enough to land a huge client but everything I write is trash."

Her eyebrows furrowed and the wind blew long wisps of hair across her cheek. "I thought you were a numbers guy."

"That's the problem." I wasn't sure why I was telling her but I said, "I am."

"Lemme see." She pulled my computer onto her lap, and I was torn between being offended by her total lack of respect for my privacy and charmed by how fucking comfortable she was. "I'm sure it's not trash."

I watched her read it, wondering what universe it was that Jack's little sister was helping *me* with my homework. Her dark lashes dipped down as her eyes scanned the screen, and after another minute she said, "Email this to me."

"What?"

She pushed my laptop at me and said, "Can you email that to me? It's a great start but you don't have any voice in there—no *you*. It sounds like a robot wrote it instead of someone who really wants their business. I'll change it to what *I* would write—with track changes turned on—and then you can either accept them or decline them."

"What's happening here?"

She rolled her eyes. "I'm being helpful . . . ?"

"But why?" Livvie was never nice to me. "We don't do that."

Her pink lips were curled up into a tiny smile as she dusted off the fabric of her skirt and said, "You caught me on a good day."

"By the way," I said, needing to get back to familiar territory, "is that dress just a bunch of bandannas tied together?"

"No, it's not, jackass." Her eyes narrowed but I could tell she wasn't mad. She stood and said, "Maybe you should stop thinking about my dress and focus on whatever cabana wear you're sporting today. Does your grandpa know you raided his storage unit?"

"Come on, Livvie." I stood and stepped closer to her, crowding her on purpose because I knew it bugged the shit out of her. "Don't lash out irrationally just because you burned up all your good clothes. We both know that I look sexy as hell in my luxurious vacation wear."

I did a little spin, and was rewarded with a lip twitch that told me she wanted to laugh when she said, "We both know you only like it because it makes you look shredded, attention hound."

"Don't be snarky." I tousled her hair and laughed at her, because she talked about my body like it disgusted her. I wasn't the arrogant asshole she thought I was—that I let her believe I was—but I also was pretty sure the sight of my chest didn't gross anyone out, either. "Just drink it all in, Marshall."

THREE HOURS LATER, I got an email from Liv.

Colin—

You never emailed your letter, but I remembered the gist of it. Sadly, the control freak in me couldn't let it go, so I drafted a version. Use it if you want, delete if you don't.

Liv

What the hell? I hadn't bothered her with it because (a) I didn't want her to feel obligated, and (b) I wasn't sure a business proposal was something she had any experience with, but she'd done it anyway. I clicked on the attachment, unsure of what to expect and worried I was going to have to lie and tell her I'd use it.

But once I started reading . . . holy shit. She nailed it.

She'd taken my sterile words and made them sound personal yet professional. She managed to exude warmth while totally wielding the subtle power of persuasion.

She had to have spent a couple hours working on it because it was perfect.

I stacked my hands on top of my head and blew out a huge breath of relief. It was ready to go now.

Because of Olivia.

I responded to her email:

Liv—

This is incredible and you're my hero. I owe you BIG TIME! Thank you x 100.

Colin

8

Olivia

THE MINUTE I WOKE UP THE NEXT MORNING, I GRABBED MY phone and pulled up the newspaper online. Seeing my column in print with the cool professional logo made it feel official, almost as if someone else wrote it. I read it three times before jamming my bare feet into running shoes and running down to the c-store on the corner, where I purchased five copies of the newspaper. I had no idea what I'd do with all of them, especially since no one actually knew the column was mine, but it somehow felt important for me to collect them.

I was so excited that I had to text Mr. Wrong Number, even though he hadn't responded to any of my texts since brunch the day before.

Me: I know you don't know any of the details and you're suddenly mute, but I don't even care because

I'm so excited! Remember that opportunity I told you I landed by lying?

I waited ten seconds before texting: Oh, that's right—you're not there. Well, anyway, that opportunity happened and today is the first day!

I didn't wait around for a response, because I knew he wouldn't text back.

When I got back to the apartment, Colin was sitting at the breakfast bar, reading a copy of the paper while eating a bagel in a pristine gray suit and a black-and-white-dotted tie. He looked like *GQ* and smelled like sin, and he raised his eyes when I walked in.

I was his hero—which made me feel like the world's most incredible writer—so I gave him a little smile.

Jack was eating a bowl of cereal over the sink and said, "I'd tell you that we already have a subscription to the paper, but they only give us one and clearly you need more."

I shut the door behind me and toed off my shoes. Shit. How to explain my stack of dailies? Thankfully I didn't have to because Colin set down his bagel and said, "I read your piece about the new restaurant. Nice job. Made me hungry for steak."

"Thanks." I gave him a grateful look and was excited that I had something tangible running that day. I'd been so excited about the 402 that I'd totally forgotten about the bistro intro. "Perhaps my parents will finally believe that I've got a job now that there's a byline."

He picked up his cup. "They'll be so proud."

Jack made a derisive snort; he knew my mother.

"That I wrote a five-hundred-word piece about a restaurant that puts bourbon in every dish? Hardly." I reached over and snagged Colin's bagel, taking a tiny bite of the burnt side. "But they'll be appeased for now."

I set down his bagel and regretted my decision as Colin watched me closely. That was clearly some sort of healthy peanut butter, and it made me want to scrape off my tongue with my finger, but that would totally destroy the badassery of my move, so I had to swallow it down without gagging.

He said, "Hey, I read that 402 column you mentioned, by the way, and you were right."

My heart started pounding. Not because it was my secret identity and I didn't want Jack to catch on, but because Colin read the words that mattered to me. I kept my eyes on his bagel, half-scared and half-desperate to know his thoughts. "Yeah?"

He shoved the last big piece of bagel in his mouth and chewed before saying, "Yeah. I couldn't care less about parenting, but that article was hilarious."

I tried, I really did, but I couldn't stop myself from beaming. "Told you."

Jack dropped his bowl into the sink and grabbed a half gallon of orange juice, unaware of our unspoken conversation.

Colin gave me a mischievous grin—a twinkly-eyed conspiratorial smile—before dusting off his hands and walking his plate over to the sink. While he rinsed it off, he asked, "So are you working here today or at the coffee shop?"

"Here, I think." I was too afraid of Hooters-loving runners

and sexual healers to hit the coffee shop so soon. "But I won't invite any kids over today, scout's honor."

His eyes squinted as he glanced over and said, "Didn't you get kicked out of the Girl Scouts?"

Jack muttered, "After the second week."

"Shut up, Jack." Man, I'd forgotten about that. "It wasn't my fault that girl hit her head on a pipe and passed out. All I did was innocently bounce my Super Ball. The rest was a series of chaotic accidents."

That made Colin slide into a grin. "A walking, talking, chaotic mess, even back then."

I rolled my eyes. "Don't you have a job to get to?"

"I do." He went into his room, and emerged a few seconds later with a buttery-soft leather messenger bag over his shoulder. I didn't know how he managed to look so flawless, so perfectly gorgeous, but my stomach got a little light just looking at him.

"You look like a banker, Beck."

He raised an eyebrow and smirked. "And you look like you've completely given up, Marshall."

"Well," I started, letting my eyes stroll over the edges of his face and the soft curl of his bottom lip, "Have a day, then."

He turned his attention toward the exit and said, "You have a day, as well."

With that, he left, and I stood frozen, staring at the door for a solid thirty seconds. Wondering what it would be like. What *he* would be—

"What the hell was that?" Jack was staring at me with his

nose scrunched up like I stunk. "You guys don't hate each other anymore?"

I shrugged and took his orange juice. "We do, just not as much as before."

THINGS GOT SCARY good after that.

The column took off. Over the next couple weeks more billboards went up, ads ran, and overall—holy shit—it seemed like the public kind of really liked my pieces. I mean, yes, there were definitely plenty of people who thought the 402 Mom was mouthy and too sarcastic, but the majority seemed to dig her.

I couldn't believe it.

I was so professionally satisfied, it was as if a match was lit under my keyboard. The combination of real-life reviews and interviews under my actual name, crossed together with the utter creative release of the 402 columns, left me marveling at the fact that I was getting paid to do *that* for a living.

Like, seriously? It was unbelievable.

When Glenda sent me flowers to congratulate me on our success, I cried for an hour. Partly because I had such intense guilt for deceiving her, but mostly because I was so unbelievably happy that it stressed me the hell out.

Because it was me, Olivia Marshall.

Smooth sailing was not sustainable.

The only complaint I had was that Mr. Wrong Number had disappeared completely. I still texted him as a way to talk to myself, to throw my ideas out into the void, but I was pretty sure he was gone forever.

Why did it even bother me? He was a stranger, for the love of God. My shit was finally together-ish, so I should've been good, but at night, when I couldn't sleep, I lay in bed and wondered what'd happened. Was it me? Was I annoying? Was I too much?

Or was it him? Was he married? Murdered? Running for political office?

I was starting to accept the fact that I'd never know, but there was a tiny part of me that just couldn't seem to get over it. Like, I *missed* my stranger friend, which was stupid but it couldn't be denied. Thank God everything else was suddenly clicking, or I might've been completely devastated.

Colin

"Marshall."

Olivia looked up from her computer. "What?"

She was curled up on the sofa, wearing those stupid flannel pants and staring at the laptop with her glasses halfway down her nose. Her hair was up in what I could only guess might've been a bun at one time, and she was gnawing on the end of her pen.

"What're you doing?" It was midnight, Jack had gone to bed, and I was barely staying awake as I watched the news. Liv, on the other hand, looked hyper-focused. "Your fingers aren't flying so I'm guessing you're not writing."

"Nope." She uncurled her legs and stretched them out on the ottoman. "I'm looking at apartments. I've gotten so comfy in your condo that I kind of forgot all about finding a place, and I'm mere days away from you physically removing me from the building."

"I'm not a monster. I'll let you stay a whole extra day if you're nice to me."

She threw me a look and said, "I don't need your favors. I just need to find a decent place that doesn't require too big of a deposit."

"Still building up your cash stash since the fire?"

"Bingo. I make enough to pay the rent, but don't have a crap-ton to put down."

"Could you maybe borrow from your parents?"

"I'd rather live on the streets." She kept scrolling through apartment listings as she said, "I borrowed a hundred bucks from them the night I came back, and my mother has literally mentioned it every time we've spoken."

"Did you fail to pay them back?"

"Nope—I know the way she works, so I actually paid them back a hundred and fifty dollars."

"Didn't buy their silence?"

"Not even for an hour."

That made me laugh, because her mom was a real piece of work. I adored Nancy, but the woman reminded me of a *Seinfeld* character. I sat down on the arm of the sofa next to her and looked down at Olivia's computer screen. "One Hundred Eighth and Q? I thought you loved living downtown."

Since moving in, I was pretty sure she'd spent more time staring out at the city than doing anything else. She was like me in that, her absolute adoration of downtown life.

"I can't afford it, moneybags; everything down here is crazy expensive, so I'm afraid it's the burbs for this girl."

"This building has loft studios; did you look at them?"

"I think so . . . ?"

"Here." I pushed her over and sat down beside her, stealing her laptop.

"Hey!"

A few clicks, and boom—there was my building. I hovered over the studio floor plan. "See? They're studios, but the loft is like the bedroom so it feels more like a one-bedroom."

"Look at those high ceilings." She squinted and leaned closer, her body leaning against mine as the smell of her shampoo—my shampoo—came at me. "Wow, those are amazing!"

I just shook my head; her excitement made me miss Misdial. Even though it was Olivia and I saw her every day, I missed what I thought it'd been.

"And not too expensive. I'm sure they require a crazy deposit, though." She frowned.

"You should just apply; you never know."

She gave me side-eye and nudged me with her elbow. "I can't believe you want me to live in your building so badly."

I reached out a hand and pushed, toppling her over on the couch. "I was being nice, but now that you mention it, perhaps having your Liv luck in the building isn't the best idea."

"Nope, it's too late now. I'm sending in an application."

"Please, God, no."

"Oh, I'm here." She grinned and pushed my leg with her foot as she stayed horizontal. "If they accept me and I can afford it, I'm going to be here all the time. In fact, I think I'll request an upper floor just so I can drop stuff down onto your deck."

"Typical."

She sat up and pushed up her glasses. "I might even train pigeons to crap on your fancy patio furniture."

"As if you could."

"You don't know." She yanked back her computer and clicked on the "Apply Now" link. "This is pointless, but I'm doing it just to make you regret trying to help me."

That made me laugh. "Why, exactly . . . ?"

"I have no idea." She grinned, and something about the intimacy of the smile she was giving me made me notice her full lower lip. "It's just the knee-jerk way I've always related to you."

"I get that." I got up, adding distance between us because the last thing that I needed was to fall under the spell of her funny charm and forget all about who she actually was. *Jack's sister, Jack's sister, Jack Marshall's little baby sister, dipshit.* "Call the office in the morning and talk to Jordyn. She's great and can give you a tour."

"Jordyn, huh?" She waggled her eyebrows in a ridiculously cheesy way. "Sounds hot."

"And incredibly pregnant." I turned off the TV with the remote, dropped it on the coffee table, and said, "G'night, Liv."

My bedroom door was almost closed when I heard her say, "Sweet dreams, Colin."

And just before I plugged in my phone to let it charge overnight, I shot off a quick email to Jordyn in the leasing office. I wasn't meddling, because Olivia was definitely not my problem, but if she needed a recommendation in order to get an apartment she loved, I was good with doing that.

Besides, I still owed her for the kick-ass letter.

And hell—the quicker she found a place, the quicker she was out of my hair, anyway.

9

Olivia

I SPENT THE ENTIRE NEXT DAY LOOKING AT APARTMENTS, but the problem was that I looked at the one available studio in Colin's building first. It was tiny but ridiculously perfect: new appliances, new flooring, cool ceilings, and the loft had a changing area and tiny half bath, so it felt like way more space than it actually was. And, of course, it had a view of the city that made my soul feel alive. The rent was doable, too, but their income requirements would probably knock me out of the running.

There were a couple others I checked out in the downtown area, but they were dumps *and* I couldn't afford them. So I went farther out into the suburbs, looking at super-basic old vanilla apartments, and before I knew it I was two blocks from my parents' house.

Talk about your bad omens.

But since I was in the neighborhood, I decided to swing by.

"Ma?" I opened the front door and went inside. My parents never locked the house until bedtime, so I never had to worry about having a key on me. "Where are you?"

"Basement."

I ran down the stairs, expecting to see her watching TV by herself, but she was actually surrounded by four ladies from church. Ellie, Beth, Tiff, and that crotchety one with the ever-narrowed eyes who'd always watched me like I was about to steal the collection baskets.

"Oh. Hey, everyone." I gave them all a smile and wished I wasn't wearing skinny jeans and a tank top that said *Summer Girl.* Now that I had a paying job, I needed to go shopping for clothes, but working remotely had kept me lazy and entirely unconcerned with my wardrobe. "How are you guys?"

"What are you doing here, hon?" My mother looked at me suspiciously and added, "You didn't lose your job already, did you?"

"Why?" I clenched my fists to keep myself from being snotty in front of her friends. "Why would you think that?"

"Because it's the middle of the day, dear," she said, her eyes moving over me from head to toe as if cataloging every failing, "And you're dressed like a scrub. Do you need some money to go shopping?"

More clenching. "No, Ma, I have money. But thank you. I just haven't had time to shop because I've been working so hard."

There. Boom.

"Oh, that's right—your father's been saving your articles. He really liked the story about the steakhouse that boozes up every dish."

I felt beads of sweat on my nose as my mom's friends looked at me like I was a disappointment.

"I tell you what," Mom said, leaning closer to Tiff, "I don't know what the paper is thinking with that new cartoon mom thing. Have you guys read that?"

Now my forehead was sweaty, too.

She continued. "After all the commercials, I thought it was going to be good stuff, but it's some young smart-ass who likes to be funny instead of helpful."

I rolled in my lips and inhaled through my nose.

Tiff said, "Oh, now, Nancy—I thought she was hilarious."

Beth said, "Me too."

"It was definitely different." Ellie tilted her head a little and added, "But I enjoyed it."

The crotchety one just looked at me, still trying to decide if I was a felonious troublemaker, but I didn't care. She could kiss my ass, because the rest of them dug my work.

"Listen, I've got to get going. I'm apartment hunting today, but since I was close, I thought I'd stop by and say hi." I pulled my keys out of my pocket. "Tell Dad, too, okay?"

My mother pursed her lips. "You could tell him yourself if you ever called us on the phone."

"I don't call anyone." I gnawed on my lip. "I hate talking on the phone."

"Who hates talking on the phone?" My mother looked at

her friends as if she were speaking about a sociopathic murderer. "I swear, your generation has completely forgotten common courtesy."

I forced a smile on my face. "Well, this discourteous girl has to go. I'll talk to you later, Mom."

"You should come by for spaghetti on Sunday."

"Okay." A courteous spaghetti Sunday. Sounded awesome. "Bye."

I looked at five apartments after that, then stopped at Target for a few groceries and two non–high school outfits. By the time I got home, it was almost dark and I was exhausted. I put away my groceries, then immediately changed into pajamas and parked myself on the couch. Jack was at Vanessa's, his new "friend," and Colin seemed to already be asleep because it was quiet behind his door, so I had all night to rule the living room.

Which was good because even though I was slowly getting caught up on *Marriage in a Month*, I still needed to binge three more episodes before I'd be up-to-date. I lay down and turned it on, but I was distracted by my phone and social media. I psychotically checked the comments when the *Times* posted one of my articles, and by "psychotically checked," I meant refreshed the page every three-to-four minutes.

I was on my fiftieth refresh when I noticed I had a voicemail. I usually didn't even listen to messages, because, like I'd told my mother, I hated talking on the phone. But it was a number I didn't know, so I clicked on it.

"Hi, Olivia—it's Jordyn in the office. Just wanted to let you know that your application was approved. Please call me tomorrow and we can talk about signing the lease and setting up your move-in date. Thanks."

What? I couldn't believe it. I listened to the message again. Holy shit! I was seriously going to live in the perfect loft apartment, for the same rent as all the suburban dumps I'd looked at that afternoon?

I ran over to Colin's door and quietly knocked. "Colin?"

I didn't want to wake him up, but I *so* wanted to wake him up. I was beyond excited but because of my lack of friends, I had no one to freak out with except him.

He pulled open the door, wearing an unbuttoned dress shirt and nice pants, and there was an undone tie hanging around his neck.

"Guess what." I pictured the apartment and couldn't help but squeal. "I got the apartment!"

"Shut up—for real?" He gave me a wide grin that was like the role model for all other smiles. "Congratulations!"

I squealed again and then we were hugging. It was a total friend hug, a hug of supportive congratulations, but as soon as it commenced my brain was shorting out from the feel of his hands wrapped around my waist.

The smell of his neck.

The bumpy musculature of his shoulders.

I pulled back, but when I did—holy damn—his blue eyes were hot. I licked my lower lip, about to blabber some bullshit small talk, when his hands came up to my face and his mouth came down on mine.

No drift, no lean, no subliminal staring at each other's mouths as if to suggestively remind the other that kissing existed. No, this was decisive.

My fingers curled into the white cotton that covered his

shoulders, and his mouth ate at mine like it was a ripe fruit and he was starved for its sweetness. Had been starved for an age. His lips were wild and aggressive, teasing and biting and making me purr into his mouth, but the way he held my cheeks left no question that all of the choices were mine to make.

I turned a little, backing against the doorframe so he could lean all of his body into mine.

And he did.

It was fire and passion and starvation, and I wanted to wrap my legs around his waist and make the dumbest possible decision I could make.

But.

"Colin." I panted his name through biting kisses. "What are we doing?"

"Fuck, Liv." His eyes were dark and intense as he fed me razor-sharp kisses that rubbed his day's stubble against my skin in the most delicious way. "I have no idea."

I put my hands on his biceps—good God—and squeezed. "We should." That tongue, *shit*. "Probably stop."

"I know." His teeth dragged over my earlobe and I felt it everywhere. "Why the hell am I kissing the biggest pain in the ass I know?"

I dug my fingernails into his skin as his mouth did wicked things. "Because I'm irresistible, you cocky dipshit."

"Says you."

His mouth was back on mine then, and the doorframe was digging into my back as our bodies were pressed so tightly together that I could feel every. Single. Inch. Of. Him.

Oh, holy hell.

"Colin. Really." I freed my mouth long enough to repeat, "What are we doing?"

That was the exact second we heard Jack's keys in the lock, so we jumped apart. I blinked fast, as did he, and he said, "Let's not make this weird, okay? We were both excited and kind of forgot ourselves. No big deal, right?"

I nodded and touched my lips, trying not to look at the bare chest that'd just been pressed against me. "Right."

Jack came in, slamming the door behind him as he carried a bag from Taco Bell over to the table. He barely shot us a glance as he sat down, so I murmured a "G'night, you guys" and slipped away into my room.

Colin

Holy shit. Had that really just happened?

I changed out of my clothes and threw them on the chair by the window, too wired to be bothered with putting them away. I paced my room like a caged animal, freaking out over my stupid punk-ass move.

I'd kissed Olivia.

I had kissed the little sister of my best friend like a total asshole. Why? Oh, yeah—because she had *hugged* me. I was such a big dumb oaf that the smell of perfume on her neck and the feel of her hands on my shoulders had made me lose my shit.

Fucking weak much?

Jack would kill me if he ever found out, and that would be

the total right move, by the way. I'd seen him go apeshit over harmless little pricks sniffing around his sister's back when she was in middle school, and I knew it'd be no different today.

Hell, if Olivia were my sister (praise Jesus that she wasn't), I'd react the exact same way.

The worst part about it was that even as I cursed myself for my stupidity, I couldn't stop thinking about the *way* she'd kissed me back. Because it'd been *exactly* the way she'd said it would be when she'd texted Mr. Wrong Number. She liked it hot and heavy and up against the wall, right?

Her kiss was definitely a preview of that unholy hotness.

After another hour of mentally kicking my own ass, I laced up my shoes and went for a run. Clearly my mind wasn't going to get tired, so maybe if my body did, sleep would eventually come and save me from my thoughts.

10

Olivia

"I CANNOT BELIEVE WHAT I'M HEARING."

"I know," I said, carrying two glasses of prosecco over to the table. Sara was unboxing our food—fried ravioli and a loaf of focaccia from Caniglia's—and staring at me as if I'd grown a second head. I gave her a sheepish grin and murmured, "I can't quite believe it myself."

She'd called last night, right after the kiss and smack-dab in the middle of my mental freak-out, to see if I wanted to grab food and catch up sometime. I said something desperate like "can we tomorrow, please?" and thankfully, she was down for a quick happy hour. I hadn't planned on telling her about the kiss, but the minute she'd walked into the condo and asked how I was, I'd blurted out the whole thing over our first bottle of wine.

"So, um," she said, looking like she wanted to laugh as she

opened the carton of ravioli that the delivery driver had just dropped off, "does this mean there's something brewing between you and Mr. Beck?"

I sat down and picked up a ravioli. "No, no, no, I was excited so I hugged—"

"Stop." She shook her head and snagged a few ravioli for herself. "In no normal situation does a friendly hug end in dry humping against a doorframe. Try again."

That made me snort. "It was way sexier than dry humping, Sara."

She coughed out a laugh and said, "For real, though—you know I'm right. There has to be something crackling if you were both sober and a yay-I-got-the-apartment hug turned into foreplay."

"Okay." I dropped the ravioli back onto the plate—it smelled weird—and reached for my wine instead. I said, "I suppose there's . . . an *awareness* between us all of a sudden. Sexual chemistry, I guess. But I also know that he doesn't really like me."

Her eyebrows went down. "What?"

"I mean, I guess he *likes* me now," I said, taking a sip and picturing his heavy-lidded gaze from the night before, "but that doesn't mean he respects me. He just sees me as a shitshow dipshit."

Sara took a bite of one of the breaded appetizers and just looked at me while she chewed.

"I'm dreading seeing him, to be honest." I ran my finger along the stem of the wineglass. "He's probably beating himself up for doing something so stupid."

"You haven't seen him since the kiss?"

I shook my head, a little embarrassed by the fact that I'd spent extra time on hair and makeup that morning, just in case I saw Colin. "When I got up this morning, he was already gone."

As if on cue, the sound of a key in the lock came from the entryway, and my stomach went wild with butterflies. I felt a little light-headed and took a deep breath, trying to look cool and casual.

Sara smirked, raised her glass, and gave me a tiny nod of support. "Cool and casual. You've got this."

The door opened, and Colin walked in.

Dear God.

Did the man ever look less than perfect?

I allowed myself one second to do a lustful inventory—blue eyes, stylish suit, wide chest, broad shoulders, Adam's apple—before turning my attention to the focaccia on the table. I leaned forward and unwrapped the loaf as I said to Sara, "I can't believe they still have this bread."

I felt it in my peripheral vision when he looked over at us. Noticed us.

"They told me when I called in the order that my timing was good, because apparently they sell out in fifteen minutes or less every single day." Sara set down her wineglass and—bless her—smiled like we were having the greatest time. "Is it really that good?"

I pulled off a hunk and set it on my plate before pushing the rest of the loaf toward her. "Oh, yeah."

"Hey." Colin set his messenger bag on the table next to the door, walked into the kitchen, and gave me a weird look. His eyes moved all over my face and I wondered if he'd been expecting a reaction over the kiss or something, because he looked like he was trying to find answers to a thousand questions.

"Hey," I said, glancing at Sara and trying not to grin as she gave me a discreet look. "This is Sara, by the way. Sara, this is my brother's roommate, Colin."

Colin's mouth curled into a warm, friendly smile that made my stomach feel light and he reached out and shook her hand. "Nice to meet you. Although . . ."

Sara tilted her head and smiled.

"Didn't we go to the same high school?" Colin let go of her hand and put his in his pockets. "You look really familiar."

I could tell Sara was charmed by the fact that he remembered her, and the two of them immediately launched into a recollection of their shared study hall and some kid named Gerbil who used to sell beef jerky under the table.

The wine was starting to give me a warm, glowing buzz, which made it impossible not to fall into a shitty grin as he behaved like Prince Charming. When they finally finished walking down memory lane, I said, "Sara, did you know that Colin has a Purple mattress?"

She sputtered out a tiny laugh. "Is that right?"

Colin's eyes narrowed and he looked at me the same way he had before, like he was trying to figure something out. He swallowed and gave a polite nod, coupled with a smile. "Guilty as charged."

"Consider me jealous," Sara said.

I tilted my head and squinted. What was he doing? Where

was the know-it-all, cocky smart-ass? I said to Sara, "Y'know, he is *never* this nice."

"What?" Colin's gaze was back on mine, and he rubbed a hand over his jaw. "I'm nice."

I rolled my eyes and picked up my bread. "Only because I'm moving out."

Sara said, "He's a man. Nothing makes a man quite as nice as when he's getting his way."

I laughed and Colin gave a half smile as he scratched his eyebrow.

"He'll probably fall asleep cackling the day I actually leave," I giggled, raising my glass to my mouth and finishing what was left.

"In a flawless suit, no doubt," Sara laughed, but shot him a kind smile.

Colin looked amused as he walked over to the counter and picked up the bottle of wine. He looked at Sara and asked, "Can I get you a refill?"

"Yes, please," she said with tipsy enthusiasm.

He brought the wine to the table, and as he asked Sara something about where she lived, I wondered what was up with him. I squinted as he was incredibly polite, treating her to a sweet, genuine smile.

Why was he being so nice?

It made me uneasy.

I watched him refill her glass, but the sight of his luxury watch peeking out from under his cuff distracted me with a gut-punch flashback of the way it'd felt when he was holding my face and a strand of my hair had gotten pulled between the links.

It'd felt like nothing. A pull that didn't matter because his fingers were on my skin, his mouth on my mouth, his breathing heavy, and his body pressing mine into the doorframe.

God.

He laughed when she said something about her baby, and it was impossible not to find him to be the most charming man on earth.

What the hell was he up to?

Colin

I listened to Sara—baby, husband, house in West O—but my mind was on the girl in my periphery. It was taking extreme self-control not to look in her direction. I'd tossed and turned all night after the kiss, plagued by guilt and also a nonstop replay of the kiss, so at five in the morning I'd finally gotten up and just went into work.

Where I spent half the day with my head in my hands, trying to stop thinking about it. I needed to have a minute alone with her to make sure we were cool, but I also didn't want to be alone with her. What was wrong with me?

"Excuse me—waiter?" Olivia cleared her throat, and when I swung my gaze her way, she was giving me a wine-drunk smirk. "I could use a refill, as well."

"Of course, ma'am." My blood went instantly hot as I looked at her red lips and the lipstick print on the rim of the wineglass. *Shit, shit, shit.* I swallowed and poured, unable to come up with a single comment.

What were words again?

I felt her watching me, and when I looked up from her glass, to the sprinkling of freckles on her nose and cheeks—how had I never noticed those before?—her eyebrows were knit together. Her eyes were narrowed, her head was tilted, and she was blinking fast.

She looked absolutely confused.

Same, Marshall.

Hard same.

11

Olivia

A WEEK LATER WAS MOVING DAY. OR, TO BE MORE SPECIFIC, moving *evening* because I'd had to wait all day for the polish on the fancy wood floor to dry. Since it was the middle of the month, they'd prorated my rent, so I had no reason to wait to move in.

I still hadn't had a chance to thank Colin for giving me a reference, mostly because I'd been avoiding one-on-one conversation with him since the kiss. Except for the weird happy hour with Sara, he seemed totally normal since it happened, behaving the way he had since I'd moved in.

Entirely unaffected.

I did my best to act normal, as well, but the sight of him brought the memories flooding back, making me hot and bothered and struggling not to stare at his incredibly talented mouth.

I grabbed the big box I'd filled with clothes and slid it into the living room. Jack was watching TV, and Colin was nowhere to be found.

"I can't believe that we literally only have to move one box and an air mattress." Jack came over and carried the box to the doorway. "Best move ever."

"Yeah, everyone should be so lucky as to have a fire burn all their belongings." It was probably a testament to my pathetic-ness, the fact that I still had no real *stuff* to move.

"Colin already went down because he wanted to measure something."

"What the hell would he want to measure?"

"I don't know, I think he liked your flooring planks or something like that."

"He's so weird."

"Yeah." He gave me a smile and said, "I'll get the box if you've got the air mattress."

"Cool." We loaded them into the elevator before riding down to my floor. *My floor*—I was beyond excited. I very nearly ran down the hall when we exited the elevator, bouncing off walls with my rubber raft, so excited to be back in that pretty apartment.

"You're such an idiot," Jack laughed before attempting to race me down the hall while carrying a huge box.

The door was ajar and I pushed it open with the air mattress. "What the hell are you measur—"

"Livvie!" Dana ran at me and grabbed the air mattress. "This place is amazing!"

"Dana, what are you doing here?" After she took it from my arms, I could see that Will and the boys were there, alongside Colin. There was also a stack of pizzas and a twelve-pack of beer on the counter. "Oh, my God, are we having a party?"

Colin laughed with my brother, and my cheeks got hot.

"We got you two stools for the counter as a housewarming gift," Dana said, grinning and pulling me toward the kitchen area, "but if you hate them, we can totally do an exchange."

"They're perfect." They were tall and the exact same shade of wood as my cabinets, and they each had a big red bow on the back. "I love them."

Brady ran over and raised his arms for me to pick him up—which I did, of course—and Kyle made a face and mouthed the word *poop* at me because he knew he wasn't allowed to say it but also knew he could use it to make me laugh.

"You guys, I can't believe you brought me pizza." I was seriously touched that they'd come over for my moving day. I opened the top box and snagged a gooey piece of cheese. "Wanna help me unpack box?"

Will's eyebrows went together. "Box?"

Colin's mouth slid into an easy smile and he explained, "Because of the fire, the only things she had to move all fit in one box."

"On-brand for Queen Dipshit, I'd say," Jack muttered.

Colin and I shared a secret smile, but before I could get light-headed, Kyle was running up the stairs to my loft and beers were being opened. It quickly became a laid-back gathering of friends instead of a moving thing.

We drank beers on the floor and ate pizza, reminiscing and

telling stories and warming the walls of my pretty new home. In spite of the shitshow that I was, the first evening in my new place was made-for-TV perfection.

When I went out on the balcony to show Kyle the lights, Colin followed us.

I raised an eyebrow. "You want to see the lights, too?"

He put his hands on the railing and looked out at the city. "Actually, I wanted a second to thank you."

Kyle squealed something about a train and ran inside, closing the patio door behind him and leaving Colin and me alone in the moonlight. It felt quiet, even though the sounds of the city surrounded us. I put my fingers on the iron deck railing and said, "For moving out?"

His eyes crinkled at the edges and he said, "For that letter you fixed."

I rolled my eyes. "You already thanked me, Einstein."

"I know that." He leaned closer and teasingly bumped my shoulder with his. "But today the client signed the contract."

I gasped. "Oh, my God, you got the deal?"

"Yup." He smiled and nodded. "I got the deal."

"That's incredible!" I was instantly filled with adrenaline, beside myself with excitement that something *I'd* done to help Colin had, well, actually helped. "Congratulations!"

"It's not a big thing," he said, looking at something just past my shoulder, but I could tell by his expression that he was trying to act like the deal didn't matter.

I could also tell that it totally did.

"Well, big or small," I said, bumping his shoulder back, "way to go."

Kyle came back outside and my brother followed. They were taking off because Brady was getting tired, and I pretended to be bummed as everyone gathered their things and made their way to the door, but the truth was that I was excited for everyone to leave.

I'd never lived alone before, and I couldn't wait to get started.

I hugged everyone and said my thank-yous, rolling my eyes at Colin when he gave me an eyebrow waggle before ushering them all out my very adorable front door.

The minute they left, I ran around the apartment. I danced to Prince on my phone. I watched the city from my very own balcony. I envisioned the furniture I was going to purchase after a few more paychecks, and I even bought a cheap desk online from Target clearance.

It wasn't until hours later, when I was finally lying on the air mattress up in my loft, that I started to calm down. I was kind of in a blissful haze of happiness, but it was keeping me from sleeping. After tossing and turning for an hour with no luck, I texted Mr. Wrong Number.

Colin

Miss Misdial: I know you're dead to me, but I can't sleep and you're the only one I have to bug.

I sighed and just stared at the phone; when was Liv going to stop texting?

Miss Misdial: I just moved into a new apartment and I think I'm too excited to sleep. It's the first time I've ever lived alone.

I wouldn't have guessed that. She was so independent that I would've assumed somewhere between high school and now she'd had her own place.

Miss Misdial: I wish you weren't in a coma, because I need your half of our idiotic banter to make me sleepy, dammit. A tiny part of me wants to say something to you like "I didn't do something, did I?" but I'm not some kind of pathetic whimpering girl so screw you if you're sensitive.

I felt like total shit for ghosting her. It had to be done, but I hated hearing her sound insecure about it.

My phone buzzed again. Good lord, she wasn't going to go away.

Miss Misdial: Tbh the main reason I can't sleep is that I'm sleeping on an air mattress. A night or two while camping is fine, but I've been on this thing for a month now. It seriously takes me like a solid minute to sit up in the morning because my back is so sore.

No wonder she'd napped on my bed.

Miss Misdial: I'm contemplating throwing it off my balcony and just sleeping on the floor.

I could see her doing that.

Miss Misdial: But the weirdest thing about night in my apartment? Thank you for asking, oh comatose one. The weirdest thing is that since I don't have a TV yet, it's deathly quiet. Like I could hear a cockroach if it were running around. Which it's not because my apartment is dope, but still—I could if it were.

Aw, hell. I don't know why, but the thought of her lying on that shitty air mattress with no furniture made me feel like trash. So much so that I lost my fucking mind and opened the drawer on my nightstand, pulling out my old iPhone. I'd stopped using it years ago, after I transferred all my calls to my work phone, but I'd never gotten around to disconnecting the line.

Olivia

My phone buzzed and my heart nearly leapt out of my chest.

And then I saw that it wasn't Mr. Wrong Number. It was a number I didn't know at all, and I hated how disappointed I was. I opened the message.

How's the new apartment, loser?

That made me smile and text: Who is this?

I got up and went down the stairs. I was thirsty, and though not really in the mood for a Bud Light, it was at least cold. I was opening the fridge when my phone buzzed again.

It's Colin. Duh.

My half giggle was loud in the empty apartment as I grabbed a beer and shut the door.

Me: How would I have known that? Have we ever texted each other before?

Colin: You're in my contacts, so I assumed it was mutual. Maybe Jack used my phone sometime.

Me: Sure. Just admit that you miss me already.

Colin: What's to miss? Your noise? Your mess? Your ability to dirty every towel in the bathroom and leave them all on the floor?

Me: On that note, can I borrow your conditioner in the morning?

Colin: Now you're asking?

Me: I'm not your roommate anymore.

Colin: You never were.

Me: Oh, that's right. I was your unwanted houseguest.

Colin: I thought you forgave me for that.

Me: Yeah but I want to use your crème rinse, so . . .

Colin: You do know now that you live alone you're going to have to go shopping for things you actually need, right?

Me: Sigh. Yes.
Colin: It's not so bad.
Me: Says you.
Colin: So you never answered my question. How's the new pad?

I took the beer and went out on the balcony. It smelled like summer and was still hot, and I adored that if I leaned just right I could see the glowing neon lights of Pazza Notte, my absolute favorite restaurant. I texted: Ridiculously perfect. Btw, did I ever thank you for giving me a reference?

Colin: I assumed that was what the kiss was all about.

I almost dropped the phone off the balcony. I didn't know what the hell to say or why he would bring that up and my heart started racing at the mention of the—

Colin: Relax. I was just messing but you went radio silent fucking fast.

I rolled my eyes but laughed.

Me: Screw you, Beck.
Colin: I think you wanted to.
Me: Um, if I recall, you were the instigator.
Colin: You might be right, but you were all in, Livvie. Admit it.
Me: I wasn't disgusted. How about that?

Colin: How about if your brother hadn't come home, I think we might've . . .
Me: Don't say it.
Colin: Totally ended up in my bed.

"Oh, my God." I opened the door and went back into the dark apartment, freaking out and nearly running up the steps to the loft.

I bit down on my lip and texted: You might be right.

Colin: We both know I'm right.

That made me giggle; Colin was fun to flirt with. Who would've guessed that?

Me: So, um, can I have a thirty min nap tomorrow?
Colin: Seriously? I thought my bed was mine now.
Me: I still can't sleep well because of my raft bed, jackwad. I'm only asking for thirty when you aren't home. Don't be stingy with your Purple.
Colin: Fine. You can have thirty, but you owe me.

I dropped down onto the air mattress, giggling yet again with full-on butterflies in my belly. I rolled onto my side, pulled the sheet over my shoulders, and closed my eyes, wholly disgusted with myself for having cliché butterflies.

Me: Swear to God I'd do almost anything to get some alone time with that mattress. We have a deal.

Colin: Btw, you do know that your brother can never know about what happened, right?

I pictured Jack yelling at Milo, my middle school boyfriend, when he walked in on us kissing in the backyard.

Me: Duh. He'd kill us both.

Colin: G'night, Olivia.

12

Olivia

"THIS WAS SO FUN, OLIVIA."

I smiled and wanted to be struck by lightning. Glenda had called and invited me to lunch to talk about the column, and it'd been really nice for a while. We had delicious pizza at Zio's and the woman was hilarious, but then she started talking about her kids. Asking about mine. Each time I gave a vague answer and then pulled an *ohmigosh, is that Tom Brady over there?* type of distraction to lead the conversation away from our offspring.

But it was a screaming reminder that eventually, the whole thing really *was* going to go down in flames. It was only a matter of time, but instead of focusing on the downfall, I was concentrating on enjoying the ride.

"I know—we should do this again soon." I finished my Diet Pepsi and pushed the glass up on the table. "Thanks for inviting me."

"Oh, my God—Glenda! I thought it was you!" A girl who looked around my age came over and hugged Glenda. She shot me a nice smile—man, the girl had perfect teeth—and said to Glenda, "How *are* you?"

The two of them caught up for a second, so I nibbled on the tiny piece of crust left on my plate until they were done. I kind of wished I'd ordered two slices instead of one. After they hugged and the girl walked away, Glenda turned her beaming face to me.

"I'm so sorry, Liv; she used to intern for me and I haven't seen her in ages."

"Oh, my gosh—no big deal at all."

Glenda said, "So where were we?"

I honestly couldn't remember. "I think I was thanking you for taking me to lunch."

"Well," she said, sitting back in her chair, "I just wanted to do something nice because we're all so happy with the column. It's exactly what we wanted but more. Bob thinks you've got a solid number of nonparents reading your articles."

"Really?" I had no idea who Bob was but I wasn't about to ask. If "Bob" thought people liked it, I was a happy girl. "That's so awesome."

She hugged me when we were leaving the restaurant, and said, "I knew I was right about you, Olivia. Congratulations on your success."

I couldn't stop smiling for two blocks as I walked home, blown away by my good fortune. But by the third block, I started to worry. It was just too good to be true—things didn't work like that for me. Someone was going to find out it was me or that I didn't have kids; I just knew it. And they would tell Glenda and everything would be ruined.

It was only a matter of time.

My phone buzzed.

Colin: Did you nap on my bed?

I smiled and responded with: It's only 2:00.

Colin: So?

Me: So only drunks and frat boys nap early. I'm headed home right now, and I'll probably snuggle into your bed soon after my arrival.

Colin: Where are you now?

Me: Just had lunch with my editor.

Colin: Wow, fancy.

Me: I am, in fact, the fanciest.

Colin: Restaurant?

Me: Zio's.

Colin: Did you get the New York King?

Me: Why not ask me if I got the vomit-and-poo pizza? Gross.

Colin: You don't like sausage?

Me: I do not.

Colin: I would've pegged you for a meat lover.

Me: Is that some sort of ribald suggestion about penises?

Colin: Now who's gross, perv? I literally meant you seem like someone who enjoys foods that were once animals.

Me: I don't like meat mixes that are squirted into casings.

Colin: You really have a way with words, Marshall.

Me: Don't I know it.

It was weird how comfortable it was, texting with Colin. I didn't really know how or why, but the back-and-forth was so good that I didn't miss Mr. Wrong Number for once.

Colin fell easily into his place.

Colin: Well, don't trash my bed, loser.

Me: Oh, I'm just going to eat spaghetti and meatballs in there, no worries.

Colin: It wouldn't surprise me if you actually did.

I decided to go straight up to his apartment when I got back. My beautiful pad would be waiting, but I needed to get in a nap before he returned home and I lost my chance. I still had my key, so I let myself in like I still lived there.

The place looked exactly the same, only a little neater. It'd only been a day, but I expected it to feel different already. I stole a Dr Pepper from the fridge and headed for Colin's bed, but got distracted by the sight of the office.

It was gorgeous.

No clothes lying around, no ugly mattress, and the desk was super organized. Colin had clearly moved his work stuff back into the space, because unlike when I'd occupied the room, there were file folders and Post-it notes all over the glass surface. I didn't know what it was, but there was something about seeing his businesslike handwriting that made me a little . . . impressed.

Weird, right?

I walked into his room, and it looked exactly the same as it had during every previous nap session. His bed was made, the charcoal comforter perfectly straightened with the pillows just right, making it look like an advertisement. The dark wood of his nightstand and dresser gleamed as if just dusted, and it smelled like pine.

And Colin.

I kicked off my shoes, knowing it was going to take me approximately thirty seconds to fall asleep once I climbed on top of that king-sized cloud and laid down my head. I dragged the edge of the comforter up and over me before setting my phone alarm for forty minutes, but fifteen minutes later my phone was ringing.

"Mfhello?" I sat up and blinked, trying to work through the shock of being woken up.

"Hey, Olivia—it's Jordyn in the office. I just wanted to let you know that the guys from the furniture store just brought your key back so they're all finished."

I scratched my head and said, "What?"

"Nebraska Furniture Mart. They just delivered something to your apartment."

I got off Colin's bed and fixed the blanket. "My apartment?"

"Um, yes; was that not okay?"

I picked up my purse and shoes from the floor and started for the door. "I mean, it's okay, but I didn't order anything. Are you sure it was my apartment?"

"Listen, Olivia, someone is here to see an apartment so I have to go." Jordyn sounded irritated now. "Let me know if there's anything else I can do for you, okay?"

"Oh." Maybe my desk had shipped early and she was confused about the store. "Okay."

As I rode the elevator, I realized it couldn't be the desk; I'd ordered that the night before and it was shipping from a warehouse in Minneapolis. Maybe Dana had exchanged the stools or something. I stepped out at my floor and just hoped I didn't owe money for furniture that wasn't mine.

Colin

"I can't believe you actually made it for once." Jillian leaned back in her chair and crossed her arms, grinning as our parents exited the dining room. "Mom's going to be insufferable for months now, reminiscing about the time her little Colin actually joined us for lunch at the club."

To be honest, I couldn't believe it myself. I usually avoided doing anything with my parents at the club, but when my mother, who had just recovered from a heart attack, called the night before, I'd caved and agreed to grab a quick bite with the family.

"Dad won't be joining her in those fond memories, though, will he?" I signed the ticket and handed it to the server, wondering why my family liked the place so much. It was dark wood and old money, formal and pretentious, and my mother and father made it a habit to share a meal there at least twice a week.

"That's because you never just shut up and let him talk."

Jill was good at that. She'd always let my father go on and on without her saying a word because she knew it was futile; I, on the other hand, wasn't so good with acquiescing. "Well, it pisses me off that everyone does that. He's like the fucking king and it's ridiculous. Who gets to say things like 'only members of a fraternity and out-of-work actors have roommates at your age' and get away with it?"

"Now, now, Colin, you have to understand." She drained the last of her wine and set down the crystal glass. "He's lashing out because he misses his little prince."

"I think our patriarch made it abundantly clear that I am not that."

"True." Jillian snorted. "But you argue with him about everything."

"I only argue with him about the things that matter to me, and when he intentionally comes at me, I refuse to just sit there and take it."

My dad was a decent guy. He went to mass every week at St. Thomas, worked hard, took his wife on nice vacations, and told funny jokes on the golf course.

But he and I had been in a perpetual standoff since I was in the eighth grade.

Public school versus private; I'd picked the wrong one at the ripe age of fourteen. After I graduated junior high, he'd wanted me to go to Creighton Prep, but I'd used my mother-son bond to get her on my side and we'd demanded my public education. He caved because he was far too busy to waste time arguing with my mom, but until the day I graduated, the man never failed to point out the terrible education I was receiving every time I wasn't able to instantly answer a pop quiz question.

Then it was state university versus Notre Dame; to this day he felt betrayed by my refusal to attend his alma mater (and my grandfather's alma mater and my grandfather's father's alma mater). He'd tried holding back the funds to keep me under his thumb, but when you scored a perfect 36 on your ACT, the scholarships flowed like water. I'd been able to flip him the bird and go away to college at the University of Nebraska with Jack.

But my ultimate sin was not going into law. He and the Becks before him had spent their entire lives working to build a prominent and thriving practice. In his mind, I was going to let their dream die off because I chose to "fiddle" with numbers like a middle-class accounting clerk instead of stepping up and choosing a proper career.

But I just couldn't. I'd watched my dad and my uncles and my grandpa spend every day of their lives working for power. They didn't love their work, but they adored what their work gave them. Respectability and influence, wealth and connections.

All I wanted was to be a regular guy who actually enjoyed his job. I loved the challenge of numbers, so why not do that for a living? That crazy way of thinking made me, the guy with a master's in mathematics, the black sheep of the family.

Honestly, that was why I'd never taken a penny from them after college. I'd worked my ass off to support myself, to buy nice things like the condo and my car, just to prove to the world that my father's opinion about my career was dead wrong.

I made my own success without the help of the esteemed Thomas Beck.

"Well, it's fun to watch." Jillian grabbed her handbag from the floor and said, "I wish you'd come more often."

My phone rang and I was a little disappointed; it felt good hanging out with my sister, and I didn't want to be interrupted. She was a lawyer and liked the Beck life, but she'd somehow managed to keep her feet on the ground enough to understand what I was trying to do, too.

I pulled the phone out of my pocket, but when I saw it was Olivia, my mood brightened and I lifted the phone to my ear. "Marshall."

"Beck." She cleared her throat. "Um, there's a bed here."

I leaned back in my chair and imagined what her reaction must've been when it showed up at her door. It'd been a crazy idea, giving her a bed, but she didn't have one and I *did* owe her for that letter. "Where?"

"You know where. In my apartment."

"And you're not talking about your raft?"

"You know I'm not." I heard her trail off and mutter, "Although, come to think of it, I have no idea where that thing went."

"Focus, Liv."

"Why is there a bed here that looks exactly like yours?"

"Well, I'm sure it isn't *exactly* like mine. Mine was a special order."

"Do you know anything about the bed in my room? Focus, Beck."

"Yeah." Was this supposed to be fun? Because this was fun. I glanced at Jill and she was watching me with a tiny smirk.

"Turns out I'm not a huge fan of people napping in my room, so I thought this was the best solution."

"You bought me a million-dollar bed exactly like yours so I won't nap in your apartment?"

"You're not listening, Marshall; it's *not* exactly like mine. I'd never drop that kind of coin on someone who could accidentally spill a vat of nacho cheese on it at any given moment."

I heard her snort out a little laugh. "Okay, so, what does this mean? Do I have to let you nap on it?"

"I'm not into slumming."

"Then why did you do something that nice?"

"It wasn't me being nice. You helped me land a huge client when you didn't have to." I rolled my eyes at Jill like the caller was ridiculous. "This was just me paying you back."

"I see." She sounded happy and confused. "Uh, this isn't like a sex thing, either, right? Like you bought me a bed, so now I have to sleep with you on it?"

Well, shit—like I needed *more* visuals of Liv in bed. I'd gone from finding her the most annoying girl on the planet to being inexplicably obsessed with her. She still irritated the hell out of me, but I couldn't stop thinking about the way she rolled her eyes and the way her face got that intensity to it when she was typing one hundred words per minute on her laptop.

I lowered my voice and turned away from the table. "It is *not* a sex thing, though gratitudial favors will not be turned down should you feel inclined."

"Gratitudial?"

"That's right."

I heard her laugh again. "Well, I *am* incredibly gratitudial,

Colin. This was the nicest surprise and I think I'm going to take a second nap on my very own bed the minute I get off the phone."

"Did you already take—"

"Oh, yeah. Your bed was amazing, by the way."

I started laughing; of course she had.

Then she said, "You should come down and see it after you get home; my bed is stunning."

No way was I going down to look at her bed. I needed to put a lot of distance between my libido and Jack's little sister.

Jack's little sister, Jack's little sister, Jack's little sister.

I said, "Mine's better."

"Well, after I nap I'm going to eat leftover pizza on my deck and shop for sheets and blankets, so it's pretty much going to be like a party all night down here on six if you change your mind."

"I will keep that in mind," I said, knowing I wouldn't.

"Well, goodbye, then, Colin."

"Goodbye, Liv."

The second I ended the call, Jillian said, "Holy hells, Col—who was that? You're positively beaming."

I rolled my eyes and stood. "As if I'm telling you. Are you ready?"

She stood and pushed in her chair. "If you don't give me the story by the time we reach our cars, I'm keying your Audi and calling our mother."

"Fine." I gave a chin-nod to one of my father's golfing buddies as we walked out of the dining room. "I'll give you the short version, but you have to promise not to laugh."

"I'm afraid I can do no such thing."

13

Olivia

I LOOKED OVER AT THE DOOR WHEN I HEARD A KNOCK. I WAS sitting on a stool, watching an old episode of *New Girl* on my laptop and eating leftover pizza, and after seeing Zooey Deschanel look so damned adorable, I'd pulled out my makeup bag and attempted to re-create her look.

It hadn't worked.

I had on bright red lipstick that looked kind of good but super trampy, like I was the kind of woman who would eat a Popsicle hyper-sexually in an obnoxious attempt to arouse all the menfolk. My eyes were lined in black and I had the wings, but I looked more like I should be in an eighties rock video than an adorable show with Nick Miller.

To make it worse, I was wearing my old softball pants because I saw them in the box and remembered how comfortable they were and wanted to see if they still fit.

"Who is it?" I stood and tried gauging how long it would take for me to sprint up to the loft and change my pants really fast. Colin had said he wasn't coming by, and no one besides my brother and Dana even knew where I lived.

"It's Colin."

Of course it is. "If you've come looking for gratitudial favors, just keep walking."

"I brought bedding."

I undid the locks and opened the door a crack, leaving on the chain. He was wearing a black T-shirt and jeans and—holy shit—those glasses. It was like he was trying to look like a hot nerd or something. I said, "Bedding for my bed?"

He tilted his head. "What else would I bring bedding for?"

Dear Lord. "Hang on."

I shut the door and started undoing the chain. "You need to promise not to say anything about the way I look."

"This should be good."

I pulled the door open, and his face immediately split into a wide grin. "Well, what do we have here?"

"Bite me."

He walked into the apartment with an armful of bedding, his eyes all over me as he grinned like I was a moron. "What *is* this, though? Like . . . Cher meets Taylor Swift . . . ?"

"Cher?" I grabbed the pile from his hands and set them on the island. "What part of this says Cher?"

He put his lips together as if trying to stop himself from smiling. "I just thought all the makeup and . . ."

He gestured to my hair and face.

"Whatever." I put my hands on my hips and tried for the

cool I would surely exude if I weren't wearing softball pants and a Coors Extra bro tank. "So do you want to see it?"

He gave a little laugh and his eyes dipped over me, but this time I felt it. This time it was flirty, not mocking. "Oh, yeah."

There was a lot in his *oh, yeah*, but I chose to ignore it. "Grab the beer out of the fridge and you can come help me make the bed."

I didn't even look at his face as I grabbed the stack of sheets and went upstairs. I hadn't meant it to sound suggestive and had no idea why I'd invited him to help me make my bed. What the hell even was that? Thankfully he had no comment, and I heard the refrigerator open, so I knew he was actually obeying.

When we got upstairs, I was a little embarrassed that there was an empty beer can on the floor beside the bed and an open box of Froot Loops. I was tempted to kick them into the closet, but it's not like my bad habits were any secret to Colin.

I set the stack of sheets on the half wall that overlooked the rest of the apartment, and ran my hand over the pristine whiteness of the fabric. "Oh, my God, Beck, are these sheets linen?"

He emerged from the last stair and—oh, mama—his handsomeness took the air out of my lungs. Something about those tortoiseshell glasses on the bridge of that strong nose really worked for me.

"So what?"

That made me smile. "So you're such a diva, Beck."

His mouth was firm but his eyes were amused. "It's summer, Liv—linen is perfect. Light and breathable so you don't get hot, but they feel heavier than a traditional sheet. You'll love them."

I knew he was right, because I'd lied; when he'd gone to Boston, I *had* slept under his covers. I hadn't known it was because of the sheets, but I'd been enamored with the feel of the cool bedding on my skin. "I promise to return them after I buy some."

I'd ordered a sofa and a TV from Amazon earlier in the day, so why not add bedding? I had a stable job now, after all.

"Consider them a gift. I washed them after I bought the set, but they've never been used."

"Um, thanks." I unfolded the bottom sheet—*of course Colin had folded it perfectly*—and shook it out. "But I'm still not sure why you're doing these nice things for me. It's so unlike you that I'm a little terrified."

"First of all, it's not unlike me. I'm a super-nice guy."

"Except to me."

"Granted." He stepped over and grabbed an end, pulling the sheet toward the bed. "Second of all, this is my insurance policy that you never return. If all it takes is a mattress and a sheet and you're forever out of the nest, it's a tiny price to pay."

"See?" I moved with him toward the bed, holding my end and being a little distracted by the sight of us doing such an intimate, domestic thing together. "That's exactly what I needed to make myself not feel guilty about being a charity case. You're actually kind of being a jackass by buying me a luxurious bed just like yours, then."

"It is *not* just like mine," he muttered, tucking his side under his corner of the mattress, "it is a much cheaper version."

"Sure it is." I tucked the sheet around my corner of the mattress, then moved down toward the foot of the bed with sheet in hand.

"Believe what you want, Marshall."

"Oh, I will, Beck."

He grabbed the top sheet from the stack and shook it out while I cracked open a beer. I watched in amusement as he not only laid it over the mattress but went around the bed four times, straightening the sheet and tucking in all the corners.

It was so white and crisp that it looked like a hotel bed.

Then he tossed a pillow on the mattress and just stood back to survey his work.

"Thank you so much." I couldn't be nonchalant anymore because my heart was overflowing with warmth for Colin. "I don't care if getting my irritating ass out of your apartment was the reason. This is like the nicest thing anyone's ever done for me."

He swallowed and I was transfixed by the sight of his throat moving. Such a solid, tan, masculine column of neck.

"Everyone deserves presents sometimes."

"Wow." I blinked. "I hadn't expected *that* to come out of your mouth."

"What's that supposed to mean?"

"Nothing." I grabbed the beer and started down the stairs. "You just don't strike me as the gift-giving sort."

"You calling me cheap?" He followed me down, his voice right behind me. "What the hell is that?"

"Not cheap," I said, setting the beer on the island and turning to face him. "Just a little too cerebral to think of thoughtful gifts."

Just like that we were close. He took another step, bringing us even closer. "I'll have you know that I am an amazing gift giver."

"Is this where you're going to tell me what an amazing lover you are? Spare me the orgasm count, Beck."

That made him smile, but it was a slow one that started in a naughty look and turned up to full-on sexy. "Fine."

"Fine."

"But you know I'm a numbers guy."

"Come on, Beck, don't."

He gave a little chuckle. "I wasn't going to."

"Good."

"But we both know."

"The number?"

"The sheer possibilities of my numbers."

Now I was giving the chuckle. "I think I need another beer."

His hot blue eyes just stayed on me for a minute, pinning me in place as we both let our minds drift to a sexual place. But then he cleared his throat and said, "I'm going to take off and let you get to your bed."

"Thanks." Disappointment slithered through me. I hadn't consciously known I'd wanted this sexual tension to go somewhere, but I was full-on bummed that he was leaving. I smiled and said, "I guess you really *didn't* get the bed so we could bang one out."

His jaw clenched before he turned and walked over to the front door, seeming in a sudden rush to get out of there. I followed him, and just as he put his hand on the doorknob he said, looking back at me, "You and me, Liv? We wouldn't need a bed."

My eyes were on his, the rest of everything falling away. "No, we wouldn't."

His hand gripped the door handle. "But that would be a terrible idea."

"The worst."

The air was so electrified that it felt like we were panting as we watched each other. He said, "I should go."

"You should."

He turned, pulled open the door and I heard myself say, "Unless."

Colin slammed it shut and turned around. "Unless . . . ?"

I shrugged and stepped forward, suddenly fully committed to this terrible decision. "Unless we were to lay down some ground rules."

"Like?" He took his own step forward and his lips were just above mine, his eyes so heavy lidded and intense that it was almost intimidating.

"Like, um," I started as his teeth nipped at my bottom lip, making my breathing choppy, "this means nothing, no strings, no one ever knows it happened, and no weirdness."

"Fuck, I love your rules."

"And," I said as we kind of started kissing around our conversation, moving back into the apartment, "no romance."

"Genius." He put his big hands under my ass and picked me up, and I happily wrapped my legs around his waist. "God, I've been dying to eat off your red lipstick since I got here."

"If you're wearing those sex-nerd glasses, you're welcome to eat whatever you want."

His eyes crinkled at the edges. "Pervert."

"Maybe." He started full-on kissing me then, with all the

power of his tongue and teeth and lips and breath. My hands went up to his thick hair, and all ten fingers sunk in.

"By the way," he breathed, lifting his mouth off mine, "your polyester baseball pants are like the biggest fucking aphrodisiac."

"Shut up, you ass, I didn't expect—"

"I'm so serious, Livvie, you don't even know."

His words made me glow on the inside, and I licked at the corner of his mouth as I reached for the bottom of his shirt.

"I thought you hated my abs."

"Shut up and help me."

He carried me over to the island and set me down, and I was almost breathless in anticipation as he grabbed his shirt and pulled it over his head. Yes, I'd seen his chest before, but I'd never been able to ogle out in the open. I stared up at him through sleepy eyes and said, "Oh, my God."

He was defined to the nth degree, his body all tanned skin and hidden strength.

"Gross, right?"

I nodded and whispered reverently, "So, so disgusting."

I ran my hands up his pecs, and then things ignited. It was like we both got greedy for everything we weren't doing yet. I pulled off my shirt and he was toeing off his shoes, and then his hands were unsnapping and mine were unbuckling.

As opposed to some drawn-out exploration of each other's bodies, this was a race to the main event. We needed to feel and had no time to spare for half measures like foreplay. Hands were everywhere. Mouths were fused and unwilling to part.

I whispered into his mouth, intending to say, *Are we sure*

about this? but instead saying, "Condom," to which he muttered something in the affirmative that required his hands to go rummaging while I continued sexually dominating his mouth with my own.

Could a person die from this? I felt like I was going to die as my heart raced and my breath hitched and my every molecule was buzzing with electricity and writhing and attuned only to Colin Beck. He grunted when I used my heels to pull him closer to me, and he cursed into my ear when I bit his shoulder.

And then—finally—he was there, hot and tense and so unbelievably *right* inside me that I unintentionally dug my nails into his shoulder blades. I'd always thought the fingernail thing was cliché, but in that moment, I was physically incapable of retracting my claws.

I forced my eyes to stay open so I could look at him. His nostrils were flared and his jaw was clenched, those rowdy eyes glued to mine as his body made me feel unbelievable things. It was so unreal—so deliciously good—that the kitchen, the apartment, and the entire world disappeared. Time dropped away as we caught fire on the granite countertop, and I wasn't sure if seconds or hours passed as Colin made me burn. My entire existence was right there, where we were together, and nothing else mattered.

"Oh, holy fuck, yes, Liv," Colin rasped as he breathed against my mouth, "Come on—"

I said through gritted teeth, "Don't rush me."

Which made him chuckle and growl into my ear, "I would never rush you, Marshall. Take all the time you need, because I could stay in here for fucking ever."

His words sent me tumbling, which clearly affected Colin because he groaned something that sounded a lot like *holyshit-motherfuckingfuck* into the space between my neck and shoulder and squeezed my ass so hard I was sure there'd be marks.

When he finally lifted his head, he gave me a crooked grin. "Did we just christen your new kitchen?"

"We did." I grabbed my shirt from where it was dangling on the faucet and said, "Someday, when my mother swings by without calling first and sets her purse on this very spot, I will smile, knowing just how upset this scenario would make her."

Colin

What in the holy shit have I just done?

I opened Olivia's fridge and grabbed one of the three remaining cans of beer from moving night and tried to stay cool, but the truth was that I was freaking the hell out.

I had sex with Olivia Marshall.

I had *sex* with Olivia, Jack's annoying little baby sister.

What had I been thinking? Jack was going to kill me, and it was the absolute right thing to do. I felt like the world's biggest asshole. I'd been determined to *not* come down and see her new bed, but somehow, after work, my dick had convinced my brain that I could drop off bedding and then just leave.

Idiot move right there.

As soon as Olivia came out of the bathroom, I was going to convince her we'd made a huge mistake, beg her to keep quiet, and get the hell out of there.

Shit.

Maybe I should move. To another country.

I was mid-chug when she came out and I nearly choked.

Because . . . *shit.*

She was wearing just her tank top, which hit right at the top of her thighs, and her long, dark hair was a mess. She absolutely looked like she'd just climbed out of bed, and she kind of took my breath away, especially when she gave me a total Olivia smirk.

"We need to talk, Beck. Let's get some air." She turned her back to me and walked toward the living room, so I dutifully followed. I clenched my jaw so hard it hurt as I forced my eyes to stay up, looking at the back of her head—instead of her perfect ass—as she walked.

"I'm glad you said it," I muttered, trailing after her as she opened the sliding door and stepped out onto the dark balcony.

As I closed the door behind me, she leaned on the railing and looked out at the city. I denied my discipline and let my eyes dip, but it was too dark to really see anything other than the curve of her backside.

Shit.

"I don't know what we were thinking in there," she said, her voice a little gruff in the darkness, "but I'm sure we both agree that it was a huge mistake."

I sat down on the deck chair that'd come with the apartment and said, "Agreed."

"I'm sure we also agree that Jack can never know what happened."

"Never." The sound of a car horn honked from below, and

I crossed my arms over my chest and wondered how she wasn't freezing out there. It was an unseasonably cool night, yet she stood there in panties and a tank top as if it were a hot summer's night.

"Good." She cleared her throat and turned around, a smile on her lips as the light from inside her apartment shined on her face. "So, um, you should probably take off now so we can put this mistake behind us."

For some reason, the smile pissed me off. Even though I'd been planning on saying to her exactly what she'd said to me, the way she was grinning and telling me to leave just hit wrong. So I said, "I *could* take off right now, but I don't know if I feel like it."

"What?" Her eyebrows slammed together like I knew they would.

I tilted my head and let my eyes stroll all over her. *Shit, shit, shit—not too smart.* "Think about it. The mistake has already been made—we had sex. So . . . if we were to have sex again on the same night, it still counts for the same mistake."

She blinked fast, like she was thinking, and she crossed her arms. "No, it doesn't."

"Are you saying each time counts, then?"

"Yes." She stacked one foot on top of the other and stood like a flamingo, which was somehow hot.

"So if we were to go up to your loft right now and have sex four times and then decided to come clean, you're saying we'd have to tell your brother, 'Hey, we had sex four times' instead of 'oops, we had sex.'"

She rolled her eyes but I could tell she wanted to smile. "Don't be an idiot."

"So you concede my point."

"Kind of." She did smile then, shaking her head a little. "I agree that sexual mistakes are probably on a *per session* basis, as opposed to *per orgasm*, but that still doesn't mean—"

"Come here, Marshall." She was only about two steps away from of me, but it wasn't close enough. "You're too far away."

Her smile changed, slid into something sexy as she dropped her arms to her sides and closed the gap between us. Except she kept coming, stepping in between my spread knees so I had to look up at her.

"So here's what I'm thinking." I put my hands on her waist and squeezed, and then—holy shit—Olivia climbed onto my lap like it was totally natural.

"Lay it on me."

I was done. Any indecision was gone as she smiled and teased me. I said, "If this is our one and only 'session,' aren't we cheating ourselves by not showing our best work? I mean, don't get me wrong, I really liked our counter work—"

"As did I."

"But I have more to offer. I've got some skills I'd like to showcase."

That made her laugh. She crinkled her nose and said, "So basically you want to make sure I know just how good you are before we never do this again."

"Exactly." It was tough not to laugh, too, when she was looking at me like that. "Don't you? Or maybe you don't have skills . . ."

She rolled her eyes. "Trust me, I have skills."

"I don't think I believe you."

"Really, Beck?"

She leaned closer and whispered something so incredibly dirty into my ear that my fingers reflexively tightened on her back. I didn't know if she could do that with her tongue or not, but I was all in on finding out.

"Son of a bitch, Marshall." I stood, threw her over my shoulder in a fireman's hold, and opened the door. "Let's go."

She squealed my name.

"That's right—say it," I said around a laugh as I smacked her squirming ass and headed for the loft, which made her cackle.

One thing about Olivia that I'd forgotten before she came back to town was that she was always fun. Whether she was falling on her face or being a brat, she'd been quick to laugh since the day I first met her. I still remembered that I'd gone home with my school friend Jack, and his weirdo little sister followed us around the entire time singing songs from *Annie*. To this day I could hear her howling out the damned words to "Maybe."

But as someone who grew up in a very serious family, I found her laugh a little addictive.

I charged up the steps, and when we got to her room, I dumped her on the bed. She was giggling, wild hair everywhere, and then she leaned up on her elbows, cocking an eyebrow. "Ready to show me those skills?"

She was all legs and tank top and sexual promise, and I had no idea how I would ever see her the same again. The smell of her perfume, the green hue of her eyes, the tilt of her pink mouth; it all worked together to destroy me.

"Born ready, sunshine." I climbed onto the bed, crawling up her body on my hands and knees.

When her eyes were right under mine, she blinked up at me and swallowed.

She had less bravado than she let on.

I remembered her texts to Mr. Wrong Number about only wanting it fast and furious; did the slow burn of intimacy scare her? Her long-lashed gaze pulled me in, and I think I muttered something like *God help me* before I lowered my head and kissed her, a hot, slow kiss that shot fire all the way through my body as she wrapped her arms around my neck and moaned into my mouth.

I kept at it, feeding her slow intensity while wondering why it mattered that she was letting me. With every long-drawn-out scorch of a kiss, I felt like I was winning something by her wanton participation.

Closed eyes, deep sighing breaths—damn.

I didn't want to push my luck, though.

"Marshall." I pulled back and watched as her emerald eyes fluttered open.

"Hmmm?" She smiled up at me with an unfocused gaze and moved her hands up to the back of my hair.

"Quit distracting me with slow kisses." I bit down on her lower lip and grabbed her ass in both hands. "I've got skills to showcase."

"It's about time," she said, breaking into a wide smile and giving my hair a tug before reaching between us to grab the hem of her shirt and pulling it up and over her head. "I was falling asleep."

"Is that right?" I touched her then, and she gasped out a breathy "Well, I was about to."

It turned explosive, with the few items of clothing we'd had on dissipating in an instant. The long kisses turned into a frenzied meeting of mouths—teeth and lips and tongues, crashing, dragging, biting as we flipped all over her new bed, our bodies fitting together so fucking perfectly that I swear to God I lost my hearing for a few minutes.

Everything disappeared but the urgent electricity crackling through that loft.

"That's a nice move," she bit out as I drove her a little higher up on the mattress.

"You like that?" I nipped her neck with my teeth and did it again, earning me a fingernail scrape down my back before she sunk all ten claws into my ass.

"Definitely a solid maneuver," she panted.

"Thanks," I managed, but it was taking every bit of my control to hold back. "I got you, Liv."

She let her head fall back as she moved with me, absolutely unaware of how mind-fuckingly perfect her skills were. I wanted to tell her, but I'd lost the ability to do anything but grit my teeth and hold on for the ride.

14

Olivia

COLIN FELL ASLEEP AROUND THREE; I COULD HEAR IN HIS breathing that he was out.

My back was against his chest and his arms were wrapped around me, and I was kind of in shock over just how incredible the night had been.

I mean, Colin being good at sex was no surprise; I'd somehow known he would be. But he'd been sweet and funny and a tiny bit romantic, too, which was one hell of a surprise. The way he'd held my face while he was kissing me, the hot look in his blue eyes—my stomach got light when I thought of it, and he was still in my bed, for God's sake.

The night was a mistake—of course it was—but it wasn't a mistake I'd regret. It'd been too good. If Colin were any other guy in the world, I'd be freaking out at that very minute and daydreaming about him becoming my boyfriend.

Thank God I knew better.

Even though he'd surprised me with his sweetness, it was still just sex. Just the two of us responding to the chemistry, and now it could never happen again. In real life, we never would've connected in a relationship sort of way, so this had just been us getting in a few more good rolls before the sun came up.

I smiled and burrowed my head deeper into the linen pillowcase that smelled like Colin's laundry detergent. Who would've thought the greatest sex of my life would be with Colin Beck?

I closed my eyes and let the quiet sound of his breathing lull me to sleep.

MY PHONE.

I sat up in bed, waking up as my phone chirped from where it was charging on the floor. I was confused for half a second before I looked down and saw that I was sprawled out across a very sleepy-looking Colin.

Who was smirking at me.

Shit. One look at his face and the events of the night before came rushing back.

Holy balls.

It'd been an incredible night, but Colin had made me feel too much. I felt my cheeks get hot as he grinned and I said, "Hey, you."

He raised an eyebrow. "Good morning."

The phone was loud, and I had to crawl over him to grab it. Part of me was glad for the distraction, because I needed to get my thoughts together and be cool about Colin. I glanced at the display—it was Glenda.

"Oh." I stole the sheet, wrapped it around my body, and moved to sit at the foot of the bed in case Colin wanted to go back to sleep.

"Hello?"

I watched Colin climb out of bed and grab his pants from the floor, stepping into them, and it almost felt too intimate for me to witness.

"Olivia, it's Glenda. Listen, I'm just going to get right to it."

Her voice sounded weird—pissed—and my stomach dropped. Something was very wrong. I scrambled off the bed, grasping the top of the sheet before running down the stairs to take the call. I didn't want Colin to hear. "Oka—"

"Beth with human resources is also on the line, just in case we require assistance, okay?"

Oh, my God. "Um, okay."

"It's been brought to our attention that you don't have any children. Is this true?"

My ears started buzzing and I felt queasy. "Um, technically *yes*, but if you'll let me ex—"

"So you completely fabricated two children in order to get this job, is that correct?"

"No!" My heartbeat was going bonkers as I tried to think of a way to explain. "I mean, kind of yes. God. It started as a tiny misunderstanding, and then I didn't know how—"

"We cannot have a parenting columnist who isn't a parent." Glenda sounded so cold that my throat hurt. "But bigger than that, one of our core values at the *Times* is integrity, Olivia. Dishonesty is absolutely unacceptable and will not be tolerated."

I blinked fast and felt both cold and hot. And also like a terrible human being. I tried not to cry. "I'm so sorry. Do you think we could get together and—"

"We have no choice but to terminate your employment." It was clear Glenda didn't care to hear my side of it, and I didn't blame her. "Beth is going to take over the call and give you information on COBRA and your NDA. Take care."

Just like that Glenda was gone, and the nice HR lady started going over my nondisclosure agreement. I listened as she explained the legal recourse of telling secrets, and it made me think of my own secrets.

How the hell had they found out?

I hadn't told anyone other than Colin that I was the 402 Mom, but he wouldn't tell, right? I mean, who the hell would he tell? He was too busy—and too self-absorbed—to tattle to the newspaper about my dishonesty.

I could still hear his words on the balcony. *You really think in a town like Omaha it's not going to come out?*

As if on cue Colin appeared, skipping down the loft steps, looking like expensive sin. He could've been in a brochure for a country club that very second, in his bare feet and tailored pants, throwing out his good haircut and bone structure like tangible pheromones.

But as I laid eyes on all of that sophistication, it hit me—he *was* the one who told. He had to be. I was positive he hadn't called the paper and ratted me out or anything like that, but I was equally positive he'd probably laughingly recounted to my brother or some of his rich-boy buddies the story of his idiotic friend who was pulling off an idiotic ruse.

He'd probably seen the billboard and told the story.

Dammit, I'd *known* everything was too good to be true. The job had been too good to be true, and so had my "friendship" with Colin. What the hell had I been thinking, trusting the guy who told me in sixth grade that my makeup looked like something a drunk old lady would paint on her face?

I turned away from him and listened to the details of how to continue my insurance before the HR girl officially terminated both me and the phone call. The second I hung up, Colin stepped into my line of sight and said, "Who was that? What's wrong?"

I just shook my head and blinked fast, but tears fell as I managed, "It's . . . God. It's just . . . *of course*."

He took a step toward me and I held out my hand. "Listen, Colin. Can you just go?"

His eyebrows were crinkled like he was worried. *Yeah, right.* His eyes traveled all over my face as he said, "Yeah, but maybe I can help."

I croaked, "You can't."

"But maybe there's a—"

"You've already helped enough, okay?" I wiped at my eyes but my voice was throaty when I crossed my arms and said, "Thanks for sexing me up, *Col*, but you need to leave."

"Col?" He leaned back a little, like I'd taken a swipe at him, and said, "What just happened?"

"What just happened?" I sniffled and another stupid tear

fell, but I didn't feel sad anymore. I was on-fire pissed, and I narrowed my eyes at that jackass. "I trusted Colin Beck, that's what happened. I just got fired, that's what happened."

"What?" He looked confused. "You got fired?"

"Yeah, as it turns out, they don't like it when their parenting columnists aren't parents."

"Oh, shit. They found out?" His eyebrows went up. "Wait. You don't think that I—"

"Of course I think that, Colin. You're the only one who knew."

He looked speechless for a second—*sucks getting caught, bro*—and then he said, "Livvie, why would I—"

"Because you're you, Colin!" I dropped my arms to my sides and wanted to scream. "You're an arrogant asshole who has always mocked me for your own entertainment. I'm sure you thought it was hilarious that I was lying about my job, so you probably shared the story with your douchey country club friends over golf and caviar or something."

He looked stunned by that. "Is that really what you think of me?"

"For sure it is. Just wait till you tell them about last night, right? Your dad will probably call you a chip off the ol' block and buy the whole place a round." I jerked the sheet around my body and said, "I'm going to shower. Please be gone by the time I get out."

I SLOWLY OPENED the bathroom door and listened.

Nothing.

All was quiet, which meant that Colin had left, thank God.

I'd held it all in while I showered, just in case he was still there and wanted to talk, but now that I had visual confirmation of his absence, I lost it.

I broke down into full-out ugly crying as my quiet apartment forced me to face all of the terrible facts. I'd lost my job, trusted a jerk, slept with said jerk, and now I had furniture that I couldn't afford on the way and a fab new apartment that was way out of my price range.

Which was zero, by the way.

I pretty much bawled for the next hour, overwhelmed by everything I'd just lost.

Then I got pissed.

Because almost as bad as the ruination of my burgeoning career was the thought of Colin in one of his fancy suits, tipping back martinis with women who looked like Harper and saying, "I know the girl who writes that. She's the one who burned down her apartment—remember her? Yeah, she's a total screwup who doesn't even have kids."

Insert a fancy lounge full of rich professionals laughing.

Shit.

I stripped the bed of Colin's sheets and jammed them into a trash bag. At first I was going to leave them on his doorstep, but knowing my amazing luck, Jack would find them and I'd be totally hosed, so I decided not to. Ultimately I took the bag down to the dumpster and threw away a perfectly lovely set of expensive linen sheets.

By late afternoon I was out of emotion. I got in that sterile, detached mood that always hit after saying, *Screw everything.* I applied for a few content jobs and sent an email to one of the online companies that'd offered me freelance work before I'd been hired by the *Times.* They were all crappy, creativity-free positions, but they'd at least pay the bills.

I walked down to the market on the corner and purchased a dinner of hot dogs, a box of Frosted Flakes, and Diet Coke, and once I got home, I didn't know what to do with myself. It was such a quiet apartment with no TV, and I was getting sick of mindlessly messing with my phone. I had a bed and two barstools—that was it.

Empty, like me at the moment.

I kept thinking Colin would text an apology, but of course not. He probably didn't even care.

Jackass.

I forced myself not to think about the night before—no good could come of that—and after lying on my bare mattress for an hour with no sleepiness to be found, I sent a text to Mr. Wrong Number.

Me: I know we don't know each other, but we DID have an actual friendship and you could've at least said goodbye. Right now everything in my life is in the trash and I'm kind of alone, and I could really use an anonymous friend. Sucks that you suck so badly.

I plugged my phone into the charger and shut off the light.

Screw him, too.

Boys sucked.

But then my phone buzzed. I looked down at it in the darkness.

Mr. Wrong Number: I can't tell you why I disappeared, but it was nothing you did and I'm so sorry for leaving you alone. I know you're mad, but if you need to talk, I'm here.

I wanted to stay mad but the truth of the matter was that I needed to talk. I desperately needed to talk to someone who didn't know me or my situation. I turned the light back on.

Me: What would you say if I told you that I slept with my brother's best friend, got fired from my job for lying, then found out that my brother's best friend was the one responsible for airing the secret that got me fired?

Colin

I stared down at the phone in my hand and didn't know what to do. Hell.

Because I was torn between feeling really bad for Liv, and being really pissed at her. It sucked that she got fired from a job she loved, especially when she was so good at it. I knew her well enough to know she was hurt and also stressing the hell out over paying rent on the new apartment.

Which was why I'd sent that apology text from Mr. Wrong Number.

But.

How could she think I'd tell? That was ludicrous in and of itself—like, who the fuck would I tell?—but her quick accusation had shown exactly what she thought of me. After living together for a month, I'd thought we'd become friends in our way.

And then the sex.

So I was shocked speechless when she basically said I was exactly like my father. Shit, I wouldn't have even guessed she'd known or remembered my dad, but apparently she did and assumed I was his country club mini-me. My worst goddamned nightmare.

You've been a busy girl, I responded.

Olivia: In the worst possible way.

I wasn't going to ask any questions. I just needed to make her feel okay and then I'd return to ghosting. I texted: That sucks.

Texting bubbles and then—

The sex was unreal. Like, porn stars would probably be jealous of how good we were.

Dammit. I agreed wholeheartedly, but it was wrong for me to see that when it wasn't intended for my eyes. I responded with: Wow.

Olivia: Right? I mean, it was going nowhere and we'd already agreed that it'd never happen again, but sleeping with him was like the MOST fun. That is, until I woke up to the worst morning of my life.

I couldn't stop myself. I texted: How do you know he's the one who told?

Olivia: No one else knew.
Me: You sure?
Olivia: Absolutely. And he's totally the dickhead type to ruin me for fun.

I sent one more text before turning off the lamp and going to bed, frustrated that I couldn't do anything to help the absurd situation.

Me: Well at least the sex was good.

15

Olivia

"HONEY, SLOW DOWN ON THE PANCAKES."

I rolled my eyes while chewing with an overfilled mouth.

My mother said, "Don't roll your eyes at me. You're twenty-five years old, for the love of God."

I breathed in through my nose and looked across the table at Dana, who looked like she was trying not to laugh. I'd joined the whole family for Sunday breakfast at IHOP, and though the pancakes were delicious, the company was working on my last nerve.

The minute I'd walked in, my mother said, "Did you really get fired already?"

It'd been a week since it all went down, so I supposed I should thank my lucky stars that she'd given me *that* much time. The hostess eyeballed me like I was a loser while I explained to my mother the "misunderstanding" that had transpired between me and my former employer.

To which she'd responded with, "You *had* to have known they thought you were a parent if they hired you to be a parenting columnist. Come on."

My mom was a lot of things, but stupid she was not.

I sat at the other end of the table, by Dana and Will, hoping she'd move on, but my mother just yelled questions louder in my direction. "So how are you going to afford your fancy new apartment?"

As if that weren't crappy enough, Kyle and Brady were at Dana's parents' house, so I didn't even have my little buddies to play with.

"You guys seriously do this every Sunday?" I shook my head at my brother and his wife, in awe of their patience, and muttered, "Is it worth it? I mean, pancakes are good, but come on."

"It's just because you're her favorite." Will took a sip of his coffee and said, "You're her baby girl, so she's always been a little more micromanagerial with you."

"That's just a lie—Jack is her favorite."

"Right?" Dana smiled and leaned her chin on her hand, clearly just enjoying a kid-free meal. "Jack can do no wrong in her eyes."

She leaned closer over the table and said, "Are you okay, by the way? If you need any help with rent or something, I'm sure we could—"

"I'm fine." She was the nicest, and I felt like the absolute biggest loser in the world that she thought it necessary to offer money. "Yesterday I got a freelance job, so that'll cover me until I find something else."

"Congratulations!"

"What are we congratulating?" My mother, from the other end of the table, poked her nose right in it. "Did you get your job back?"

I sighed. "Since you asked me about it ten minutes ago? 'Fraid not."

"So . . . ?" She looked at me with an eyebrow raise.

"I got a freelance job just to cover—"

"Jack!" My mother squealed and forgot I existed as my brother walked in.

I rolled my eyes and went back to slathering my hotcakes in syrup and jamming them into my mouth, filling my cheeks just to get on my mom's nerves. It was so typical of Jack to show up late and make my mother absurdly happy, while I had been early yet still was treated to her criticism. I focused on my lake of syrup and ignored her excited chatter until I heard her say, "And he brought you again—how nice!"

I glanced up, expecting to see Jack's new squeeze, but my pancake turned to concrete in my throat as I saw Colin, smiling at my mother.

Shit, shit, shit. Of course Colin was here. I'd made sure to look stunning every single day of the past week on the off chance I'd see him in the elevator, but on the morning I'd decided to skip makeup and just wear gray sweats and a *Grab Some Buds* T-shirt, there he was.

"I had so much fun last time that I would've come without him." My chest hurt a little as he gave my mom a teasing grin.

He was wearing jeans and a fisherman sweater and those mother-loving glasses, and I was torn between wanting to tackle him to the ground and do him on the disgusting IHOP floor, wanting to punch him square in the face, and wanting to just ugly cry like a big baby.

"Here, everyone scoot down." My mom was beaming at him and gesturing for my dad to move over so Colin could sit next to her. Thank God I was at the end of the table and out of scooting range, although knowing my mother, she might make me sit with the elderly couple at the table next to us if there wasn't room for him.

I returned my attention to my plate, which was in serious jeopardy of overflowing from my maple syrup ocean, and I grabbed the last pancake. I felt his eyes on me, so I dipped the whole pancake into the mess and stuffed half the thing in my mouth.

That's right, asshole—I care so little about your presence that I'm eating like the ultimate pig. Suck it.

"Livvie was just about to tell us her good news." My mother said it in a perky voice that intimated the boys had just interrupted a celebratory moment. She pointed her fork in my direction and said, "Go ahead, honey."

"Rnmupf." I held up a finger while I attempted to swallow a pancake the size of my face. The entire family, including my grandma, grandpa, Auntie Midge, and Uncle Bert, were looking at me like I was hard to look at.

Yeah, I got that.

"Oof, Liv, did you lose your makeup?" Jack teased under his breath, "Lookin' craggy this morning."

Once I swallowed—and flipped off my brother, which made my mom gasp—I cleared my throat and said, "I wouldn't really call it good news, but I got a freelance job yesterday."

"So, part time?" Auntie Midge screwed her eyebrows together and said, "Is that what that means?"

"It's not even that, I don't think," my mother said. "What is that—like, work at your own pace?"

"Good job, hon," my dad muttered, and jammed a piece of grape jelly toast into his mouth. I absently thought, *Don't let Mom see you eat that,* when she spoke up.

"Don't eat that, dear." She shook her head like he was a recalcitrant child and said, "You know that gives you the bloats."

I'd never figured out what exactly that meant, but it had haunted me throughout my childhood, the threat of his "bloats."

"My sister made a fortune freelancing." Colin looked at me as he said to the table, "It usually just means you're paid on a per-project basis."

"Really?" My mom batted her eyes at Colin and then said to me, "Is that how this is?"

I was torn again. Colin was being nice, trying to help me with the family, and I knew I should be grateful. But did he think me that pathetic that he had to jump in to make me sound good? Did he feel *sorry* for me?

Guilty, more like.

And I didn't need his pity-based help.

"Colin's wrong, actually." I looked right at his blue eyes and said, "This freelance job is super part time and the wage is terrible. You can't even really call it work."

I saw his jaw clench—good, I'd irritated him—before my

mother sucked him into a whole lot of ass kissing. I was forgotten, thank God, and when Colin got up from the table to take a phone call ten minutes later, I quickly said my goodbyes to the family and took off.

I SPENT THE afternoon writing automobile descriptions for car dealerships, my amazing new shitty freelance job. I kept falling asleep on my stool, so I took a break and went onto my deck to watch the rain. It was depressing and cold—usually my favorite—and seemed appropriate for my situation.

I snuggled into the chair, the chair that I'd shared with Colin, and I stared out at the wet cityscape. I needed to find a way to get my mojo back, to feel excited about the future. If I'd been able to bounce back from Eli and the fire, surely I could bounce back from Colin and the firing.

Right?

I needed to make something happen.

I scrolled through my contacts and clicked on Mr. Wrong Number. I knew it was a risk, especially since he'd just come back, but I was done waiting around for things to just fall into place.

I was going to do it, consequences be damned.

Me: I know what we've said from the beginning, but I think we should meet. I'm sure there are a thousand reasons why it shouldn't happen, but I don't care anymore. I will be at Cupps (coffee shop) Friday night at 7pm. Hopefully you won't ghost me again.

Colin

Fuck.

What in the hell was she doing to me? To herself? I stared at the phone, sitting on my desk as I worked on the real estate budget for next year, and couldn't quite believe it. Her life was shit right now, so how was getting stood up going to help her? She had to know that I—he—wasn't going to show, right? I mean, after all the ghosting, she really thought this guy would show up in person?

Shit.

I hadn't expected her to be at the Marshall breakfast—she never went—and something about the way she'd looked at me while inhaling soggy pancakes messed with my head.

It was almost like I missed her, and that wasn't remotely okay.

Jack's sister, she was Jack's fucking sister, dammit. *Your best friend's sister, you moron.*

Surely it was just the unbelievable sex messing with my mind. Olivia was just Olivia Marshall—klutzy little smart-ass—and there was no way I could miss her.

Fuck, no.

I took off my glasses and rubbed my eyes. I didn't like the thought of Liv being stood up, but it was her own damned fault for proposing we meet. Mr. Wrong Number and Miss Misdial had agreed on anonymity, and just because she was having a bad stretch didn't mean that changed the rules.

Tough lesson, but she was bringing it on herself.

Olivia

"That sounds terrible." Sara motioned for the bartender to refill her glass and said to me, "But if it pays the bills, I'd totally write car descriptions."

"And that's where I'm at." I crossed my legs and took a chug of my rum and Coke. I hadn't felt like venturing out when Sara had called to invite me to happy hour, but what else did I really have going on? Usually at that hour of the day, I went out on my deck and pathetically watched the commuters—who still had *their* jobs—make their way home.

I hadn't left the apartment since IHOP three days before, though, so the still-functioning part of my brain accepted her invite and forced me to shower for my own good.

"You'll get another job in no time. You're a great writer." She leaned back on her stool and shook her head. "I still can't believe you were the 402 Mom. I really loved your articles."

"Thanks." It felt good to hear that, even after the hellacious crash and burn.

"So listen. I had an ulterior motive for happy hour." She crossed her arms and said, "Are you dating yet, post-Eli? Because my brother-in-law is adorable and single, and I think he would love you."

Yeah, I hadn't told her about Colin and all the sex.

I took another drink. The thought of dating made me want to pull out all my hair. Not because I was hung up on that dickhead with the big mouth and smoking bod, but because I wasn't ready.

When Colin had started giving me long, slow kisses that night, I'd started feeling claustrophobic, terrified of falling under the influence of romance. Thankfully he'd kicked it up a notch, but it had reminded me that I was in no shape to pursue any entanglements. The only exception was Mr. Wrong Number, and that was only because we already sort of knew each other. "Thanks, but no thanks. I don't think I'm ready."

"Maybe you won't know you're ready until you actually go out with a guy." The bartender set Sara's glass on the bar in front of her and she smiled at him before continuing with, "You're probably just scared because that Eli dude was horrible."

Eli. She'd referenced Eli and . . . *nothing.* I hadn't realized until that very moment that Eli had lost his power. When had that happened? Suddenly he was nothing anymore; like, I didn't get any sort of feeling at all at the mention of his name.

It was a breakthrough. Maybe having sex with Colin had been some sort of a catalyst for emotional change.

I mean, I still thought he was a giant prick, but maybe he'd served a purpose.

Other than sexual gratification, of course.

"What is going on in that head of yours?" Sara was grinning, staring at me as I realized I'd completely zoned out. "You look a million miles away."

Part of me wanted to tell her about Colin, to get her perspective on the whole thing, but I was too embarrassed. I still felt like an absolute idiot for trusting him to be decent. Instead I said, "So remember that Wrong Number dude I was talking to? I think I'm going to meet him for coffee."

Colin

"Nick."

Nick DeVry, whose office was next to mine, popped in the doorway. "Yeah, bro?"

Nick was a nice guy. He had a lumberjack beard and dressed like a golfer, all trendy polos and pants that didn't fit quite right. "Come in here."

Nick came in and shut the door. He still had the smile of a little kid, but the guy was so smart he'd probably be CFO in five years.

"I need a nonwork favor, Nick, and feel free to say no."

"Oh, shit."

"No, nothing like that. I just want you to go on a blind coffee date for an hour."

After five beers and a lot of stewing, I'd come up with a solid plan last night. All I needed was for someone to just show up and be nice to Liv, and then she could write the whole thing off and move on. I gave Nick a half-truth about the story, saying Mr. Wrong Number was a total douche friend of mine who planned on standing her up.

"Normally I'd just butt out, but the girl has gone through a lot of shit and I feel like it could crush her. If you could just show up, say you're Mr. Wrong Number, and have a coffee with her, that'd be it. Be boring so she doesn't fall in love with you, of course. Then she'll leave feeling good about herself, and I'll buy you a new bottle of scotch."

He started to shake his head. "She must be really ugly if you're not doing it yourself."

"I told you—she knows me so I can't. She's my buddy's little sister."

"That didn't answer the question about her looks."

"She's beautiful." She was, too. Swear to God my ears had started ringing when she'd climbed on my lap out on her balcony. "But she's like a helpless, pathetic little puppy. Just make her feel good and get out."

He looked at me and I knew he was in. He was a total people-pleaser, and also super into scotch. "I'm only doing it for the Glenfarclas twenty-five."

"Where the hell am I going to find that?"

"I've got a guy." He came over and sat on the guest chair. "Write it down. Clark Ehlers. Dundee Scotch Co."

It was going to cost a lot, but I couldn't leave Olivia sitting alone in a coffee shop. I spent the next ten minutes briefing him on any pertinent info he'd need from the texts, and by the time he left my office, I was positive nothing could go wrong.

16

Olivia

I PUT ON RED LIPSTICK AND ADDED A SMIDGE OF POWDER to my nose. Not only was I sporting full-on evening makeup, but I'd even taken the time to put curls in my stick-straight hair. And the best thing—it was an unusually chilly night, which meant it was okay to pair my black dress with a fuzzy black cardigan, tights, and boots.

Because everyone knows if it's under seventy, sweaters and boots are acceptable, right?

I turned off the bathroom light and couldn't believe I was finally going to be meeting Mr. Wrong Number. I felt like I was going to puke. I was so nervous and excited, and I had to keep reminding myself that serious concerns existed about the dude.

He'd ghosted me multiple times, so he probably had weird things going on in his personal life like buried bodies, dolls made out of human hair, and a plethora of hidden wives. Hell,

I was pretty convinced he would for sure ghost me tonight. That was obviously his thing.

I reminded myself of that as butterflies destroyed my stomach on the walk to the coffee shop. He wasn't going to show, so no reason to be nervous. I took a deep breath when I got there, grabbed the handle, and opened the door.

I'd barely taken a step inside when I heard from behind me in a deep voice, "Misdial?"

I swallowed, and things went movie slo-mo as I turned around, the world turning with me as I looked to see my Wrong Number. I don't know what I was expecting, but the guy standing there was my height, with a bushy beard and a big smile. He looked like he was ready for a frat-boy golf outing as he grinned at me.

"Wrong Number?"

He nodded and smiled and then we shared an awkward half hug. He said, "I grabbed us a table by the window."

"Oh, awesome." I followed him and wasn't disappointed, per se, because he was a handsome-enough guy. But I think I'd expected to feel some sort of awareness or familiarity with him, like a major connection, and it didn't seem like that was happening.

I slid into his booth and we shared a nervous smile. I said, "I can't believe we're finally meeting."

"Right?" He nodded and smiled.

"The whole thing is just so bizarre. I mean, you were there, so you know, but still."

He said, "Right?"

Hmmm . . . two rights in one minute didn't make a wrong, but three probably would.

"I texted and asked what you were wearing, and you said my

mom's wedding dress." He gave a laugh and said, "The rest is history."

"Yep. That's how I remember it, too."

"And remember that time you pissed off that guy about Hooters?"

"I do." I waved to the waitress. "So, what is your name, Wrong Number? We can say it now, right?"

He smiled. "I guess we can. I'm Nick DeVry."

I nodded; Wrong Number had an actual name. *Nick*. "I'm Olivia Marshall. It's nice to finally meet you."

Two nervous smiles at one tiny table.

I cleared my throat. "So, what do you do, Nick?"

"I'm in finance. Snore, right?"

I smiled, irritated that the word *finance* instantly put the image of Colin in my head. "Good paying snore, though."

"It is. And you . . . ?"

"I'm a writer." *Please don't ask where I work*.

The waitress came over and took my order, and then my phone buzzed. While Nick was ordering a piece of cake, I looked at the message.

Sara: So . . . ?

Me: Seems nice.

Sara: Uh-oh. Not a love connection? Sorry, kitten.

Me: Thanks.

I put my phone in the pocket of my sweater. "So what part of town do you live in, Nick? Did you grow up here? What's your story?"

He leaned back and stroked his chin, or where I assumed his chin was under the brush. “Grew up in KC, and I live out in Millard.”

“So you’re a suburb guy.”

“That’s me.” He stopped stroking. “I’ve got hella street cred, though.”

“Oh, sure.”

His eyes twinkled. “Don’t make me prove it.”

I smiled. “Um, how would you be doing that . . . ?”

“Break dancing. Duh.”

“Um, I’m afraid I’m definitely going to have to make you prove it.”

And Nick, bless his heart, flashed me a grin, stood, and started moonwalking in the middle of the packed coffeehouse.

“I HAD A really great time talking to you, Olivia.”

“Same.”

We stopped in front of my building, and I was so ready to be done with the date. Nick was great, but in person we had none of the crackling electricity that’d existed in our texts. Like, not an ounce. Honestly, I couldn’t even imagine Nick *thinking* dirty thoughts, much less sending them in a text. Or teasing me. He was just . . . nice.

I swallowed and looked at his face—really *looked*. And he was definitely cute. I hated the stupid ick factor, because it had arrived, and all I felt in my stomach was ick for Nick.

So disappointing.

Dammit—NO. I stepped forward and put my mouth on

his. A test kiss. Maybe we'd share a kiss for the record books and it'd change everything. I wasn't above forcing things at this point—I needed a win.

Nick made a breathing whistle sound through his nose, and then he turned his head and just let go with his everything.

He kissed the shit out of me.

I didn't know if he had a grotesquely oversized tongue or if he was just trying to see if he could fit the entire thing in my mouth, but kissing him messed with my breathing. There was so much happening in my mouth that I couldn't get enough air. It was full of intended passion and an ample amount of saliva, but it just didn't work.

And it felt like I might have collected a beard hair in my mouth.

I pulled back and smiled. "Thanks again for the coffee. Have a good night, Nick."

Colin

Nick texted me after the date. She seemed nice and I think it went well.

Perfect.

I kept watching for Liv to text something to Wrong Number, but she was unusually quiet. I went upstairs to the gym and lifted, and when I got home, there was a message.

Miss Misdial: Thanks again for tonight—it was fun.

I wanted to keep it brief, so I responded with: Agreed.

Miss Misdial: About the kiss, by the way.

I read it twice, then read it again. The kiss? They kissed? Nick fucking kissed Olivia?

I texted: Yeah, let's talk about the kiss.

I waited. I paced and guzzled water while I waited. Then I fired off a text to that motherfucker.

You KISSED her? Why the fuck did you kiss Olivia?

When my phone finally vibrated, it was both of them checking in at the same time.

Nick: She kissed me, dude—swear to God.
Olivia: It was a bad idea; let's just forget I did it, okay?

I started to respond to Liv, but Nick texted again.

Nick: Why? What'd she say?

"Dammit." I texted Olivia first, as Wrong Number.

Me: Do YOU want to forget it?

The second I hit send, Nick was texting again.

Nick: Because I don't want to piss you off, but I actually thought she was really cool.
Me: NO. Off limits.

I barely hit send when Olivia responded.

Olivia: I do. I cherish our texting friendship and don't want it to change.
Nick: Can we talk about this?

Dear God, I was about to lose my shit.

I sent Nick one last text: We'll talk tomorrow, but she's bat-shit crazy with a truckload of issues; you don't want any of that. Trust me. I ordered your scotch, btw.

Olivia

As soon as Nick was out of sight, I went back outside and headed for the Old Market; I just didn't feel like going home yet. Meeting Wrong Number had been my grand solution to all the *meh* that my life had become, but after that disappointing reveal, I really just needed comfort food.

Because the *meh* was bigger than ever.

Thankfully there wasn't a line out the door when I got to Ted and Wally's Ice Cream, which was usually the case after dark—it was a hot post-date spot. I walked up to the counter, pressed my nose against the glass, and wanted it all.

"Could I please get a chocolate malt?" It was a total cliché, but I just wanted to sad eat until I either puked or fell asleep with a chocolate mustache. I moved down the line, swiped my card, and took my malt from the smiley kid with huge gauges in his ears. "Thanks."

I turned to exit the shop and almost ran—literally—into Glenda. I muttered something akin to *ohmigodsorryexcuseme* just before we both awkwardly looked at each other and quickly transitioned through the hey-I-know-you-wait-something-bad-happened-with-us-oh-this-is-uncomfortable steps.

"Hi, Olivia." She was better than me at recovering. She smiled and said, "This is my husband, Ben. Ben, this is Olivia Marshall."

I hadn't even noticed the guy beside her. I tried for a smile and said, "Um, it's nice to meet you." I cleared my throat. "Good seeing you, Glenda."

She looked so nice as she said, "You, too."

I turned and started for the door, wanting to cry because—what the hell—I missed her. But just as I grabbed the handle I turned back around and said, "Hey, Glenda?"

She'd been talking to her husband, surely about me, but she lifted her head and said, "Yeah?"

I went back over to where she was standing in line and said, "I just want to apologize. I, um, I really like you and feel terrible for lying." I knew the other ice cream customers were getting an earful, but I didn't care. "I never meant to, it just . . . I wanted the job badly enough to let you misunderstand."

Glenda gave me one of her super-nice, motherly smiles and said, "It's okay, Olivia."

"That's really nice of you to say." I swallowed. "I can't imagine what you thought when you heard. I only told one person, but he was apparently the wrong person. Regardless, it was a terrible thing to do and I'm really sorry."

"Oh. Um." She cocked an eyebrow and said, "That person might've blabbed, but it was Andrea who told me."

"Andrea?" I had no idea who she was talking about. Her husband had moved away from us and was pretending to peruse the homemade ice cream selections.

"Andrea Swirtz. My ex-intern?" She pushed up her glasses and said, "We saw her when we had lunch at Zio's, remember?"

That girl? "How did *she* know?"

"She said that she overheard us talking about the column, and her 'conscience' compelled her to call me." She rolled her eyes and said, "Apparently she went to high school with you. We all know how that goes."

I didn't remember any Andrea Swirtz, but I was going to look her up the second I got home. *What a bitch.*

"I need to get going, Olivia," Glenda said, gesturing toward her husband, "but I have no hard feelings. Take this as a learning lesson and move on, okay?"

I wanted to cry again because she was being so nice. I nodded and managed to croak out something like *sorryagainandhaveagoodnight* before taking my malt and disappearing out into the night.

I walked a block and then sat down on a bench as it hit me, the awful truth of it all.

Holy shit.

Colin hadn't told anyone.

I felt sick as I thought of his face when I'd been an absolute witch to him. Compared him to his dad—ugh. I pulled out my phone and texted him.

Me: Colin, I am SO sorry. I know it wasn't you who told and I am SO sorry I was such a bitch, especially after Sex Night.

I stood and walked down another block before checking my phone.

Nothing.

I sent another text.

Me: I know you're probably mad at me but please know that I greatly regret the way I treated you. You didn't deserve it and I am the world's biggest asshole.

I walked the rest of the way home, and when I got to the lobby I sent another message.

Me: Okay. So you're ignoring me. I deserve it, but please forgive me. I know we're dicks to each other all the time, but I went beyond our usual banter and I couldn't be more sorry. If you want to come down and talk, my door will be unlocked and I'll be guilt-eating ramen.

I hit send, but as soon as I got in the elevator, I pushed the button for Colin's floor.

I had to make him listen.

I took a deep breath before knocking at his door. *Please don't let Jack be home, and please don't let some woman be there.* I was reaching into my skirt pocket to check my phone, when the door opened.

There he was.

"Hey." His face showed nothing, all business as if I were at his door selling vacuum cleaners. He looked impatient, like he wanted me to hurry.

And so detached that it hurt to breathe.

"Can I talk to you for a second?"

He glanced over his shoulder. "Your brother—"

I grabbed the front of his hoodie and dragged him out into the hallway. "I just need a second. Please?"

He pulled the door closed behind him and I felt *something* skip through my middle as his Adam's apple bobbed around a swallow. I let go of his shirt but my hand immediately missed the solid breadth of his chest.

I raised my eyes from his throat and said, "Did you get my texts?"

His jaw flexed. "My phone's charging in the office. What's up?"

I swallowed. It was harder to say in person. "Listen, Colin. About the other day—"

"Forget it." His jaw clenched again and he said, "It doesn't matter."

"Yes, it does. I was wrong—"

"Forget it, Liv. We've covered that it was a mistake and—"

"Quit interrupting. I'm not talking about the sex, okay?"

Cue my brother, opening the door and looking back and forth between the two of us. "What're you guys doing out here?"

Colin said, "Nothing," as I said, "Talking."

But God—had Jack heard me yelling about sex?

He raised his eyebrows and smirked. "Lemme guess. Livvie wants to move back in with us now that she's jobless."

"Screw you." I was relieved he hadn't heard, but his blasé attitude about my life pissed me off. I rolled my eyes and pleaded with emotionless Colin, "Please just read my texts."

Colin

I watched her walk away, feeling gut punched. What had that been about?

"Dude, why don't you stop looking at my sister's ass?" Jack was giving me a weird look that I wasn't in the mood for.

"Yeah. Okay." I went back inside and he followed.

"What the hell would Livvie be texting you about?"

I feigned ignorance. "Who knows?"

"No, seriously. It makes no sense that Olivia would text you."

I ignored him, went into the office, and unplugged my old phone from the charger. "Dunno."

"Well, why don't you check?" He stood in the doorway, scowling at me. "Then you'll know, dipshit."

I let my arm fall to my side. "I'm good, but thanks."

"What the fuck?" He took a step into the office and said,

"I'm *good*? The right answer is 'I have no fucking idea why your little sister would ever be texting me. I better check because that's weird.' That would be a solid response."

I didn't say anything because I didn't know what the fuck to even say.

"Is something going on with you two?"

I breathed in through my nose and apparently took too long to answer because Jack's mouth dropped open. "My sister—are you kidding me?"

"Listen, Jack—"

"No, you listen." He grabbed the phone from my hand—that was the fastest I'd ever seen the guy move—and looked down at the messages, holding out a stiff arm to keep me back. I wanted to tackle him and take back the phone, but I was screwed at this point.

Regardless of whatever Liv had just texted, it was all in his face. Jack *knew*.

His eyes moved over the screen before he said, "Gah!"

He dropped the phone like it'd burned him.

"Sex Night? What the fuck is that? Please tell me you didn't sleep with Olivia." He glared at me for a solid second before charging forward and pushing me. "What the hell is wrong with you?"

He pushed me again, his face red as he spit out, "*My sister?*"

And then it was on. He pushed me again, then rushed forward and totally put his shoulder into it and laid me out. We both hit the wall before landing on the ground—*fuck, my head*—and he was muttering a whole lot of fuckery (*disgusting son of a bitch taking advantage of Liv*) as he tried to pin me down so he could hit me.

"Knock it off, Jack." I grunted and got my legs under me, flipping so he wasn't on top of me anymore, pinning him just to keep his fucking flailing limbs from knocking me the hell out.

"Will you fucking relax?" I hollered the words as I tried keeping him down, but he had a good fifty pounds on me. His knee connected with my gut, and I groaned and rolled over onto my back, giving him the total perfect angle to beat the shit out of me.

He glared down at me and pulled back his fist, and I just waited for him to hit me. Maybe the physical pain would relieve some of the guilt that'd been eating away at me since the night I'd kissed her. I braced myself, but instead of feeling his knuckles on my eye, Jack lowered his arm and panted, "What the hell, Beck?"

I shook my head. "I know, man."

"You really aren't going to fight back?" Jack looked both disappointed and disgusted as he waited for my answer, like he'd been looking forward to a fight. "You're seriously going to let me hit you?"

I just shook my head again and said, "You *should* hit me."

He swallowed and sat back on his heels. "So you and Olivia . . . ?"

I nodded, hating myself.

Jack touched the front of his tousled hair. "Dammit, Beck, I think you fucked up my hair."

"I think your barber fucked up your hair."

He smiled for a second but it didn't last.

"So, what? Are you going to dump her?" He sounded jaded, because he knew me well enough to know relationships were not my thing. He'd been there for every single fling I'd ever had. "I mean, of course you are. Did you already?"

"No." That made a bitter laugh rise in my throat as I remembered her telling me to leave. "Your sister beat me to it."

He looked a little less angry. "No shit?"

I nodded again. "She dumped me the morning after."

"Fuck," he muttered under his breath. He ran a hand over his chin and climbed to his feet. He held out a hand for me and said, "Is that why you've been an asshole for the past week?"

I grabbed it and stood. "Have I?"

"You pulled out the entire kitchen faucet because of a drip." He coughed out a laugh and added, "Like a total psychopath."

I cleared my throat. "I like the new one, though."

"Same." Jack scratched his forehead and said, "So, like . . . what? You're pissed because she was the one to end things instead of you?"

I sighed, looked at my best friend, and decided to stop lying. "I'm pissed because I kind of, I don't know, I actually really like her. Maybe."

He shook his head. "But . . . it's *Livvie*."

"I know." We'd been a team as long as I'd known him, a team in agreement of the fact that Olivia was a little pain-in-the-ass nutjob. "I can't believe it myself."

"Good God." He rolled his eyes and shook his head. "Well,

you better pick up the phone and read her goddamned messages, then. She's really sorry about something and wants you to go talk to her."

I leaned down and grabbed the phone with the freshly cracked screen, my eyes staying on Jack. "What are you saying—you're cool with this?"

"Gross. Fuck. I don't know." He made a face like something smelled bad and said, "I know you're a good guy, so if you really like her and don't plan on screwing her over, I'm not going to end our friendship over this."

I was honestly shocked to hear that.

"But I'm gonna need a brain scrub after what I read. Like, the sight of you two together is probably going to make me projectile vomit. Take this as a warning."

That made me laugh, which made him laugh, too.

"Noted," I said, feeling so damned relieved that I kind of wanted to hug Jack.

"Vomit fucking everywhere." He walked out to the living room but kept talking. "A bloodbath, only it's puke instead of blood."

"Got it."

"*The Exorcist* level of split pea ralphing."

"It's puke." I followed him out of the office and said, "I get it."

"Did you ever see that scene in *Carrie*, with the bucket of pig's blood? It'll be like that, only instead of pig's blood—"

"Holy shit, Jack," I said, laughing. "Will you shut up about the puke already?"

Olivia

My heart was in my throat when I heard the knock. I'd never been intimidated by Colin, but for some reason I was super nervous to apologize.

Probably because he'd waited an hour to respond, and then all he'd texted was *K.*

I cleared my throat and pulled open the door.

And there he was. His face was serious, hard, unreadable, and so handsome that I was torn between fear and excitement. His hair was kind of a mess, though, and he had a couple red marks on his face.

I said, "Hey. Come on in."

He walked right at me, making me shuffle backward. He let the door slam behind us as he towered just over me and said, "I've got good news and bad news."

I opened my mouth—what were words?—and closed it again. I hadn't expected him to say that.

Or to be right up in my personal space.

I managed, "Um. What's the good news?"

His face softened a little and he gave me a smirk before he said, "I've decided to forgive you."

"Oh. Good." His smile went hot—and dirty—and made me nervous again but in a different way. I cleared my throat and asked, "Well, what's the bad news?"

His smile slipped and his blue eyes moved all over my face before he said, "Your brother knows about us."

"*What?* Oh, my God!" My mouth dropped open and I couldn't stop it. "How? How do you know? What did he say?"

He turned away from me and went into my kitchen. "So what'd you do tonight, Marshall? You look nice."

What?

"Um, thank you. Went on a date." I stared at his back and begged, "For the love of God, tell me about my brother."

He grabbed two beers from the fridge and passed one to me, giving me a half smile. "Relax. Tell me about your date first."

I took the beer but instead of responding, I rolled my eyes and left the kitchen.

"I'm going outside," I said, going through the living room and out onto the dark deck, needing a little space for a split second. I had no idea what was happening, and I didn't like it.

He didn't seem fazed at all by Jack's knowledge of what happened between us, which was bizarre. And not only that, but he was seemingly not upset with me at all over my bitchery.

It felt like he was messing with me. Like the old-school Colin of my childhood, the one who toyed with me but ultimately made me feel like shit.

I turned around and waited for him so my backside was resting against the railing, and when he came through the sliding door I said, "It was just a blind date."

"And . . . ?" He dropped into my deck chair, stretching out his legs while opening his beer.

"And . . . nice guy but no chemistry." I cracked open my own can and said, "Now tell me what the hell happened with Jack."

"Well," he said, looking at me like I was some sort of a rambunctious child, "after you dragged me out into the hallway, yelled at us and then just took off, your brother beat me to my phone and read your text messages."

"Seriously?" I knew I'd texted the words *Sex Night*, so it wouldn't have been hard for him to do the math. And Jack had always been an overprotective brother, so his reaction wasn't a surprise, either. "Oh, my God, I am so sorry. What did you do? What did you say? Did you tell him it was just a onetime mistake?"

"Well, after we wrestled, because, yes, your brother wanted to kick my ass, we came to an agreement."

I looked at his calm, cool, amused face, lightly illuminated by the downtown lights, and I didn't know why he wasn't freaking out. He and my brother had gotten into a fight about this and he thought it was funny? "What do you mean, an agreement?"

He stared straight at his beer when he said, "As long as I'm not trying to screw you over—his words—he's kind of okay with this."

"Wait, what?" I didn't know what that meant. "He's okay with *what*, exactly?"

"You and me." He raised his eyes and was watching me really closely, while I tried my hardest to make my face absolutely unreadable.

Because inside I was absolutely freaking out. Like—what in the hell was happening? *You and me?* Did Colin want something with me, is that what that meant? There was a part of me that was excitedly jumping up and down at the thought of Colin wanting *something* with me.

He was funny, confident, beautiful, and downright masterful in the sack, but we'd never called "us" anything other than a onetime mistake. He was perfect and I was a shitshow. He was an Audi and I was a Corolla. Like, Colin and I made zero sense.

That couldn't be what he meant.

I looked down at my can of beer, started wiggling the pop top, and said, "He's okay with the fact that we accidentally slept together?"

"He's okay with that." He picked up his beer and raised it to his mouth. "And whatever we want to do now."

"'Whatever we want to do now'?" I stopped trying to hide my emotions and looked at Colin with every bit of the *what the hell* that was pinging through my mind. "What does that even mean?"

"It means," he said, climbing out of the chair with a lazy, sexy smile on his lips, "that he's going to be cool should we decide that maybe it wasn't a mistake."

I blinked and found myself at a total loss for words. I stumbled over "But, um, it *was* a mistake."

He stepped so close that I had to look up at him. His voice was quiet and deep in the darkness when he murmured, "Was it?"

I swallowed and I could feel my heart beating in all ten of my fingertips. A motor revved somewhere down below, and I said, "I mean, I think—"

"Can you honestly tell me you haven't lain in bed, replaying that night over and over in your mind, ever since it happened?" He lifted a hand, tucked my hair behind my ear, and said, "I've thought about it nonstop. I've become obsessed with the memory of the noises you made in the back of your throat and the way your face looked when you told me to show you my skills."

I was melting, but I still had no idea if he was just talking about sex or something more. "Colin—"

"Why not follow this for a while?" His teasing slipped a little, and his voice was sweet when he said, "Where's the harm in seeing where it goes?"

I was teetering, hovering *this* close to the edge. He had me hypnotized, mesmerized, at the thought of a full-on entanglement with him. The idea of Colin directing 100 percent of his attention in my direction was a little intoxicating and completely overwhelming.

But it was easy for him. Colin could "follow" this in a total no-harm/no-foul way because he didn't have anything to lose. Colin Beck, mathematical genius with old money and a model's good looks, could just shrug and walk away when he got bored.

I had a feeling, though, that if—no, when—he left, he'd have the power to destroy me.

"Doesn't it seem like a bad idea to you?" I looked up at him, wondering why my voice was so breathy and lacking in conviction when I knew the words to be true. "We don't even really get along when we're not having sex."

"Oh, come on, Marshall," he said, his mouth lowering so it was just above mine. "We do, too."

"Dammit," I whispered just before his lips landed on mine and made me forget my common sense. His mouth was as hot as I remembered, as perfectly perfect, and it absolutely devoured mine.

Oh, Gawwwd.

Colin kissed me like he was the hero in an action movie and our world was about to end. He kissed me like I was his greatest obsession and he couldn't believe he finally had me.

I wrapped my arms around his neck and did my best to return his favor, throwing my all into the kiss. His growl made me smile against his lips, which quickly turned into a whimper as he nipped at my bottom lip and picked me up.

"This doesn't mean anything," I said into his mouth as I wrapped my legs around him.

"Sure it doesn't," he said, just before he lowered his mouth and scraped his teeth over my neck. He took me inside and up the stairs to the loft, his grip tightening as the kissing kicked up to an even hotter level.

I swear to everything holy that Colin Beck's intense kissing could bring a woman to orgasm.

When we got up to the loft, he set me down next to the bed. I could barely open my eyes—too, too heavy—but I saw his red-hot gaze and my pulse picked up.

"Lose the shirt, Beck," I said, and his T-shirt was gone in a second. He pulled it over his head—all half naked and beautiful—and looked down at me, and I set both my hands on his warm chest.

Oh, holy Greek gods. It wasn't just that he was chiseled and tan and had that delicious tattoo that started on his shoulder and wound down his ropy arm. Those things made him ridiculously hot, but it was the faint appendectomy scar and the dusting of hair leading from his navel down south that made him deathly sexy, because it was intimate.

Up close and personal in my bedroom.

Mine.

"Any way you can remove that dress but leave on the boots, honey?" He looked at me with heavy-lidded hot eyes, like I was the sexiest being he'd ever seen, which made me feel like the sexiest being on the planet. His deep voice rumbled out, "I love those boots."

"Can you unzip me?" I turned and lifted my hair, giving him my back, happy that (a) I was wearing a dress with a perfect escape zipper, and (b) I was wearing one of my nicer undies and thigh-high tights.

Side note: I always wore thigh highs because I hated the sagging crotches that inevitably occurred with tights, but on the rare occasions I'd undressed in front of a male while wearing them, they made me feel like a damned seductress.

When I felt his breath on the back of my neck and his fingers started dragging down the zipper, I was shaking in anticipation. He barely touched the dress and it fell from my shoulders and pooled around my feet.

I gnawed on the inside of my cheek and turned around, but I shouldn't have wasted that second on nerves. The intensity in his face as his eyes burned all over my body relieved any concern I had that I didn't measure up.

"Damn, Marshall," he whispered, saying it in a way that made me shiver. "You're a fucking fantasy."

I set my hands back on his chest, needing him closer, but as he started kissing me long and deep and sliding his hands all over my body, an uneasy feeling skittered down my spine.

Because he'd ignored what I'd said.

So had I. We were both so lusty for each other that we were "following" this thing whether we wanted to or not.

And it wasn't that I didn't want to.

It was that I couldn't.

I could not do this.

Colin

I was losing her.

She was still kissing me back, but for some reason I could just tell when Olivia was freaking out. Her muscles were tighter, her hands were still, and she was just less *present.*

She was freaking out in that overactive brain of hers, slipping away from this.

From me.

I still didn't know if it was because of that fuckwit Eli or someone else, but she was skittish. I hadn't meant to be reverent and slow with her—I knew better—but I'd damn near collapsed when I saw her in stiletto boots, stockings, and black lace.

I'd felt like dropping to my knees and worshipping at the altar of Olivia's gorgeousness, but for some reason that kind of slow attentiveness messed with Liv.

So I changed the kiss, going faster, rougher, and more urgent. Eating that luscious mouth like I was a starved beast.

And I was. I *was* a starved beast in that moment.

Instead of moving to the bed, where I wanted to spread her out and kiss every square inch of her, I fed her desperate kisses while divesting her of lace and leading her over to the loft's half wall.

And thank you, God, she was coming back to me with a vengeance. She bit down hard on my bottom lip and I grunted and wondered when I'd become so in tune with Olivia. And not just in tune, but obsessed with her responses.

I pulled my mouth away and turned her around, wrapping her fingers around the railing that ran across the half wall before putting my hands right beside hers.

"Better?" I murmured into her ear, biting the soft skin on the side of her pretty neck while inhaling her scent and moving my body closer to hers.

"*Yes*," she breathed, leaning down a little and pushing back against me, shattering my mind into a million pieces.

After that we both forgot to think as we went fucking wild together.

"COLIN, STOP COOKING and sit down."

I turned away from the stove, and Olivia looked at me from her spot on the stool, eyebrows furrowed while she chewed a mouthful of pancakes. Her face had always been expressive. Even as a kid, I'd been able to tell by the chin raise when she was lying, by the crinkled eyebrows when she was confused and her mind was whirling a mile a minute, and by the eye roll if she was irritated.

Nothing about that had changed, but all of a sudden I found it charming. Her crinkled eyebrows as she waited for me to sit down so she could talk to me "about all of this" was kind of adorable.

"I'm not done." I flipped over my spinach egg-white omelet with the spatula and said, "Gimme two more minutes and then you can talk."

After the insane night together, I'd found myself wide-awake at five a.m. I lay there under hot-pink, threadbare sheets—they were horrible—for a solid twenty minutes before finally deciding to get up and make her breakfast. I knew she wouldn't appreciate a romantic gesture like breakfast in bed, but if I made her a pile of pancakes in the kitchen when she woke up, surely she'd appreciate that.

I had to sneak to my place for the food (Jack wasn't home, thank God) and then back up again a second time for pans and cooking utensils, but I'd managed to finish before she woke up.

The minute she'd walked into the kitchen, she'd blinked her wide eyes and said, "Listen, Colin, we need to talk about all of this. This is really sweet, but last night was a terrible idea and—"

"Are you kidding me right now?" I'd given her the head shake like she was ridiculous, and said, "I was starving because some sex fiend made me work up an appetite all night long. This is just food. Don't read anything romantic into it, Miss Big Head."

She'd done her whole fast-blink thing before I shoved a stack of pancakes into her hand, and said, "Eat first. Then talk."

I don't know how it'd happened, but just like that I had an

entirely different viewpoint on "all of this." We seemed like a terrible match, Olivia and I, but I'd woken up that morning thinking, *Why not just go for the ride and enjoy it while it lasted?* I'd been having one hell of a good time, and being with her was fun, so where was the problem in seeing where it could lead?

Maybe it was the relief of having Jack be okay with it. Knowing he was okay with us possibly dating made it seem like an actual possibility. And when I pictured it—us together—I didn't hate how it looked.

I slid the omelet onto one of the two plates Livvie owned and carried it over to the island. Pulled up the other stool and said, "Okay. Now talk."

Olivia

I looked across the island at Colin, and my mind went blank.

He was good at that, making me lose focus. I still had no idea how we'd ended up spending another night together. One minute I'd been saying it was a terrible idea, and the next I'd been waking up to the smell of his cologne on my pillow after a night of screamingly good sex.

"I think you're overthinking this." He set down his glass after taking a drink and said, "Haven't you ever had a fun fling? A relationship that you know probably won't lead to something concrete, but it's a damned good time while it lasts?"

"No." The thought of him having a fun fling with anyone made me insanely jealous, which pissed me off. I crossed my arms and said, "Are you talking, like, friends with benefits?"

"God, no. Your brother would actually kill me." He cut off another piece of egg. "Friends with benefits is just platonic friendship with secret sex every once in a while that no one knows about."

"And your fun fling thing is different how, exactly?" I was impressed by how cool and unaffected I sounded, when in reality I was freaking out and needed some space to work through all of this. Because I still couldn't quite comprehend the idea that Colin wanted to have *anything* with me other than sex.

"For starters, it's not a secret." He slid his fork between his teeth, and my stomach dipped as I remembered his teeth scraping over the tattoo on my back. He chewed and swallowed before continuing. "It's just like a regular relationship—I take you out, give you multiples, beg you to send pics—only we're both in agreement that once it isn't fun anymore, we walk away with no hard feelings."

My throat was dry as I swallowed. How in the hell would that ever work? It's not like we'd both find it "not fun anymore" at the same exact time, shake hands, and happily walk away. This was a recipe for an Olivia disaster.

But even as I knew that, the thought of *more* with Colin—going out to dinner and holding his hand and getting flirty sexts from him—was so damned intriguing that I was tempted. "That sounds preposterously simple, Colin."

He tilted his head. "Scared, Livvie?"

"Of what?"

He just raised an eyebrow.

"Now who has the big head?"

I was torn between giggling hysterically and crying a little as

I watched him put in his AirPods, fiddle with his running watch, and then leave the apartment like it was normal and he'd be returning later.

Had we really just decided to do the thing?

What the hell?

Five minutes later, as I was still freaking out, Colin texted me.

Colin: Three things: 1. Don't freak out. 2. Send me a pic. 3. Can I take you to dinner tonight?

I smiled in spite of myself and texted: 1. I'm not 2. Perhaps later 3. Depends. Where are you going to take me?

His response was immediate. Name the place, Marshall.

I'd barely gone out at all since moving back, so I had no idea what a good dinner-date restaurant would be. I remembered Dana telling me that she and Will got a $150 gift card to Fleming's and it didn't even cover their dinner, so I shot for the moon.

Me: Fleming's.

I expected him to balk or redirect me to the bar and grill down the block from our building, but he just responded with:

Oh, I see—it's like that. I'll pick you up at 6.

I laughed at his response and set my phone down on the counter. That seemed a little early for someone like Colin; he seemed like a dinner-at-eight kind of guy.

Just as I thought that, my phone buzzed again.

Colin: You still eat early, right?

I set my phone down again and gnawed on the inside of my lip. He remembered from when I lived with him that I ate early? Perhaps I'd underestimated him.

17

Olivia

I WASN'T PROUD OF IT, BUT I POUNDED THREE GLASSES OF wine while I waited for Colin to arrive.

I just needed to calm my nerves, which was weird in and of itself.

Because I was completely relaxed around Colin; I was used to being with him. But I just didn't know if Date Colin was going to be different from Regular Colin. I'd known him for a large portion of my life, but this was uncharted territory.

The wine worked, though, and I was relaxed for the most part when I heard his knock and opened the door.

"Hi," I breathed, incapable of more than a single syllable because Colin looked so good. Like, not just his usual handsomeness, but he looked *cool.* He had on slim black pants and a bomber jacket, the opposite of his usual work attire.

And he was wearing his glasses.

I sort of wanted to call off the date and just stay home. In my bedroom.

"Wow," Colin said, looking me up and down and making my skin feel hot. "You look really nice, Livvie."

I'd borrowed an off-the-shoulder red cashmere sweater from Dana, along with a black skirt and a pair of suede ankle boots that were to die for. Her clothes made me feel put-together and beautiful and I never wanted to give them back.

"So do you." I looked at his belt buckle and said, "Your abs don't look too terrible in that shirt."

"But still disgusting, right?"

I grabbed my purse and coat from the counter. "I think I've made my stance clear."

"You gave me a stomach hickey."

"I said what I said."

We were both smiling as we exited the apartment. I asked him, "Does Jack know we're going out tonight?"

"No, but he was gone when I got home. I'll tell him." He pressed the button when we got to the elevator bank and then grabbed my hand. He laced his warm fingers through mine, spreading that warmth throughout my entire body.

I giggled.

"Something funny?" He looked down at me, his lips in a tiny smile, and I giggled again.

"Don't you find this bizarre? Like, Jack's friend who told me when I was in seventh grade that my crimped hair looked like burnt French fries is holding my hand."

He gave a deep chuckle and dropped my hand. "Wait, that's you? I'm taking out the girl who ran over her own foot with a car?"

The doors opened and we got in the elevator. "Technically it wasn't my fault. The Dodge Colt always slipped out of gear."

"Sure it did."

"It *did*." I put my hands in the pockets of my jacket.

Colin turned and stepped closer to me, moving us and pressing my body against the elevator wall with his as he caged me in with his arms. "Y'know, we could have a lot of fun in here, Marshall."

"That's pretty inappropriate for a first date," I said, betraying my words with my hoarse voice as he lowered his mouth and pressed a featherlight kiss on my neck.

We small-talked all the way to the restaurant, and it wasn't until we parked that I even remembered we were on a date. Colin came around to my side of the car just as I was getting out, and as soon as I stood, he slammed the door and reached for my hand.

He threaded his fingers between mine again, and butterflies went wild in my stomach as we walked toward the door, hand in hand like a regular couple. The cool night breeze made my hair tickle my cheeks, and I glanced at him and said, "This place looks pretty swanky. Have you ever eaten here?"

Colin

Had I ever eaten there?

Um, since my parents' house was three blocks away, I'd

eaten there a hundred times. My grandparents had rented the entire restaurant for their anniversary party, and the firm had their Christmas party there every year.

The chef was my uncle Simon's golf partner.

But Liv already thought of me as pretentious, so I wasn't thrilled for her to find out that the overpriced steakhouse was where we'd had my high school graduation lunch.

I was figuring out how to answer, when loud barking interrupted us. We both turned around, and a huge furry dog was running across the parking lot toward us at full speed, his owner yelling after him over and over. The dog's tongue was lolling out of his mouth and he was clearly playing, but this mutt made a German shepherd look dainty.

Before I could move her out of the way, Liv let go of my hand and dropped to a squat, laughing and coaxing him with her arms as the monstrously large dog ran toward her.

"Liv—"

She screamed when he knocked her over, dissolving into cackles as he licked her and jumped all over her with his enormous paws. The dog's wagging tail kept smacking her as he attacked, making her laugh even harder.

"Finneas!" The owner finally caught up and reached for the dog's collar, yanking him off Olivia and leaning down to grab the leash. "Oh, my God, I am so sorry."

Finneas whimpered, sad to be pulled away from his new friend, but sat obediently when his owner told him to.

I helped Olivia to her feet. "Are you okay?"

"I'm fine." Her eyes were still squinting with laughter, and she dusted off the front of her skirt, looking down at the dog instead of at either of us. "He's just the cutest thing."

The dog owner and I shared a look, both of us wondering how she was so unfazed, before looking at Olivia, who was still cooing at the dog. She only had heart eyes for that dog.

Even in the waning evening light I could see muddy paw prints on her outfit and a hole in the right leg of her tights. She had to have seen them when she'd dusted herself off, but she apparently didn't care.

Seeing a cute dog was worth it to her?

I tilted my head and watched her as she baby talked to the dog. She was so alive, bursting with happy energy, that it was impossible not to smile. I felt like this moment with the dog explained a lot about her "bad luck."

She'd always put herself in ridiculous situations, but was it stupidity or more of a sucking-the-marrow-out-of-life kind of thing? When I'd gotten dumped in college, I'd swallowed the pain and moved on, suffering in stoic silence. But when Livvie got dumped, she had a ceremonial letter burning. It hadn't ended well, with the fire and subsequent homelessness, but I imagine it must've felt cathartic as hell to revel in that moment of pain.

Finneas and his owner left, and Livvie's smile wavered a little bit as she looked at me. "If you want to skip dinner, y'know, since I'm a mess now, I totally get it. We can drive through somewhere and just head home."

I shook my head and reached for her hand again. I was suddenly in this weird place where I always wanted a hand on her. I said, "You're stunning, Marshall. Let's go."

She blinked, surprised by my comment, and then she smiled. "God, my impeccable bedding skills have really done a number on you."

THAT WAS IT.

Holy shit.

The puzzle that was Olivia Marshall had suddenly shown itself to me.

Livvie spilled her red wine all over the table a mere five minutes after we'd been seated, but it was because she was gesturing wildly as she tried explaining to me exactly how her dad had given CPR to a cat who'd been struck by lightning.

It wasn't that she'd been clumsily oblivious to the glass, it was that she was so present in her own story that she hadn't had time to notice the expensive crystal stemware that might be in the way.

She was less shitshow and more about living in high-definition, wide-awake, full-on color. Or something more poetic than that. But once I'd seen it, I couldn't unsee it. It was in everything she did, and it was why everyone was drawn to her the way they were.

For example, after Liv spilled her wine, she didn't wave over a waiter. No, Olivia pulled a pack of Kleenex out of her purse and tried cleaning the mess herself. When I'd shaken my head at her fruitless attempts, laughing in spite of myself at her ridiculousness, she'd erupted into giggles at her situation.

When the waiter saw what she was doing, he was clearly touched. Because among the crowd of affluent, entitled customers all demanding excellence, here was a laughing minx who apologized to him profusely while cleaning her own mess.

After that debacle we played a game where I told her the ridiculous memories I had of her from our childhood, and she corrected me on how wrong I was and how things actually had been. She snorted at one point, smacking my pointing finger as I accused her of being the one who stole my purple Cubs baseball hat when I was in the third grade, and I was charmed to a pathetic degree.

We were both laughing when my grandparents appeared next to the table.

"Colin!" My grandmother smiled down at me for half of a second before looking over at Liv. *Dammit*. I swallowed a curse and stood to hug her, not happy with the timing of this little reunion.

"Grandmother." I immediately stood up. I kissed her cheek and said, "Nice to see you."

My grandparents were nice people, but very traditional. Serious. If a dog had barked in the direction of my grandmother, my grandfather probably would've driven over it with his Mercedes and complained to the maître d' to clean up the menace in the parking lot.

"This is my friend Olivia Marshall." I looked down at her smiling face and said, "Olivia, these are my grandparents."

"Nice to meet you both." She stood, and I saw my grandmother's eyes roam over Livvie's dirty sweater and the hole in her tights. She shook both of their hands and said to my granddad around a smile, "I see where Colin gets his great hair."

My grandfather laughed and teased her about how the

women in our family were responsible for turning it silver, and though my grandmother smiled, I could tell Olivia's disheveled state had captured her full attention.

"We'll let you get back to your dinner, dear." She patted my hand and said, "Come by the house this week."

"I will."

As soon as they walked away, Olivia said out of the side of her mouth, "Your grandma definitely noticed the paw prints on my sweater."

I shrugged and picked up the lowball glass of whiskey that reminded me I still owed Nick a bottle of scotch. "Who cares?"

Her eyebrows crinkled together. "You're very mellow tonight, Beck."

"Maybe it's all the sex I've been getting lately. Makes me super chill."

She rolled her eyes while laughing and pushed back her chair. "I'll be right back, weirdo."

After she disappeared our food came, and just as the waiter was filling her wineglass, my phone lit up.

It was Olivia.

Texting Wrong Number.

From the ladies' room.

Olivia: I need to talk to you. Can I call you later?

I double-checked that my phone was on silent and put it in my pocket. What in the hell? She was out with me but thinking about Nick? Texting Nick from the bathroom?

I knew Mr. Wrong Number wasn't an actual person and

that Nick wasn't attached to the number, but my gut burned at the thought of her wanting to talk to him.

Olivia

I rubbed my lips together and put the gloss back in my purse. I felt better now that I'd put Mr. Wrong Number on notice, and now I could go enjoy the rest of the night without feeling so guilty.

Because from the second Colin had grabbed my hand by the elevators at our building, I'd felt like a snake. Nothing was going on with Mr. Wrong Number, but it felt wrong to have a secret textual relationship that he didn't know about.

The truth of the matter was that even though Colin might just be a "fun fling," if he were doing the same thing—if he had his own Misdial who he talked to on the regular—well . . . that would not be okay with me.

Even though technically we'd never talked about exclusivity.

I was sad to lose Mr. Wrong Number because he'd really meant a lot to me since I'd come back to Omaha, but the combination of the no chemistry with Nick and the out-of-this-world chemistry with Colin left me without any doubt that it was the right thing to do.

Before leaving the bathroom, I scrubbed the paw prints off my skirt and sweater and removed my tights, tossing them into the garbage can.

Done and done.

When I got back to the table, Colin's eyes dipped down to

my legs and he smiled. There was something about the way he noticed little things—my missing tights, how early I liked to eat dinner—that made me feel like I mattered to him.

Even if only temporarily.

Colin seemed a little quieter when I came back. He was still charming and entertaining, but I felt like something was a little off.

Maybe he didn't get along with his grandparents and seeing them had upset him.

Maybe he was embarrassed that they'd seen him with a girl who looked like she'd been dumpster diving. I wanted to break this weird feeling, so when we got in the car, I turned toward him in my seat.

"Okay. Question. Did you ever think about me before I moved in with you guys?"

He gave me a weird look out of the corner of his eye. "What?"

I giggled and looked out the window. "Let me give you an example. Even though I hated you because you were a jerk, there was a time your senior year when you crashed at our house. I had to go into Jack's room at like five in the morning, looking for my charger, and there you were."

He glanced over at me and just shook his head slowly.

"You were sound asleep on the air mattress, wearing just your boxers, and, well, this klutzy nerd about had a heart attack."

He slid into one of his deep chuckles that warmed me from the inside. He squinted his eyes at me and said, "You little pervert!"

"Guilty. I can still remember *exactly* what those plaid boxers looked like." I grinned. "Now you go."

"Not a chance." He hit the blinker and slowed as he merged onto the east ramp. "I plead the Fifth."

"Oh, come on—give me something. There wasn't one tiny moment of attraction in all of our years?"

"Not doing this," he laughed.

"Well." I crossed my arms over my chest. "Now I wish I hadn't been quite so forthcoming with mine."

He tilted his head and laid on the gas, making me smile as that slinky little car moved forward like it'd been shot out of a cannon. He said, "Okay, well, remember when you got kicked out of the dorms?"

"I still have nightmares about those fire sprinklers." I turned in my seat and said, "Wait—did you think I was hot when you came over for dinner?"

"Settle your ass down." He grinned at me and then looked back at the road. "When I came over to your house for dinner, there were two things about you that I've always remembered. One, college turned you into the most incredible smart-ass. You finally had a comeback for all the shit I threw your way."

"Ooh, sexy."

He chuckled, knowing I was disappointed. "The second thing was that you rolled your eyes after literally everything I said."

"You seriously don't have *any* little confessions about finding me hot?"

He laughed again and I could tell I'd cheered him up—he thought this was hilarious. But I couldn't believe he'd never once looked at me sideways. He explained, "I thought your eyes were very green when you rolled them. And you had the longest eyelashes."

"Stop. I don't need your compliment charity."

He gave me a whole minute of silence before saying, "So you've spent all these years picturing me asleep in my underwear."

"You wish," I said, mortified.

"You literally said those words, Livvie."

"Says you."

"What is happening here?" He laughed out the words, and I was a little shocked to realize that going on a date with Colin was *really* fun. We morphed into our usual banter until we exited the interstate, and then he got quiet. When he finally pulled in the underground garage and drove into his spot, he said, "Listen. About this thing we're doing."

"I'm not moving in with you, Colin," I teased. "We've already done that, and I need my space."

He ignored my joke completely and said, "Regardless of how casual it is, we're seeing each other exclusively, yes?"

"Um . . . are you asking or telling?" I honestly didn't know what his answer would be, but he seemed intense about it and that made me feel . . . I don't know . . . some kind of way.

"You went on a date the other night." He put the Audi in first gear before letting out the clutch and pulling up the emergency brake.

"Well, that wasn't a *date* date," I fumbled, feeling guilty about Mr. Wrong Number. "And we weren't—"

"I know." He looked over at me, and I saw his jaws clench slightly. "But I didn't like it."

My heart kicked up as his eyes pulled me in. He'd been jealous? Over me? I tucked my hair behind my ears and said, "I'd never even met—"

"I didn't like it." The smell of his cologne found its way to my nose and filled me with hot memories of his skin as he looked into my eyes.

"Well." I cleared my throat, shaken by whatever the hell was happening, and said, "Let's agree to be exclusive until we're done with this, then."

His lips curved into a smile, but it didn't hit his eyes. "You always have to add the 'until it's over,' don't you?"

"I do."

"Fine." He turned off the car and opened his door. "Little shit."

That made me laugh again, and as we stepped into the elevator, I grabbed his hand and slid my fingers between his. That made him look down at me in surprise, and his face was so sweet I kind of thought I was going to melt.

The second the elevator doors closed, Colin's mouth was on mine and he slammed my body against the wall with his. Not hard enough to hurt me, but deliberate enough to make me instantly weak in the knees. His big hands held my face, his fingers partially in my hair as his mouth did its thing.

Sweet holy heaven, I was defenseless.

His hard body pressed against me and I dug my hands into his hair, needing as I breathed him, tasted him, felt him in every nerve ending in my body.

"Mm . . . button." I pulled my mouth free but that just made him bite my neck, which made me moan, "God, isn't there an elevator stop button, Col?"

He lifted his head long enough to say, "You want to stop the elevator?"

I looked into his eyes, and he looked disoriented and disheveled and absolutely delicious.

I just nodded.

Which made his nostrils flare and his eyes ignite.

And then the damned elevator dinged.

I jumped out of his arms and ran a hand over my hair as the doors opened and yes, we were still just in the garage. A man in hospital scrubs smiled at us as he got in and pushed the button to my floor.

Awesome. Apparently we were neighbors.

I looked down at the floor as the elevator went up. If I looked at Colin I'd either laugh, shrivel up in embarrassment, or just jump on him, witness be damned. Not that I particularly cared what my doctor neighbor thought of me, but my terrible clearly-about-to-have-sex-in-the-elevator neighborly first impression was a symptom of a bigger problem.

I couldn't say no to Colin anymore.

No matter what I said about us, all he had to do was touch me or kiss me or flirt in that deep, sexy tone, and I would follow him into a fathomless ocean and I literally couldn't swim. (Ask my mother—she was still pissed that she'd paid for five years of childhood swimming lessons where I'd refused to go in the deep end. That was her legendary beef with me.)

But it wasn't just that Colin had the upper hand in this whole fling, it was that I had *no* hand.

Not even a strong pinkie finger.

I glanced up and he was leaning against the wall, just staring at me with a look so scaldingly hot that my muscles all turned to jelly. I swallowed before returning my gaze back to the floor.

This just wouldn't do.

I looked at the illuminated elevator numbers out of the corner of my eye—two more floors.

And as we rode up those last two floors, I came up with a plan of protection.

See, the problem, in my opinion, was that all of it was too much at once.

If it were just sex, I could handle it because it was purely physical.

If it were just a date, I could handle it because it was purely fun.

If I kept them separate, I thought I could somehow manage to keep feelings from growing too big and overtaking everything else. I was already in way deeper than I should be, but with a little tweaking, maybe I would be okay.

Colin

We stepped out of the elevator behind the guy, and I wondered if he'd been able to feel how badly I wanted to wring his fucking neck. Technically he'd done nothing wrong, but Liv had just told me to stop the elevator.

She'd wanted to have sex with me in the elevator, and I'd damn near dropped to my knees when the power of her nod landed a killer punch to my midsection.

"I had a great time tonight," Olivia said, smiling over at me as we walked down the hall toward her apartment.

"Same," I growled, barely able to talk from how badly I wanted her.

When we got to her door, she took her keys out of her purse and turned toward me, so her back was resting against the door. "Thanks for the incredible dinner. Text me later, okay?"

I was confused for a second, but then I saw the telltale blink. The biting on the corner of her lip.

She was nervous.

But the hell of it was, I didn't know *what* she was nervous about. Was she nervous I'd be mad she wasn't inviting me in? I wasn't mad, but disappointed didn't even come close to describing how I felt.

Or was she still nervous about our relationship? Was her skittishness the driving factor here? I swallowed and looked at the freckles on her nose, wanting to figure out exactly how she ticked.

"Yeah, I'll text you." I moved a little closer to her then, but only kissed the top of her head. "Thanks for dinner, Marshall."

WHEN I GOT to my condo, I threw my keys down on the counter and pulled my phone out of my pocket. What a night. Who would've thought Olivia Marshall would be capable of turning me inside out? As soon as I thought that, a message lit up my phone.

Olivia: Stellar date, Beck. Really choice. ☺

I laughed and didn't even know how to respond. Agreed. The choicest.

"Dude, did you see the end of that game?" Jack, who I hadn't even seen all sprawled out on the couch, got up and grabbed his beer. "Crazy."

I couldn't even remember what game had been on that night. Once I'd picked up Liv, nothing else but her was on my radar. "I missed it. What happened?"

"Won with a walk off in the twelfth." He dumped his can into the recycling bin and went over to the fridge. "What'd you do tonight?"

I immediately felt like trash as I pictured Olivia in the elevator. "Not much. Just grabbed a bite."

"For fuck's sake, Beck." Jack rolled his eyes at me over the refrigerator door and said, "You can tell me if you were with her."

"Yeah." I sighed and dropped down onto one of the stools. "I was with her."

"No shit," he muttered. "You're dressed like a douchebag on the prowl. If you *weren't* with her, I would have questions."

"It's called style. You should try it."

"I do just fine without your bullshit tailoring."

"Listen." I dragged a hand through my hair and hated feeling like such a lowlife. "You do know that in my whole life, until she came back and moved into the building, I never, ever thought about making a move on your sister, right?"

He closed the door and brought two beers over, hopping up on the counter and handing one to me. "I know."

"I still don't know how this happened." I took the bottle and couldn't even remember bratty Olivia anymore. The only Olivia I could picture now was the one who'd rolled around in the parking lot with a dog the size of a wolf, with a laugh that ran down my spine like a fingernail. "Swear to God. But I am so fucking sorry."

"Col." Jack popped the bottle top on the wall and said, "Livvie is a huge pain in the ass, but she's an adult. She can do whatever she wants."

I was still shocked that he was being understanding about the whole thing. We sat there for a few minutes, just drinking our beer, and then I thought, *What the hell.* I tried to sound casual. "So, what was that Eli guy like?"

Jack started laughing. "Oh, my God, you are so adorable I want to pinch your fucking cheeks. Look at you, all insecure about the ex."

"I'm not insecure about the ex, you shit. I'm just curious."

"Sure. Okay." He did his stupid little half smile, clearly not believing me. "No one really knows what happened with that dude. She met him right after she moved to Chicago and fell madly in love, full-bore Olivia-style. Moved in with him like three months after they started dating."

I hated Eli.

"He was nice enough, I guess. They seemed good together the few times I visited, but then again I pretty much just talked to the guy about beer."

"Of course you did."

He gave a little laugh and took a drink. Then he said, "Livvie thought they were going to get married. I talked to her a few months before she moved back, and she was all excited because he was working on some secret project with one of her colleagues. She thought it was a whole big proposal deal, that maybe they were planning for some epic romantic thing to happen at her office."

Shit. She told Mr. Wrong Number that she'd been cool about her boyfriend working on something with her coworker, and then he'd cheated with her.

Ouch.

"The next time I talked to her was when she called and said her building was burning down and she needed a place to stay. So . . . your guess is as good as mine."

Poor Liv. I mean, obviously I was glad she hadn't ended up with that prick, but that had to have hurt, thinking you were getting a proposal when you were actually getting cheated on.

"What was he like?"

"Fucking sweet as hell you are." He shook his head. "I don't think I've ever seen you so insecure in my entire life. Just be yourself, sunshine, and she will love you as much as I do."

I started laughing. "You're such a dick."

He grinned before saying, "You got no worries. He had a beard, bad hair, and shitty taste in music."

Why did that make me feel better—what was I, a fourteen-year-old boy? "What'd he listen to?"

"He had a Felston playlist on Spotify."

"Felston?" I made a face—we hated that shit. "What a pussy."

18

Olivia

THE NEXT COUPLE WEEKS FELL INTO A WEIRD, UNPLANNED routine. I filled out job applications and wrote boring car descriptions while Colin went to work, and then Colin would call on his way home to see if I needed anything. I always came up with something—food, trash bags, a growler of O! Gold from Upstream—just so he had to come visit me.

And visit he did.

Every night he came into my apartment, loosened his tie in that way that I loved, and spent the evening hanging out with me. We ate together, watched TV together, and used each other's bodies in the most delightful way. Like clockwork, he gathered his stuff around midnight and went back to his place without ever pushing to stay over.

It was perfect.

If it weren't for the fact that I was terrified he was going to break my heart, I'd say things with him were about as close to perfect as they could possibly get.

I was sitting out on the balcony with him one afternoon after he'd left work early, both of us reading as the threat of autumn cooled the air, when my phone rang. I didn't know the number, but still picked up and said, "Hello?"

"Hi, is this Olivia Marshall?"

I glanced at Colin and stood to go inside. The last thing I needed was him hearing me get a call about an overdraft charge or something, although I was pretty sure my account was still in mediocre shape. "This is she."

"Hi. This is Elena Wrigley, the editor of *Feminine Rage* magazine."

I opened the slider and went inside, trying to sound unaffected and cool. But that magazine was my favorite; it was like *People* combined with *Teen Vogue* combined with *McSweeney's*. I managed to find my voice and deliver a perky "Hey."

"I got your application for the content writer position. Do you have time to talk?"

I walked over to one of the stools and sat down, terrified to get excited. "Of course."

"I'm going to be honest with you. I got your application because recruiting was going to pass it to the content editor, but then they read about the fire. The story actually cracked me up, and I fell down a rabbit hole of finding information about you."

"Shit." *Dammit. I just said* shit *to a potential employer.* "I mean, um—"

"No, it's a totally appropriate response." She was laughing, so I let out a breath. "I have to ask you, though, Olivia, if you have a sense of humor about these things or if they're sore subjects."

"I definitely can laugh at myself. May I ask why?"

"Of course. But I don't want to offend you, so please jump in if I am."

"Okay." I was intrigued.

"We used to have an advice column called Ask Abbie. It was super popular because Abbie was kind of bitchy, but also hilarious and good with the advice."

"I remember," I said. "I loved reading it."

Colin opened the door and came inside, carrying my book along with his.

"You read it? Awesome." She sounded happy, which was encouraging. "She left, and we've been trying to figure out what to do with it. It was all about her voice and her personality, so we didn't want to just shove someone else in her place."

"That makes sense." I was trying not to get excited, because it couldn't be what it sounded like, right?

"But when I read about the fire and the flooded dorm thing, I thought, how hilarious would it be to have an advice columnist who, on paper, is kind of a mess?"

I didn't take offense, and the idea *was* a little funny.

"I also had a tip that you were the writer behind the 402 Mom, which, by the way, was a really great column."

I wanted to say thanks, but probably wasn't allowed to, so I made a noncommittal sound.

"Thankfully, I went to college with Glenda Budd at the *Times*, so I was able to call her and poke around."

Oh, my God; she'd talked to Glenda.

"And while she couldn't confirm the 402 Mom thing, she was able to tell me that the writer always met her deadlines, provided exemplary work, and was a delight. Glenda was sad to see her go."

"She said that?"

"She did. Now." She cleared her throat. "How do you feel about embracing your bad luck? Making it your strength?"

Colin gestured that he was going to go, but I shook my head. I wanted to tell him all about it when I was done.

"Can you stay like five more minutes," I whispered.

He looked surprised and said, "Of course."

He went over to the couch and sat down, grabbing the remote like he was at home in my apartment.

I said, "I've spent my entire life laughing at myself and my bad luck, Elena; that's kind of my sweet spot."

She started talking, brainstorming, and we just clicked. As opposed to 402 Mom, this would be capitalizing on who I was, adding my own ridiculous anecdotes into the column. We talked for an hour before she asked if I could come in the following day for a formal interview.

When I finally got off the phone, I went over and plopped down next to Colin. "I am so sorry that took so long."

He muted the TV. "Shut up. Tell me all about this job."

And I did. It was Colin, so I should've played it cool and acted like it was no big deal so he couldn't mock me later, but I'd pretty much left guarding myself from him by the wayside. I told him every detail, and when I was finished he said, "Just make sure you get what you're worth."

I crossed my arms. "Well, I don't exactly have a lot to bargain with."

"I know, but your writing speaks for itself." He said matter-of-factly, "Don't let them think they can have you on the cheap; you're too good."

I leaned against him and said, "Oh, my God, you're so incredibly into me it's a little pathetic. You think I'm so great and—"

I couldn't finish because he pushed me down onto the couch, got on top of me, and shut me up in the very best way. By the time I was breathing heavy, he lifted his mouth and gave me a wicked grin. "Why do I even like you when you're such a pain in the ass?"

I grinned back. "You're just a glutton for punishment, I guess."

19

Colin

I WAS PATHETIC.

Jack was staying over at Vanessa's, so not only was I making dinner for Olivia, but I was really looking forward to having her stay the night. I'd casually brought it up, expecting her to balk since she seemed to like our strict no-sleepover arrangement, but she'd shocked me by saying that she wanted to.

For some reason, inviting her to my condo as . . . whatever the hell she was now, felt like a big deal. I'd lived with her for a month, but we'd never shared the space as anything more than friends who didn't really like each other.

Things had changed. A lot.

My phone vibrated, which meant that she was probably home. She'd been offered the job after her interview—no surprise there because it was a brilliant idea and she was a great writer—but she'd texted that she was sticking around for a while to meet the staff and tour the building.

Olivia: Just got home and I'm starving. What time is dinner?

Me: DON'T EAT.

Olivia: Well if we aren't eating for like an hour, I'm going to nibble or I'll starve.

Me: No nibbling. Dinner will be ready in ten minutes.

Olivia: Oh, thank God. I'll be right there.

I'd come to the realization on my run that morning, after being sexually harassed by Liv from her balcony as I'd stretched, that things were kind of serious. I mean, technically not, since she'd yet to call me her boyfriend and still hadn't invited me to stay the night, but they were serious for me, and I suspected for her, too. She was the first thing I thought of when I woke up in the morning, the last thing before I fell asleep. I would blow off anything to be with her, because everything was brighter when Olivia was around.

She was funny, messy, clumsy, smart, and the sexiest human I'd ever met.

The toughest thing to swallow was that neither of us had changed. Liv was exactly the same as she'd always been, but I'd never looked hard enough to see all the amazingness around the mess. And I suspected it was the same for her, too, because God knows I was just as big of an ass as I'd ever been.

"Knock, knock." She walked in and immediately kicked off

the shiny black pumps that made her legs look ridiculous. "What are you feeding me?"

"Pepperoni casserole. Tell me about the job."

"Um." She opened the fridge and grabbed a Vanilla Bean Blonde before hopping up on the counter beside where I was slicing the garlic bread. I glanced at her and she grinned before popping the top on the wall bottle opener and taking a sip. "I'm terrified because it sounds unbelievably perfect."

"Money's good?" I didn't want to minimize the importance of liking the job, but she was so passionate about the role she'd probably work for free.

"Not Colin Beck good, but yes." Her smile was so big it was almost a laugh. "I'll be making more than I was at the *Times* and the benefits are better."

"Atta girl." I set down the bread knife and wiped my hands on the towel I'd set on the counter. "When do you start?"

"Tomorrow."

"Tomorrow?" I leaned my head down and kissed her happy mouth. "That's soon."

"They asked when I could start, and I was half-joking when I said tomorrow, and they were all 'awesome,' and I was all 'awesome,' and it was amazing."

I laughed with her—it was contagious—and went over to take the casserole out of the oven. "If you want to sleep at your apartment tonight, I totally get it."

"Oh, my God, Beck, if you think you're getting out of letting me sleep in that bed of yours, you've got another thing coming."

I pulled out the bubbling pasta pan and set it on the stove. "So it's about my bed, then, not me?"

"I mean, you're an orgasmic bonus, but yeah—I've missed that king-sized dreamboat." She took another sip and added, "Besides, you get up at like five thirty so I'll have plenty of time to scuttle home and get ready."

"Isn't scuttling what cockroaches do?"

"Among other vermin, yes." She hopped off the counter, put her hands on her hips, and said, "Do you want me to, um, get out some dishes or pour some . . . cognac or something?"

"Cognac or something?"

She rolled her eyes and opened the cupboard where the dishes were. "I don't know what people like you do when you have dinner dates. Multiple forks and brandy snifters? Cloth napkins and flaming appetizers?"

"Y'know, Marshall," I said, never sure if she actually thought I was a pompous prick or if she was just messing with me, "just because I have a good job doesn't mean I'm automatically a douche."

Her face turned toward mine and she raised an eyebrow. "Then how do you explain your jack-off corkscrew?"

Now I rolled my eyes and muttered, "Touché."

She set the dishes on the table and it reminded me of the night she'd made spaghetti and meatballs for Jack and me. She'd been nervous and irreverent, babbling as she served the food and owl-staring at me as I'd tried the first bite, and I'd been absolutely charmed by her.

Until she'd outed herself as Misdial before the night had ended.

God, that seemed like years ago.

We lost ourselves in the food and conversation after that. Liv launched into a story about how she'd broken her heel in a sidewalk crack on the way to her interview, and then she fetched the shoe from the entryway to show me how she'd repaired it by chewing six pieces of bubble gum. She asked about my day and made me describe every detail of my office so she could picture me in it whenever we texted.

I felt a little bit like Olivia; I was terrified because it seemed unbelievably perfect.

Olivia

"Marshall." Colin's voice was deep and sleepy. "Let's go to bed."

"Hmm?" I opened my eyes and there he was, looking down at me and smiling as I was all snuggled up against his chest on the couch. "I must've dozed off."

"Think so?" he teased.

I sat up and stretched. "What time is it?"

He glanced at his watch. "Five after ten."

"Ooh, so late."

"You've got a big day tomorrow." Colin shut off the TV. "You need a good night's sleep."

I climbed to my feet. "Can I borrow something to sleep in? I don't feel like going back to my place right now."

"Sure," he said, grabbing my hand and pulling me with him toward the bedroom.

It was weird, going into Colin's room *with* him. I'd been in there alone many times, but following his tall body through the doorway and inside his lair was a brand-new experience.

He hit the wall switch and the bedside lamps turned on, infusing the room with warm light. Man, I loved his room. It was sleek and modern, but still had that cozy feel to it that made you want to snuggle under his heavy comforter and watch movies all day.

"Do you want actual pajamas," he asked, pulling open a drawer, "or would you rather have a T-shirt?"

"Seriously, look at your drawers." I walked over to him and peered over his shoulder at the clothes neatly folded in his dresser. "That attention to detail is obscene."

"I'll show you obscene," he murmured, holding up a T-shirt for me. "Does this work?"

I nodded and took it, weirdly nervous all of a sudden.

But before I could overthink it, his phone rang. He pulled it out of his pocket, glanced at the display, and said as if he was asking permission to answer, "It's my sister."

"Take it."

He lifted the phone to his ear. "Hey, Jill. What's up?"

For some reason, I found his friendship with his sister adorable.

He said, "Oh, yeah. Let me get you his number."

Colin went out into the kitchen, so I took the time to change into his shirt and steal a pair of thick socks from his top drawer. I wasn't sure whether or not he slept on a certain side of the bed, but I pulled back the blankets and climbed in the left side of the bed.

"Just call him and tell him there's a tire vibration, and he'll take care of it."

He walked back into the bedroom, and the expression on his face shifted when he saw me in his bed. "I can't talk, Jill. Gotta go."

He hung up and dropped his phone on the bench at the foot of his bed. "Am I a terrible person if I tell you I fantasized about this exact thing when you still lived here?"

That made me strangely happy. "You did not."

"Swear to God." He pulled the sweater over his head and tossed it toward the hamper, then reached for his belt, grinning at me as he unbuckled, unzipped, and let the pants drop to the floor, stepping out of them. "Once you told me you'd napped in my room, I couldn't get rid of the idea of you in my bed. I imagined discovering you sound asleep in here . . ."

"And . . . ?" I rolled onto my side and propped my head on my hand.

"And I'd wake you up, but you'd be in the middle of a *very* naughty dream."

"Of course I would." I was obsessed with the thought of him fantasizing about me. "You little pervert. I bet in your fantasy I thought you were part of the dream, right? So I pulled you down on the bed . . . ?"

His teeth flashed. "Something like that."

"Why didn't you tell me this the other night when I was *begging*?"

"You were asking about before you moved back." Instead of crawling on top of me like I would've expected—and wanted—Colin tossed his pants on the chair, climbed under the covers next to me, and switched off the lamp.

It was so . . . habitual. Ritualistic. It felt like we were a couple climbing into bed, the same as we did every other night. He turned toward me and said, "Are you going to shut off that lamp or what, Marshall?"

"On it." I turned off the lamp, plunging the room into total darkness.

"Much better," he breathed, his body moving closer as he pulled the comforter up and over us. The weighted blanket cocooned us together, and I felt like the air was sucked out of my lungs because one minute I was fine, and the next his hands were cupping my cheeks and he was dropping the softest kisses over my face.

Featherlight, reverent, and sweet. I looked up at his face, the eyes I could still see in the darkness, and I felt the warmth. Not the heat of sexual need—that wasn't new to either of us—but real warmth, almost as if he really cared about me.

I took a deep breath and waited for the panic to arrive, but I think my body—brain, heart, lungs, nervous system, all of it—knew that Colin was safe and was slowly lowering the protective wall I'd carefully erected. I relaxed into the soft bedding, every muscle in my body melting into his perfect linen sheets as he literally made me shiver.

His lips settled on mine, and I let my fingers slide over his muscular shoulders, but instead of the wildly intense kisses I was well versed in, the ones that made me moan into his mouth, he gave me slow, drawn out, and hot. Wide, openmouthed artistry that curled my toes and made me dizzy before he descended into nibbles and nips, licking at my lips before trailing down my neck and moving south.

I got lost in shaky sighs as he worshipped every bit of me with his mouth and hands. The darkness heightened my other senses and I felt everything *more.* His lips on my skin, his breath on my flesh, the warmth of his strong fingers as they made me pant for him. He worked his slow magic again and again, building over and over, until I thought his thorough madness was going to kill me.

"Colin." I wasn't one to beg, but I would if I had to. "Come *on.*"

"So impatient," he growled, moving back up my body. And when he hovered over me, I felt light-headed just looking at him. Through the darkness I could see the heavy-lidded desire on his smirking face and it took my breath away.

Because beautiful Colin Beck, with the perfect everything, looked like he'd never wanted anything more than he wanted me at that moment. His hair was sticking up from my hands, his nostrils were flared, his eyes were on fire, and in that moment I knew I was wholly his.

His fingers threaded through mine and he pushed them down, so our adjoined hands were lying on the pillow, one on each side of my head. He lowered his mouth and kissed me, a long, deep kiss that spoke of things more potent than passion.

"Colin." I exhaled his name and wanted to tell him, but then he slid inside me, clenching his fingers around mine as he moved and destroyed my ability to form coherent words. My fingers grasped his, squeezing, as he proceeded to completely obliterate any remaining doubts I had that I was madly in love with him.

FIVE A.M.

It was a ridiculous time of day to be awake. Colin wasn't even stirring yet and he ran at five thirty every day like a psychopath, so it was absurd that I was up. But I was so stoked to start my first day at the magazine that I couldn't sleep another second.

And I was glad to have a few minutes alone without him.

Every time I'd picked up my phone to text Mr. Wrong Number since our dinner at Fleming's, I hadn't really known what to say, and I'd blown it off. We hadn't been dating or anything, so it seemed oddly egomaniacal to send a bizarre type of breakup text, especially when he'd sort of done that by ghosting me more times than I could count.

But I needed to do it.

I needed to be officially free and clear, because God help me, I was totally in love with Colin. I'd tried to guard my heart and keep it from happening, but it'd been no use. I'd lain in bed for hours last night, trying to explain away my emotions, before finally realizing it was all thoughts and words.

My heart was his.

And God, it seemed like he felt the same. I wasn't going to say he was wildly in love with me, but there was obviously something between us that he liked because he kept coming back and making me happier with every passing day.

And last night had felt . . . downright magical.

I sat down on a stool and texted Mr. Wrong Number.

Me: I know it's early, but since you mostly just ghost me I figure it doesn't matter.

Send.

Me: It was great meeting you and you have no idea how much our texting meant to me in the beginning.

Send.

Wait, did that sound weird, saying *in the beginning*? I supposed it was too late to worry about it because I'd already sent it.

Me: But I'm seeing someone now and it feels wrong to keep texting you, like I'm having a secret relationship or something.

Send.

Colin's phone lit up, catching my eye as it charged in the dark kitchen. It was probably a reminder to be perfect or an eat-more-protein notification. He used his phone to über-organize his life, whereas I used mine as just a texting machine.

Me: Good luck with everything, and thanks for being a friend when I didn't really have any.

Send.

Colin's phone lit up again.

Me: Thanks for everything.

Send.

Colin's phone lit up again.

I got up and walked around to where his phone was plugged in. I was sure it was just a weird coincidence, but I texted: Um.

Send.

My ears started ringing, my stomach dropped, and everything got blurry for a second when the notification window popped up on his phone.

Miss Misdial: Um.

Colin

I opened my eyes and reached for her, but she wasn't there.

Holy God, Olivia Marshall woke up before me? What time was it?

I sat up and could hear her scuttling around in the kitchen. It sounded like she was pacing, probably with her lip between her teeth as she imagined everything that could go wrong on her first day. I stood and got a pair of shorts and a T-shirt out of the dresser; she needed a distraction or a pep talk, maybe both.

Might have to blow off the run that morning.

I was pulling my shirt on when I walked into the kitchen and saw her face. She was leaning against the refrigerator, her cheeks red, her eyes glassy.

"What's wrong, Livvie?" I took a step toward her—God, had something happened with the job already?—and she held out her hand to stop me.

And in her hand was my phone.

"Why do you have Misdial messages in here?" Her voice cracked and she blinked fast. "I keep trying to figure it out, but nothing makes sense. How in the hell would you get my messages?"

I felt my insides drop as her face begged me for a feasible explanation that I did not have.

I said, "Why do you have—"

"Don't you *dare* pull the cheating boyfriend bullshit line and ask why I have your fucking phone, Colin. Have a shred of decency here."

She was right, but I had no idea what to say. "I know this is going to sound crazy, Liv, but I am actually your wrong number."

She just stared at me for a minute, unmoving, like she was trying to reconcile the facts. "I think you're forgetting that I *met* my wrong number. So unless your name is Nick and you know how to break dance, you aren't him. Try again."

Shit. How the hell could I make her understand? I said, "I swear I'm telling the truth. Nick met you for coffee because I asked him to. Can we sit down and talk about th—"

"No!" She dropped my phone onto the counter and crossed her arms. "Just make me understand what this is all about."

"Hell." I rubbed the back of my neck. "I'm your wrong number. It was a total weird coincidence for both of us; I was as shocked as you when I found out. I tried ghosting you and ending it but—"

"Oh, my God . . ." She stared at me. "When did you realize it was me?"

No way was I answering that. "I don't know, Liv, a while back—"

"Tell me." Her voice was deep and low, like it was holding back a wall of emotion as she said through gritted teeth, "Because we both know that you remember the exact second you found out."

"Liv—"

"When, Colin?"

"The night you made us spaghetti and meatballs, okay?" I stepped closer, needing to make her understand. "I was—"

"Wait. That was *months* ago." She stepped away from me, her eyes darting around as she attempted to catch up. "You knew that long ago? Holy shit. You didn't ghost me, you liar. You texted me all the time."

"No, I—"

"You texted me when I was on a date, you texted me when *you* were on a date, you texted—" She broke off with a gasp. "Oh, my God! Have you been reading every single message I've sent when I was talking to myself?"

I opened my mouth but she kept going, her eyes wild as everything came back to her. "And is that why we had such great sex from day one? Because I'd talked about it with Wrong Number so you just dialed it up because you already knew how to get me off?"

"Liv, no—"

"Our first time was on the kitchen counter!" She was exploding, but anger didn't take any of the hurt out of her face and it was killing me. God, I just needed her to understand.

"That was just a coinci—"

"Oh, my God." She smiled and let out a hollow laugh, but her eyes were filled with tears. "I bet you felt like the king when you read that you were the best sex of my life. Oh, my God, this must've been hilarious for you."

"It wasn't. Shit. This isn't how it was."

She tilted her head and narrowed her eyes. "So tell me how things went down with Nick. Did you tell him you were already screwing me so you couldn't mess it up with honesty and needed a fill-in?"

As I watched her cry, I knew it was never going to be okay. "God, no. Liv—"

"No." She walked over to the doorway and grabbed her purse and shoes. "Don't call me that like we're close. I'm not *Liv* to you anymore."

I moved toward the door and put a hand on it. "You have to let me explain."

"No explanations, remember?" She shook her head and swiped at my hand to remove it from the door. "We said when we got bored we could just walk away, right? Well, I'm bored."

I swallowed down a knot of fear in my throat as I heard the finality in her words. I leaned down so our faces were at the same level; I needed her to see me. "We both know that's not true."

"Really?" Her eyes narrowed and she said, "All I know is that I had a relationship with some random number, and then he catfished me by pretending he was someone else while also using my messages to get in my pants. Get out of my way because I have to get ready for work."

"Please. God." I didn't want to beg, but I felt desperate when I said, "Just let me explain."

"I don't even care, Colin. Goodbye."

She slammed the door behind her when she left, and I felt like she took all the oxygen in the apartment with her.

Olivia

"Sometimes vendors come in on Fridays. Last week, they said it would be Chick-fil-A."

"Yay, right?" I smiled at Bethanne, the other girl going through new-hire orientation with me, and tried not to let our lunch break get at my emotions. After sobbing through the shower that morning, I'd steeled myself. That asshole wasn't going to ruin my first day, so I forced him out of my mind and focused on the new job.

Of course, it wasn't helping that he'd been blowing up my phone all morning until I finally had to turn it off. His initial text had confused me at first because it came from Wrong Number, but then I remembered that was Colin's actual number.

Prick.

"Yeah, I swear I could eat it for every meal." She pushed her long blond hair back and said, "So do you have any kids? Husband? Boyfriend?"

Before I could even flounder for a response, she said, "I got engaged a week ago today."

She shoved her huge square diamond at me. "Look at this thing."

"Wow," I said, forcing my lips up into a smile. "You marrying Jeff Bezos?"

She giggled. "He did good, right? But I don't even care about the ring. I just want to spend every day forever with him."

"Aww." I swallowed—or tried to—but my throat felt like it had a rock lodged inside of it.

"It's so cliché to say I'm marrying my best friend, but God, I just adore him."

"Nice."

"Like, I want to hang out with him twenty-four seven, all the time."

"Enough, okay?"

"What?"

Shit, I hadn't meant to say that out loud. The words had clawed their way out of me, and I hadn't been able to stop them on time. I pulled on what felt like a smile and said, "Kidding."

"Oh."

I nodded and thought I was smiling.

She said, "Ohmigod, what's wrong?"

I shook my head. I tried to tell her it was nothing, but it sounded like a moan or a cow braying.

"Oh, sweetie, what is it?"

I couldn't see. Holy shit, tears had made the world—and the break room of *Feminine Rage*—float away from my line of sight.

"Will you excuse me?" I got up and tried to escape to the bathroom, but I tripped over a chair at the next table that I couldn't see and tumbled to my knees as the chair crashed to the ground loudly beside me.

"Shit," I muttered, scrambling to my feet as fast as I could before I died of mortification.

But I got up too fast and couldn't see the tray-carrying man to my right through my blurred vision, so I sent his tray sailing into the air when I popped up and headbutted it with a loud *bang*, causing macaroni to rain down upon the man and me.

I gave up hope for salvaging my dignity and literally ran

toward the restroom, though the pools of tears that'd taken up residence in my eye sockets were so unrelenting that I had no idea if I'd entered the men's or the women's room.

Not that I gave a shit at that moment.

Once I locked myself in the bathroom, I looked at my reflection in the mirror and wanted to punch Colin Beck in the face as hard as I could. My first day on the job and not only did I have macaroni in my hair, but I had the black sludge of both eyeliner and mascara running down my face.

And even after doing an incredibly thorough job with half a roll of toilet paper, I looked like a person who'd just escaped a traumatic accident. Especially since there was also a huge red knob on my forehead from that guy's lunch tray. I desperately wanted to just wait it out in the bathroom until after the bell rang, but then I remembered that this wasn't high school and I needed to get my hysterical ass out there if I were going to keep my dream job.

God, I really hated Colin.

BY THE TIME I got home from work, I had no more tears. I'd been in a lethargic funk all afternoon and I just wanted to collapse. But when I went up to my room, the sight of that bed made me want to vomit.

A smart person probably would've been content with the fact that they'd at least scored a kick-ass bed from that asshat.

I was not a smart person.

I wrestled that mattress off the bed, sweated and groaned as I navigated it down the stairs, almost passing out by the time I got in the elevator with it. Thankfully a nice guy was already in there and asked if I needed help, so he and I dragged it up to Colin's door. He started to prop it against the wall across from Colin's condo, but I shook my head and told him it needed to block the doorway.

"I'm sorry, what?"

"It has to."

After he moved the mattress, I said, "Thank you so much for your help."

He looked at me like he thought I was batshit crazy and said, "Forget about it."

I repeated the same thing with the box spring but without a helper, and by the time I was finished, I was covered in sweat. I hoped Jack wasn't the one who had to come home and deal with it, but the bed that prick had bought was no longer my business.

It wasn't until midnight that I remembered I'd shut off my phone, and as soon as it powered up, I saw message after message from Colin come through. That made my body find another store of tears, dammit, and I was just done. Without reading any of his texts I sent: For the love of God, if you ever cared about me at all, please stop texting. I can't do this.

He immediately responded. Just let me come down and talk to you.

I closed my eyes as the tears burned.

Me: I guess I'm blocking you, then. Bye.

I cried as I blocked him because it felt supremely final. It was closure, the circle of life as I shut down the original Wrong Number from ever texting me again.

But because I was a glutton for punishment, I spent the next few hours rereading our transcript from the beginning. Who needed sleep anyway? But Gawwwd, there were so many embarrassing things I'd texted to Wrong Number, things I never would've wanted Colin to know.

I was beyond angry and disgusted with him, but worse than that, I was devastated to lose him. It probably meant I was weak, but all the little inside jokes and easy banter we'd shared had blossomed into something huge and full, and now they were gone.

It was like that line in *You've Got Mail.*

"All this nothing has meant more to me than so many somethings."

20

Colin

"YOU LOOK LIKE SHIT, COL."

"Language, Jillian." My mother glared at my sister before giving me a big smile, twisting her pearls in multi-ringed fingers. "Sit down, sweetie."

I dropped into the chair across from my father and reached for the drink menu. Sure, I'd pregamed in the lounge, so I had a decent buzz rolling, but from his stern expression, I got the impression I'd definitely need more. I asked, "Do they have appetizers here? Like mozzarella sticks?"

My sister snorted and my dad said, "We're not at an Applebee's, Colin."

"I wish we were, because I think I'm in the mood to try karaoke."

Jillian's eyes widened, and I could tell she was trying to discern whether or not I was drunk. I wished I were, but sadly I was sober enough to see the fight brewing in my father and the odd disconnection on my mom's face. I decided to dial it back and said, "Kidding, you guys."

My dad gestured for the waiter to bring him a scotch before saying to me, "So how's business?"

"Good." I did the slow nod and said, "Having a hell of a good year."

He nodded. "Fantastic. Too bad it isn't your business; not really *your* good year at all."

"That is so true, Dad."

"Been promoted lately?"

"Since the last time you asked me a month ago? Let me think." I tilted my head. "Nope."

"Ha ha, funny man." My dad crossed his arms over his chest. "It just seems like you've been stuck in this position for a while."

"I'm not stuck; I love my job."

"Said the stuck guy." He looked at me for a long minute, narrowed his eyes, and said, "You don't get to the top by loving your job, Col. You get to the top by—"

"Can you guys knock it off?" My sister rolled her eyes and said, "As exciting as it is to talk about Col's horrible, awful, unthinkable job as a very successful financial analyst, I would like to hear about the girl he's been seeing."

Just like that, my throat was frozen and I couldn't swallow. "Not now, Jill."

"No, we'd like to hear all about this girl, sweetheart." My mom was beaming at me when she said, "Your grandfather called her delightful."

"I'm not doing this."

My dad said, "You can't indulge your mother this one time?"

"Damn it."

My mom whispered, "Language, Colin."

I took a deep breath. "I'm not seeing her anymore, so it doesn't matter."

Jillian mouthed, *I'm sorry*, and I just shrugged. My father, however, took the opportunity to make me feel like shit.

"What happened with this girl? Your grandmother thought it might be serious."

I looked down at the linen tablecloth. "Turns out it wasn't."

"Who ended it?"

"Dad, I don't think that's any of our business." Jillian spoke up but he ran right over her.

"Why not? We're family." He turned his full attention on me and said, "Tell us why you broke up."

I needed another drink, because I could tell my father was in the mood to press it. I thought about coming up with something good, some mature, boring reason, but then I thought, *Screw it.* It *was* family, so why not be brutally honest?

"Well, we were doing the whole friends-with-benefits thing and it was really great. She's smart and funny and a real fireball in the sack, so everything was clicking, y'know?"

"Knock it off, Colin," my father warned, looking at the table next to ours to see if Edward Russell was eavesdropping on our table's conversation.

"No, you said we're family and you're right; we are. You're the ones I should be talking to about this." I cleared my throat and lowered my voice. "Okay, so, we were banging it out all the time and having a great—"

"Stop it." My dad leaned over the table and pointed at me. "Stop it right now, or this dinner is over."

"Oh, no. Not dinner." I grinned at Jillian, but she looked uncomfortable. "Actually, as long as we get to have those appetizers, cocktails, and karaoke, I don't care if we ever get dinner."

Jill couldn't help herself. She muttered, "Still not an Applebee's, Col."

"Why are you doing this?" My father looked mad, but he also looked confused. "I don't understand why you'd accept the invitation if you didn't want to be here."

"I was fine until you wouldn't let the Olivia thing go."

"Honey, are you okay?" My mom looked genuinely worried, and something about her gentle tone made me feel like a child, which I hated. "I'm so sorry things didn't—"

"I'm fine."

My dad said, "You don't seem fine."

I turned my head toward him and just wanted to lose my shit. Like flipping tables, hellbeast-roaring, tearing-things-up kinds of stuff. Because I didn't want to talk about Olivia at all, but especially not with them. "Well, I am."

"Get up." My dad stood up, looked down at me, and said, "Let's go outside."

Now, my dad was an arrogant, pompous asshole, but he was never violent. He loved me and had always been a good father in his judgmental way. So I didn't even know what to say as he stared me down.

"Sit down, dear," my mom said, but my father was firm.

"Come on, Col. I'll meet you outside."

We all watched in disbelief as my father exited the dining room.

"Um." Jillian leaned her elbows on the table. "Is Dad going to kick your ass?"

"Oh, for God's sake, no." My mother's cheeks were red, and she looked at the other tables to make sure none of her Women's League friends had noticed my family's dustup. "He must want to talk to you in private."

I looked at Jillian. "What do I do?"

She shrugged her shoulders.

"Go, darling." My mother was speaking in a clipped, harsh whisper. "Go speak to him before we make a scene."

I rolled my eyes and stood. "God forbid."

"Don't worry, I've got your back." Jillian lifted her fists. "I'll be your second."

"Oh, for the love of Pete," my mother muttered.

"I think I've got this, but thanks."

I exited the dining room and went out the club's main entrance, clueless as to what was happening. I still had a buzz, so the entire situation was kind of amusing, but bubbling underneath it all was that part of me that wanted to destroy everyone who dared to mention Olivia's name.

"Over here." My dad was leaning against his Mercedes, looking down at his phone as if he were just chilling in the parking lot.

"What's the deal here, Dad?" Just like that, I was done playing games. I needed to get out of there and go home, to the apartment that'd become a cold, sterile reminder of Olivia, before I lost it. "Let's not go crazy and throw hands in the parking lot of the fucking club; I'll just leave now."

He put his phone in his pocket and scowled at me. "I want to talk without your mother stepping in to baby you."

"Oh, well this sounds promising."

He clenched his jaw and said, "Can you maybe knock off the sarcasm for five minutes?"

I wasn't in the mood for a lecture so I said, "The most I can promise is three."

"See, this is what I'm talking about."

"Well, you weren't really talking about *anything* yet, actually—"

"Come on, Colin, shut your obnoxious mouth, will you?"

Now he looked ready to explode, and I kind of wanted him to. I felt a restlessness pulsing under my skin, a tension that made me hungry for confrontation as he gave me his disappointed glare.

Still, he was my father.

I took a deep breath, counted to five, and said, "Consider it shut. Please continue."

He looked at me for a minute, like he was waiting to see if I meant it or not. Then he gave me a sarcastic half smile. "Was that so tough?"

I rubbed the back of my neck. "A little . . . ?"

That made him grin, and we were good again in our own dysfunctional way. He leaned against the car and said, "You don't seem okay, Col."

I nodded. "I know."

"Your mother is convinced this Olivia girl broke your heart.

I don't know if that's true or not, but I think this might be a good time for you to step back and reexamine your life."

I didn't like the sound of that, but I just said, "Think so?"

"I do." He rubbed a hand over his closely trimmed beard and said, "When things don't go as planned, we can either pout and behave like a reticent child, or take some time to reconsider our choices. Ruminate over what we've done in our past, and how best to move forward in our future."

I couldn't nod politely—I couldn't give him the satisfaction—because that would make him think he was getting through to me. It was immature as hell, but I just stared back at him with a straight face. I'd let him talk because he was my father and I respected him, but that didn't mean I'd let him think he was winning.

He said, "You've been living your life like you're still in college, Colin. You have a roommate. You're working in someone else's finance department. You're getting dumped by your roommate's little sister. Does that sound like adult behavior?"

"Yes."

"No." He stroked his chin, the way he always did when he was working toward putting the exclamation point on his argument, and said, "Ditch the roommate, Col—you're not in a frat. Leave the easy job behind and take your place at Beck. Trust me, it will feel good to stop this juvenile rebellion and settle into your grown-up life."

"Listen, Dad—"

"And for the love of God, I think it's time to stop dating around. Find a nice girl who wants the same things as you and get serious."

The rage was coming back. "I *did* stop dating around—that's what Olivia was."

"No, she was convenient." He said it like I was a clueless child who had no idea what I was talking about. "She was living with you, for God's sake. Low-hanging fruit like everything else in your life. Make an effort to be *more*, Colin. To be better."

I opened my mouth to go off, because I was fucking done, but I had to swallow my words when Brinker Hartmann, one of my dad's buddies, approached with a huge grin on his ruddy face.

"Well, if it isn't the young Mr. Beck. It's been a while since we've been graced with your presence. How are you, Colin?"

I tried for a smile. "Good. Leaving, actually."

My dad, who was clearly about to ditch my mom and sister for his friend's company, said, "Are you going to go tell your mother you're leaving?"

I glanced toward the club. "She's sitting near the bar, so sure."

They both laughed, but my dad's eyes were serious. I started walking away and he said, "Think about what I said, Col."

"Oh, I will," I said without looking back. "Just as soon as I'm floor-licking drunk."

Olivia

I opened the magazine and flipped to my column, Oh, Olivia!, totally geeked out to see my headshot and my words on the slick, glossy pages. Who would've ever thought I'd be writing an advice column? I started reading, even though I already knew every word.

Dear Oh, Olivia!

I walked in on my boyfriend with another girl, but he says he's sorry and won't stop begging me to come back. We were technically "on a break" that weekend after a fight, so in a way it wasn't cheating.

I want to get over it and get back together because I do love him, but every time I look at his face, I'm triggered and have a flashback of the awful sex-face he was making when I walked in on them. Totally brings on the ick factor and I find him repulsive.

How do I forget that face? Help!

Oh-no-that-O-face
Athens, GA

Dear Oh-no-that-O-face,

Take it from a girl who once walked in on her boyfriend eating cake off his side piece's incredibly flat stomach; the ick factor isn't going away anytime soon. ICK! You can't unsee that I'm-about-to-orgasm nose flare and heavy-lidded gaze any more than I could unsee my man's tongue lifting frosting out of her belly button.

So, so ick.

Now, my story was a little different from yours because instead of begging me to forgive him, my boyfriend actually thanked me for introducing him to the love of his life. I won't tell you where his body is buried, but just know that I eat cake there sometimes when the weather's just right.☺

Seriously, though, the thing that matters is how YOU feel about him. If you genuinely love the man and want a future with him, I suggest therapy. I'm sure if you talked this through with a professional, you could eventually forget that gaping I'm-almost-there expression and have a happy life together. Check it out, and good luck, Miss O!

Love,
Olivia

It made me happy. Writing was the only thing that made me happy anymore, because it was the only thing that distracted me from thinking of him. I'd written more since that horrible morning than I had my entire life, because the minute I stopped typing, that jerk came into my head.

I'd never thought my heart could hurt more than it had with Eli. I'd been blindsided by his betrayal, absolutely shocked that he and I hadn't been on the same page. But after the breakup, I'd been able to see the cracks. We'd been living two separate-but-parallel lives for a pretty long time, and I'd been blind to it.

Colin, on the other hand . . . everything had been movie perfect. I hadn't wanted it to be, but our relationship had been better than everything I'd ever daydreamed about.

But now it was tainted.

I'd never know if any of those seemingly perfect moments

were genuine, or if they'd been the result of his manipulation of what I'd shared with him via Wrong Number.

And that just sucked.

Colin

"Here's your key, man." Jack handed me his copy and looked around my condo. It looked exactly the same, of course, because he'd contributed nothing to the decor except his shit in the guest room, but it was weird that he was leaving after being my roommate for so long.

He'd decided to move in with Vanessa, which was probably best for both of us. I would have my place to myself, and he would have a shot at a happily ever after. I'd rather die than have my dad discover I no longer had a roommate, but since he hadn't spoken to me since our dinner, odds were good that he wouldn't find out for a while. I took the key and said, "Thanks."

"If you ever need a place to stay, y'know, feel free to shoot me a text." He grinned and put his hands in his pockets, and I noticed for the first time that he and Olivia did the same nose-crinkle thing when they smiled. "Although I guess I don't have an air mattress anymore. Stupid sisters ruin everything."

When Jack asked me what'd happened with Olivia after a night when I'd gotten way too hammered, I figured the least I could do was let her tell him. That way, she could throw it whatever way she wanted.

I'd said, "Livvie should be the one to tell you," and then I think I'd actually hiccuped.

I'd expected him to kick my ass for hurting her, but he had hugged me, instead. My patheticness must've been crystal clear on my face because he'd said, "Fuck, man," and swallowed me in a bear hug.

Thank God I had Jack. If I'd lost them both, it would've been too much. I said, "So it'll be BYOAM?"

"Yep." He laughed. "Bring your own air mattress."

"You going to Billy's for the game Saturday?" I hoped he said yes because I didn't want an awkward goodbye.

"You know it."

"See you Saturday, then."

Jack nodded. "See you Saturday."

After I shut the door, I turned on some music and went into my office. It'd been a month now since Olivia found out the truth, and I'd given up trying to change her mind. She'd blocked my calls and wouldn't let me into her apartment, and she'd even taken the huge bouquet of flowers I sent—my last-ditch effort—and left them on the table in the lobby, where they slowly died a little more each day.

I hadn't seen her face since that morning, and it was killing me.

But that was that.

It was done.

I'd read her column a few times and it was amazing. I was happy that she'd landed a job that seemed perfect for her. It was funny and self-deprecating and so incredibly Olivia that I'd had to stop reading it because I missed her too much.

I logged into my laptop and started working, but everything felt wrong. Maybe it was just because Jack was gone and I was alone, but everything felt *off.* Things should've been back to normal—Liv and I hadn't even been officially a thing to begin with—but the world was just shit now.

I leaned back in the chair and ran a hand over my chin. Jillian thought it was just because I'd never been dumped before. She thought the shock of being a dumpee was making this rough on me, and it probably had next to nothing to do with the actual girl.

She was so wrong.

I started thinking about that morning again, like I always did, thinking about all the things I wished I'd said. They wouldn't have made a difference in us staying together, but perhaps I'd feel less shitty about the whole thing if she'd have let me explain.

I went to her magazine's website and clicked on the Oh, Olivia! page.

It seemed like a pathetic, incredibly lame thing to do, but I clicked on the form to submit a letter. I probably wouldn't end up sending it, but it might prove therapeutic, right? I stared into space and tried to come up with words.

Dear Olivia,

I did the unthinkable–I fell for two women.

One was charming, witty, and smart, and the other was beautiful, passionate, and more fun than anyone I've ever known. I could've spent a lifetime talking to each of them, listening to their wildly entertaining takes on the world and getting lost in their contagious laughter. I've never felt as alive as when I was with them, and I can't stop dreaming about wild green eyes and tiny freckles. Dogs and elevators and pepperoni casserole.

They turned out to be the same woman, so there's no doubt that she's the one for me, but I think I ruined everything by being a coward. Do you have any advice as to how I can convince her–this wonder woman who can repair a broken heel with six pieces of bubble gum–to give me another chance?

I'd do anything for another shot because I'm crazy about her.

–Robot Brain, Omaha, NE

Olivia

"It's for sure him." I took a big gulp from my glass of wine and still couldn't believe it. I'd read and reread that submission all afternoon, obsessed since the minute it had hit my inbox. I ticked the items off on my fingers. "They're the same woman, dogs, pepperoni casserole, elevators—that's totally us! And I actually called him a robot brain once, so it *has* to be from him."

Sara and her husband, Trae, sitting across from me on their patio with their adorable baby as the firepit blazed between us, had stopped contributing to my conversation altogether and just watched me as I repeated the same things over and over again. *Broken heel with bubble gum. Dogs. Pepperoni casserole. Elevators.*

But I just couldn't believe it was from him.

When did he learn to write like that?

It made me cry for an hour, because I still missed him so much it cramped my stomach.

I said, "Am I drunk to consider talking to him?"

"You must be drunk for sure," Sara said and reached for the bottle. "Don't call that asshole."

Trae patted the baby's back and said, "But you'll always wonder if you should've talked to him if you don't."

"Huh?"

"I'm sorry, what?" Sara gave him a withering look that spoke volumes.

"It's only been a month, and you're second-guessing whether or not you should talk to him. As time goes on, you'll wonder more and more why you didn't just hear him out."

"Hmmm." He had a point.

He stood and grabbed the pacifier from the end table. "It can't hurt."

I ran my hand through my hair and thought about it. "It could hurt my heart, though."

"It's already hurting, honey," he said, bouncing that sweet little baby. "Just call the guy."

Well, shit. I looked at Sara, who rolled her eyes and said, "He's probably right."

I went into my contacts, unblocked Colin, and started typing.

Me: Are you robot brain?

I didn't expect him to respond immediately, but he did. Yes.

I sighed and texted: I'm sure it won't change anything, but if you still want to talk I'll meet you at Corbyn Coffee at 8am tomorrow.

I'd barely sent it when he responded.

I'll be there.

I looked at Sara and Trae and my mouth fell open. "Oh, my God. He's meeting me tomorrow morning."

Sara let me borrow a cute fall dress before I left, and made me promise to call her the second I was done. I didn't get much sleep that night, because I was absolutely torn on what to expect. And what I wanted. Half of me was envisioning him begging for my forgiveness and me accepting. That half imagined a day of worshipful sex, followed by his confession of undying love and our happily ever after.

But the other half of me was realistic. I imagined forgiving him, only to fall back into the precarious position of being wholeheartedly in love with him and in constant fear of it being temporary. I didn't think I could go back to that now, so I was clueless as to what in the world I was going to do.

21

Olivia

"HI, CAN I PLEASE GET A REFILL?" I HANDED MY CARD AND cup to the barista and took a deep breath. I'd woken at six, anxious and nervous, so instead of trying to sleep, I'd grabbed my laptop so I could get some work done while I waited.

It was 7:50 a.m.; I still had ten minutes.

Once I got my drink, I went back to the table by the window and tried concentrating on work.

"Olivia?"

I glanced up and—

"Oh, my God! Hi, Nick." I smiled, but the truth was that I wanted him to disappear. Colin would be there soon, and seeing those two together might make me so pissed and disgusted by their scheming that it'd ruin everything.

"How are you?" He gave me a big smile, and I wondered if

he thought it was funny, the way I'd kissed him. Had he laughed about it with Colin?

"Listen, Nick, I know about the whole switcheroo thing. Colin told me."

"Oh." He looked shaken. "Um—"

"Don't worry, I'm not mad." I gave him what I hoped was a friendly smile. "I totally get why he did it."

"Whew." He gave a little laugh. "It's really been bugging me, just so you know."

"No worries." I cleared my throat. "Let me ask you this, by the way. I totally understand Colin's reasons, but why did *you* agree to the whole thing?"

He looked concerned again. "Well—"

"I'm assuming you just felt bad and wanted to protect me from feeling rejected. Like Colin."

He nodded, happy for the lifeline. "I did. Colin was telling me how you'd been through a lot with losing your job and everything, and he said you were like a sweet, adorably klutzy little puppy and he just didn't want you to be destroyed by getting stood up."

"Wow." *Klutzy little puppy.* I clenched my fists and simpered, "You're so nice."

He lowered his voice and said, "Well, he did have to buy me a bottle of scotch, so I'm not *that* nice."

Did he think I'd find that funny?

He leaned down a little closer. "I actually wanted to ask you out after that, but Colin wouldn't let me. So please don't be mad that I didn't call."

"Really." I gave an Oscar-worthy performance of a genuine laugh. "You must not have wanted to very badly, if he was able to talk you out of it."

"Well, I'm asking now." He looked pleased with his answer. "Can I take you out sometime?"

"Colin not stopping you anymore?"

He grinned. "Let's just say I've figured him out. He claimed you were batshit crazy with a truckload of issues, but I should've known he was lying to keep me out of his territory."

"You do realize that referring to any woman as someone's territory is offensive, don't you, Nick?" *Batshit crazy. Truckload of issues.* I wanted to kick stuff down all of a sudden as rage started blooming inside of me. I'd actually come to terms with my emotions and decided to consider Colin's apology for the sake of possible true love.

And it was a joke. I was a joke to him, just like I'd always been.

"Whoa." Nick ran a hand over his beard and said, "I am really sorry. I didn't mean to offend you, I was just saying that I think Colin was jealous."

Always with the impeccable timing, Colin walked through the door. He hadn't seen us yet, and I was physically pained by how handsome he was as he walked inside like a movie star. Those expressive eyes, that mouth that I knew for a fact tasted like blue Altoids 99 percent of the time; it was all for nothing.

A waste of beauty.

The moment he saw me, everything else fell away. His eyes on mine—that was all that existed in the world for a long and extended second. His mouth started to slide into a smile, but then he saw Nick.

He walked over and said, "Nick. Didn't expect to see you here."

Nick glanced at me, then at Colin. "Talk about your small worlds."

I shut my laptop and stuck it in my bag. "Listen, Beck, we're going to have to do this some other time."

That got me his full attention. "What?"

I shrugged. "Nick asked me out, and I think I'm going to do that this morning instead. Maybe we'll connect next week or something."

"I think Nick means later." Colin glared at his friend. "Nick is going to take you out later."

"Whenever you want," Nick stammered.

"I don't care what you think Nick *means*, Colin." I shimmied out of the booth and lifted my chin. "I want to go out with him now."

"What is this?" He gestured to both of us and looked irritated. "You guys are talking now?"

"No, no," Nick said, kissing Colin's ass so much that I wanted to slug him, too. "I just ran into her."

I said to Colin, "Our relationship is none of your business."

"We don't have a relationship," Nick laughed, looking at Colin like I *was* batshit crazy. "Seriously."

"Oh, my God, can you take your lips off his ass for five seconds?" I rolled my eyes at Nick and said to Colin, "I actually don't want to go out with him, but I definitely don't want to talk to you. See you guys later."

I took two steps before Colin grabbed the strap of my bag and yanked me back. "What happened to talking?"

"I've spent a few minutes talking to your buddy Nick here and I've learned everything I need to know."

Colin turned his face to his friend. "What the hell did you say to her?"

Nick's face went red and he full-on dissolved, lowering his voice and saying to Colin, "I have no idea what's happening, man. You were right about her because I just stopped by her table to say hi and she lost her shit."

"I can hear you, you jackass," I said through gritted teeth.

Colin swallowed and his eyes darted to my face, then back to Nick. "Why don't you take off and let us talk."

Nick very nearly sprinted for the door while Colin and I stared each other down.

"Can we sit?" He was still holding on to my strap. "Please?"

I bit my bottom lip before saying, "I don't think I want to talk."

His jaw clenched and he raised a hand and touched my chin. "Please?"

I shook my head but wanted to push my face into his warm palm. "I just don't—"

"I love you."

Everything went quiet in the world as his words crashed into me. "What?"

He swallowed again, his throat moving hard before he said, "I love you. I know I screwed everything up and I know we were going to keep it casual, but I somehow fell in love with you. I can't believe it myself, but in spite of our lifetime of hatred for each other, I am completely lost without you in my life."

Colin

I watched her process it.

Her dark eyebrows crinkled together the way they always did when she was working through something she didn't quite understand, and she blinked fast. Her green eyes stared into my soul, seeing all of me, and I swear to God I started sweating.

Because—holy shit—what the hell had I just said?

It was one hundred percent true, but I hadn't even known it myself until the words fell out of my mouth. Dammit if I didn't feel like someone who'd just been given shocking news. It seemed like time had slowed as she looked at me, and I felt like I was going to lose my shit if she didn't say something.

Anything.

"You love me." Her voice was almost a whisper as her eyes darted all over my face.

"Yes."

"And you can't believe it yourself?"

"I can't. I mean, can you?" I put my hands in my jacket pockets to keep from touching her and smiled. "After all this time? It's pretty crazy."

She smiled back but I could tell it was fake. Something was wrong. She said, "It *is* crazy. I mean, Colin Beck falling in love with a batshit-crazy mess like me? Who could ever believe that?"

Ah, shit. "That's not what I meant."

She shook her head. "Maybe not, but it is exactly what it is. You fell in 'love' in spite of yourself, regardless of everything you know about me. You think you're in love with me and even *you* have a hard time believing it."

"Dammit, Liv—"

"Don't call me that."

"Well, then, dammit, *Olivia*." I gritted my teeth. "And can you maybe not air quote my feelings like it's a joke?"

She moved the strap of her bag to the other shoulder. "But it *is* a joke, Colin. Come on. You don't love me, just like I don't love you. We both love good sex and witty banter. That's all it was."

I had no idea what to say to that, to her utter disregard for my feelings. "You're wrong."

"I'm not." She pulled her keys out of her coat pocket. "If I didn't find out about the Wrong Number thing, you would've outgrown me by the second time I spilled something in your Audi or wore the wrong shoes to the club."

"Wow. After everything, you still really think that little of me?" I was surprised her words could make me feel so much shittier than I already did, but I guess I'd never known just how much of an asshole she thought I was. "Um, I guess that about covers everything. Later, then, Marshall."

I turned to walk out of the coffee shop, and something inside of me died when I heard her quietly say, "Later, then, Beck."

22

Olivia

THANKSGIVING DAY

"SHE ALWAYS RECOVERS FROM HER MESSES, THOUGH." MY mother stood in the kitchen in her stupid pumpkin sweater with my grandma and my auntie Midge—both in stupid pumpkin sweaters—and discussed me as if I weren't right there in the living room with the rest of the family.

"Your mess-recovering abilities are second to none." Jack gave me a smirk from where he was lying on the floor, and kicked my leg with his Nike. "So impressive."

"Shut it."

"He's right, Liv," Will said, grinning. "Unmatched."

"Hilarious. You both look like idiots in your sweaters, by the way." I wanted to ditch the family and go play in the backyard with the boys, but since it was Thanksgiving, I'd agreed to stay inside with the adults and "visit."

"You don't look cool in yours, either," Jack said to me before saying to Will, "Liv has been so damned cranky lately."

"She seriously punched me yesterday and she wasn't playing," Will chimed in.

"Can you morons be quiet, please?" I leaned forward to better hear the TV. We were watching a DVD my dad had burned of Thanksgiving episodes of a bunch of shows, and *Friends* was currently on. I tuned all of them out for most of the episode until I heard Will say Colin's name.

I kept my eyes on the TV as Jack said, "Yeah. He's taking a promotion in Chicago."

"He's selling the condo?" Will asked.

"Yeah. It's the best unit in the building, so it'll sell in like a day."

"When?"

They both looked at me. Holy shit, I'd said it out loud?

"Hello?" I waved my hands for them to hurry and answer. "When is he moving, Jack?"

"Not that it's any of your business anymore, but I think he's starting next week and staying in a hotel until he finds a house."

I blinked and felt a little light-headed. "I can't believe he didn't tell me."

Jack squinted. "You hate him. Why would he tell you?"

"I don't hate him." I stared at the TV without actually watching. He was leaving? He was leaving and wasn't even going to tell me, like we were strangers? I felt like I couldn't breathe.

"C'mere," Jack said to me out of the side of his mouth, glancing over at my mom with shifty eyes like he didn't want her to hear.

I moved down to the floor and sat beside him. "What?"

"Don't get dirty, Liv," my mom yelled, scowling and stirring something on the stove. "We still have to take the picture."

How the hell would I get dirty? "I won't, Ma."

I brought my attention back to my brother, who said, "I'm pretty sure he's leaving because of you. You wrecked him."

"*I* wrecked *him*?"

"Shhh—Geez."

We both glanced over at the kitchen, but thankfully Auntie Midge was ranting about potatoes and botulism so no one had heard my little freak-out.

I lowered my voice and said, "Is that what he told you?"

He shook his head. "He never told me anything, but I've known him forever and I've never seen him like this. Not even when he proposed to Daniela and she said no."

I rolled my eyes and forced myself not to picture his face.

"He told his sister that he can't stand to live in the same city, much less the same building, as you, knowing he can't be with you anymore. He said it's killing him."

"Shut up." My heart started pounding in my neck. "He'd never say that."

"Swear to God. Jillian texted me the other night because he said it when he was wasted." He pulled out his phone, scrolled for a minute, and then showed it to me. "She wanted to know if I knew anything."

I glanced down. She'd said it, word for word.

"Oh, my God." I got up and adjusted my sweater. "I have to go."

"What?" my mom yelled from the kitchen. "Where are you going? We eat in an hour."

I looked around and everyone was staring at me. "I, um, I have to go talk to someone."

"Oh, for the love of God, Olivia, it's Thanksgiving."

"I know, Ma." I grabbed my purse from the floor. "I'll be back."

"We're taking the family picture soon. What can't wait until tomorrow?" She looked at Auntie Midge and then said to my dad, "Fred, tell her this can wait until tomorrow."

"It can wait until tomorrow," he muttered, not bothering to open his eyes.

"It can't wait."

"What the hell, Liv?" Will asked. Even though he was a grown-ass family man, he still got all annoying when someone dared to do something he couldn't.

Like leave on Thanksgiving.

"Language, William," my mother scolded, feigning horror even though I knew she wielded the f-word like a dockworker when she was alone with my dad and thought we couldn't hear her.

"I have to talk to Colin before he leaves." I gave Jack a look that made Will say, "Holy shit, do you have a thing for Colin Beck?"

I blinked as the entire house seemed to pause and wait for my answer. My dad even opened his eyes.

I just nodded.

"Oh, honey," my mom said with a pitying smile, "I know the boy is handsome, but I don't really think he's your type."

"What?"

"He's just very type A, always has been. Driven, motivated, successful . . ." She trailed off as if that explained everything.

"What's your point, Ma?"

She just raised her eyebrows.

"I'll have you know that we were actually together for months before I dumped him."

"What?" Will nearly yelled it. "I call bullshit."

"Oh, Livvie," my mother said, sounding disappointed that I was lying like an overimaginative toddler.

"You seriously don't believe me?" I pulled out my keys and said to Will, "Screw you."

"Language," my mother gasped as my dad muttered, "Christ almighty."

"I'm leaving now," I said, running toward the door, irritated by my family but too desperate to get to Colin to care. I got in my car, put it in reverse, and flew out of the driveway, terrified he was already gone.

I glanced toward the house and saw a crowd of faces watching me, all jammed into the square of my parents' front bay window. I knew I should wave, or feel bad for ditching them on a holiday, but I put the car in drive and took off.

I had to get to Colin, and nothing else mattered.

I TOOK A deep breath and knocked again.

It was my third round of loud knocks, but there was still no answer.

Come. On.

Was he gone already? Had I missed him? I wondered if Jack knew how I could find him in Chicago if he'd already left. I knocked again and then pulled out my phone.

Maybe the thing that brought us together—and tore us apart—could get through to him.

Me: Tell me exactly what you're wearing, Mr. Wrong Number.

I slid down the wall and sat on the carpet of the hallway, without a plan but absolutely unwilling to consider what his absence meant.

He couldn't leave. He *couldn't.*

After a good five minutes, I texted: I am out in your hallway, wearing the sexiest top you've ever seen.

I sent the message, and then I took a selfie of the dumb sweater and sent it.

He didn't respond, and after ten more minutes, I stood and ran my hand over his door. I blinked back pools of heavy tears and tried one last time, just in case. There were still no sounds from within, so I cleared my throat and rested my forehead on his door.

"It sounds bizarre, but I didn't realize until today that I've forgiven you for the whole thing. As soon as Jack said you're moving to Chicago, nothing else mattered but seeing you and begging you not to go."

I blinked back the tears and added, "Unless you're dying to go. Then I'll just beg you to text me a lot and let me visit or something." I straightened and muttered, "Shit. He's probably not even home."

"He's home."

My head snapped around and there was Colin, two doors down in the hallway and walking toward his apartment in a black North Face jacket. His cheeks were red like he'd been outside for a while, and he was looking at me with a stoic face, no warmth at all in the blue eyes I'd been having dreams about for a month. My stomach dropped, and I struggled to think of words as he held me in his cold stare. I'd practiced on the way over, but the only thing I was able to come up with was "Were you really going to move to Chicago without telling me?"

I hated that my voice cracked when I said it.

"Why would I tell you?" He looked down at my stupid pumpkin sweater but didn't say anything about it. "Does it matter?"

I nodded.

His eyes narrowed. "What does that nod mean?"

"Yes."

"Yes, what, Marshall?" He gestured for me to get on with it. "Help me understand what is happening here."

I put my hands in my coat pockets. "I'm trying to apologize."

"By nodding at me."

I nodded.

"Listen, I don't know what you want from me here." His voice was gravelly as he scratched his eyebrow. "I screwed up and you walked away. I told you that I loved you and you told me I was a joke. So now that I'm moving, you're back . . . ? What am I supposed to do here?"

I had no answer, so I just shrugged listlessly.

"This is great, Liv, that you're suddenly mute, but I can't do this anymore, okay?" He shoved his hands in his pockets and said, "I know it was my own fault, but losing you turned out to be the worst thing that's ever happened to me. Everything sucked, everything reminded me of you, and I was so fucking sad all the time that I couldn't even stand to be around myself. I can't keep living like this, hoping to see you in the elevator or daydreaming like a lovesick puppy that we might run into each other at Starbucks. I love you, Olivia, but this is killing me. I have to get away from all of this."

My heart was pounding. "You still love me?"

He shook his head. "Stop it. That's not the point."

"Oh, my God, it is, too." I was flat-out crying now and I didn't care. "I love you, too, and everything has been awful for me, too. Ask anyone. I punched Will the other day for saying I was acting like a pouty baby."

He tilted his head. "You did not."

"I really did. And my mother is probably going to show up here any second now because I ditched Thanksgiving dinner to come find you."

"What?"

I rolled my eyes. "Jack said you were moving, so I just left. And we hadn't even taken the family picture yet."

"You ditched Thanksgiving dinner?"

I nodded and said, "I'd do it again if it meant stopping you from leaving."

"Holy shit, I *was* right." He stared at me, his jaw flexing, and it looked like he could see into my soul or something.

"About what?" I asked.

His mouth softened and he looked at me like he was figuring out a puzzle. "When we went to Fleming's and you let that dog knock you down in the parking lot, I realized something. You aren't a hot mess at all, Livvie. You're just this . . . this . . . human tornado who is so alive, so filled with the energy of the moment, that there occasionally is a little collateral damage."

I opened my mouth and had no words—for once.

"But all the damages are worth it. They're but a small price. I *wish* I lived in the moment like you do." He took his hands out of his pockets and stepped closer, and his palms slid over my cheeks. "You have no idea how much I admire that about you."

"Colin." I looked up at his handsome face and wasn't sure any compliment had ever meant that much to me in my entire life. "Are you saying that I'm your hero? That I'm the wind beneath your—"

He stopped my words with a kiss, one of his Colin specials that left me grasping at his shirt while he reminded me how good it'd been with us. *As if I needed reminding.* He lifted his lips just long enough to say against mine, "Say it again."

I felt like my heart was going to burst. "I love you."

He grinned down at me. "Again."

"I love you, Colin Beck."

"I love you, too, Marshall." He cupped my face and gave me the sweetest, hottest kiss, the kind of kiss that wrapped itself around you and made you feel foolishly, deliciously, unbearably loved. I let myself sink into it, no longer afraid.

I wanted to dive into every fathomless ocean with him.

And even after the smoke alarms started wailing because I passionately slammed Colin against the fire panel, he didn't stop kissing the holy hell out of me.

Epilogue

Olivia

TWO WEEKS LATER

Mr. Wrong Number: Did you know that I picture you naked like 24/7? I can't stop myself. It's becoming problematic.

I laughed and pulled the blanket up under my arms. I texted: Same. The other day I think your mother saw me staring right at your . . .

Mr. Wrong Number: Yes, baby, say it.

My breath caught, and I almost dropped the phone as I giggled. I rolled over so I was facing him and typed: You want me to text it? Or would you rather have me whisper it?

"Whisper. Now." Colin held out his hand for my phone, an eyebrow raised and an intriguing look in his eyes.

Instead of handing it over, I tossed it onto the floor and said, "I keep telling Mr. Wrong Number I don't need him anymore but he just won't let me go."

He tossed his phone beside mine and rolled on top of me. "Can you blame him? When you find your perfect Misdial, you can't let her go."

I felt his words pulse through my veins like thick honey. I whispered, "I love you, Mr. Wrong Number."

Colin kissed the tip of my nose. "I love you, too, Miss Misdial."

Acknowledgments

First and foremost, thank you to everyone who has picked up this book. This is my dream come true, this book in your hands, and I'm eternally grateful for the part you've played in my happily-ever-after. Thank you, thank you, thank you, and if I'm ever in your neighborhood, I'll be happy to walk your dog; I owe you one, after all.

Endless piles of gratitude go to Kim Lionetti, my agent extraordinaire. You were with me when the first book didn't sell, you were with me when the next one did, and you were with me when I got pulled over by the Utah Highway Patrol, texting me about offers while the dude went back to his cruiser to write my ticket. I'm beyond blessed to have you and BookEnds in my corner.

Thank you to Angela Kim, my incredible editor. From that first phone call, I knew you were the perfect person for this book, and working with you has been an absolute joy. I'm so excited—and grateful—that I get to do more books with you! (Insert cartwheels.)

Thanks to everyone at Berkley PRH; this entire process has been a pleasure. An extra-special thanks to Nathan Burton for creating such a stunning cover.

Also—Tom Colgan's plague journals deserve all the literary awards. Just sayin' . . .

To the Berkletes—especially India, Courtney, Amy, Lyn, Sarah ZJ, Sarah Bruhbruh, Joanna, Nekesa, Ali, Elizabeth, Libby, Alanna, Amanda, Mia, Freya, Eliza, Lauren, and Olivia—you guys are everything. I've heard authors give the writerly advice to "find your people," but I always assumed that excluded this awkward dork right here who doesn't make friends easily. Yet here I am, colluding with this super group of incredibly talented humans whom I consider to be some of my closest friends. *How did that happen?* Thank you for inviting me into your hilariously wonderful circle and making me cackle at my computer on a daily basis. (*Also see knotting, hands, bad Chris*)

A HUGE thanks to the Bookstagram community for your kindness and your willingness to help a noob like me. I am in awe of your voracious appetite for books and your remarkable organizational skills. I still don't understand how authors are lucky enough to have you; we're not worthy (Wayne-and-Garth style). A special scream to the delightful Love Arctually gang, all of whom I want to be my besties.

Also, thank you, Carla Bastos, Aliza Pollak, Chaitanya Srivastava, Shay Tibbs, and Indigo's amazing Dayla—I'm so grateful that BTTM introduced me to awesome people like you. And Lori Anderjaska—thank you for being the type of person who sends me random texts of dogs yelling obscenities at each other.

And the fam:

Mom, you made me a writer by fostering my love of books. It couldn't have been fun, walking six blocks to the library—rain (or snow) or shine—every week, but I'm forever grateful. I love you to the moon and back.

Dad, I miss you every day.

MaryLee, I don't deserve a sister as sweet as you and I can't wait to see your movies. It is GOING to happen.

To my kids—Cass, Ty, Matt, Joey, and Kate—you really had nothing at all to do with this book. That being said, you're the coolest people I know and we should eat spaghetti and meatballs together soon. I love you.

Last but not least—Kevin. I mean, I dedicated the entire book to you so I think that should be more than enough, but if not, thank you for not firing me that time I accidentally checked a guest into a room where there were already guests. If you would've gotten rid of this slacker desk clerk after that guy screamed at you, I never would've been able to badger you into dating and ultimately spending your life with me. That college job was kind of a life sentence, eh? ☺ I love you the mostest.

Keep reading for an excerpt from

The Love Wager

the next romantic comedy by Lynn Painter,
coming soon

"CAN I GET A MANHATTAN AND A CHARDONNAY, PLEASE?"

"Sure thing." Hallie glanced over her shoulder as she handed one of the bridesmaids a Crown and Coke, and—wow—the dude shouting his order over the way-too-loud version of "Electric Slide" was *very* attractive. He was obviously in the bridal party, all tuxxed-up and looking fancy, and even though she was on a 90-day man diet, Hallie couldn't help but appreciate the dimples and Hollywood bone structure. "You want that with bourbon?"

He leaned on his forearms and stretched a little closer to the bar as the hotel's ballroom hit peak noise level. "Rye, please."

"Nice." She reached into the gray plastic bucket and pulled a California bottle out of the ice. "Interested in trying it with orange bitters?"

His dimples popped and he raised his eyebrows, his blue(?)—yes, blue—eyes squinting. "Is that a thing?"

"It is." She poured the chardonnay and set the glass in front of him. "If you're not a moron, you'll love it."

He coughed a laugh and said, "I consider myself to be generally non-moronic, so hook me up."

Hallie started making his drink, and she kind of felt like she knew the guy. He seemed familiar. Not his face, necessarily, but his voice and super-tall height and twinkly eyes that made him look like he was down for any wild adventure.

She glanced at him as the dance floor's disco lights lit up his dark hair. Shaking the mixer and straining the Manhattan into a glass, she struggled to come up with it; *think, think, think*. He was looking back in the direction of the head table when it finally hit her.

"I know how I know you!"

He turned back around. "What?"

It was so loud that Hallie had to lean a little closer to him. She smiled and said, "You're Jack, right? I'm Hallie. I was the one who sold you the—"

"Hey!" he said, smiling, but then he set his hand on hers and gave her hard-core eye contact as he leaned closer and said, "Hallie. Listen. Let's not mention—"

"Oh. My. God." A blonde appeared beside him—*where had she come from?*—and her eyes narrowed as she looked at Hallie and said, "Seriously, Jack? The *waitress*?"

"Bartender," Hallie corrected, having no idea why or what was up the Superblonde's ass.

"You leave me alone for ten minutes—at your sister's wedding, for God's sake—to canoodle with the *waitress*?"

"Um, I can assure you there was no canoodling," Hallie

said, painfully aware that the woman's loud voice was drawing a lot of attention. "And I'm a bartender, not a wait—"

"Can you just shut *up*?" Superblonde said it through her nose and with the last word pitched an octave higher, like she was a Kardashian.

"Would you relax, Vanessa?" Jack said it through his teeth, glancing over his lady friend's head as he tried to get her to quiet down. "I don't even know her—"

"I saw you!" She was near-yelling as the DJ switched to "Endless Love," which did zero to mute the outburst. *Where was the damn Macarena when you needed it?* Superblonde—Vanessa, apparently—said, "You were leaning in and holding her hand. How long has this—"

"Come on, Van, it's not—"

"How long?" she shrieked.

The guy's jaw flexed, like he was clenching and unclenching his teeth, and then he said, "Since this morning."

Vanessa's mouth dropped open. "You were with her *this morning*?"

"Not *with me* with me," Hallie said, looking around, horrified by the implication. She worked part-time at Borsheims on the weekends, and the guy—Jack—had come into the store that morning and she'd helped him find a ring.

And not just any ring.

The ring.

The *will-you-be-a-jealous-hag-for-the-rest-of-my-life?* ring.

"She sold me this." Jack pulled the ring box out of his pocket and practically shoved it in the girl's face as he spoke through his teeth. "I bought this for you, Vanessa. Christ."

The box was closed, but Hallie knew a stunning square-cut diamond engagement ring was nestled inside. He'd seemed like a funny, charming guy when she'd helped him shop for the perfect ring, but if he thought Vanessa was soul mate material, he clearly only thought with his penis.

Or else he really was a moron.

"Oh, my God," Vanessa squealed, her face transforming into sunlight as she beamed at Jack and put her hands over her heart. "You're proposing?"

He stared at her with his eyes squinted for a solid five seconds before saying, "I'm not *now*."

Her smile slipped. "You're not?"

"Fuck, no."

Hallie snorted.

Which made Vanessa swing her narrowed, long-lashed—wow, those had to be extensions—eyes in Hallie's direction. She hissed, "Is something funny?"

Hallie shook her head, but for some reason, she couldn't make her lips straighten. She kept hearing the dude's *fuck, no* and it was just so *chef's kiss*.

Before she had a second to realize what was happening, Vanessa grabbed the full glass of chardonnay from where it was sitting on the bar, turned her wrist, and threw its contents in Hallie's face.

"Gahh!" Cold wine splashed over her face and burned her eyes. Thankfully, as a bartender, she was surrounded by towels and happened to have one on her shoulder that very second. Hallie snatched it and wiped her face. "Hey. *Van*. What is your *problem*?"

"*You* are my prob—"

"I am so sorry," Jack said, looking pathetically apologetic. He grabbed Hallie's towel and started patting her dripping neck, which made Vanessa's eyes grow huge.

"Oh, my God, she's fine," Vanessa said.

"Yeah, I'm fine," Hallie said, giving him a weird look as she snatched back the towel. "She seems great, by the way."

He leaned in closer, so all Hallie could see was his worried face and blue eyes. "You're good?"

"Yeah." Hallie blinked and felt like she needed to take a step back. He was too attractive for human eyes, especially when giving that sort of eye contact. She ran her tongue over her freshly chardonnayed lips. "Well, actually no, if I'm being honest. See, I recommend this chardonnay all the time because it's supposed to be oaky with a rich, buttery finish, but it's actually dry as hell with a bitter, stale aftertaste."

He pursed his lips.

"I've been perpetrating a lie this entire time."

His eyes crinkled around the edges and his mouth twitched. He looked like he was about to smile, but Vanessa grabbed his arm and his face changed to straight-up pissed. Hallie watched his throat move as he swallowed, and then he turned around and said, "We need to go."

Her perfect eyebrows went up. "We're leaving?"

"Something like that. Come on."

He led his pretty monster away from the bar, and Hallie mopped up before getting back to making drinks. The entire dust-up had happened over the course of a mere three minutes, but it'd felt like an eternity.

The other bartender, Julio, asked out of the side of his mouth as he poured vodka into five shot glasses, "What the hell was that?"

"Just a batshit jealous girlfriend." She moved to the other end of the bar and took an order for two whiskey sours. "I don't even know them."

"Oh, my God, Hallie Piper, I thought that was you!"

Hallie looked up and did a double-take. *Seriously, universe?* "Allison?"

Ugh. Allison Scott. They'd gone to high school together, and she was one of those girls who was technically super nice, but always managed to word things in ways that made people feel like shit. Hallie hadn't seen her since graduation eight years ago and she definitely hadn't missed her.

"Oh, my God, you are the most adorable bartender I've ever seen." Allison beamed and gestured toward Hallie's damp black tank top and black jeans. "Seriously, you're, like, a cutesy-cute drink-maker in a movie."

Allison was giving total Alexis Rose vibes, and Hallie pasted a smile on her face. "Can I make you something?"

"My boyfriend is one of the groomsmen," she said, apparently not in want of a beverage. "And when he ran over and said there was a catfight at the bar, I never in a million years would've guessed it'd be my super anal, buttoned-up friend Hallie."

Did she just call me super anal? Dear God. Hallie explained, "It wasn't a catfight, it was more like a misunderstanding between a couple and I was collateral damage."

"I caught the end of it." Allison smiled, and it was kind of Grinch-like in the slow, satisfied climb of it. "So, what're you doing these days? Besides tending bar at wedding receptions. Are you still with Kyle?"

A man behind Allison held up two empty Mich Ultra bottles, so Hallie grabbed two from under the bar, opened them, and set them down as she said, "Nope. I am finally Kyle-free."

"Oh. Wow." Allison's eyes got big, like Hallie had just declared herself a serial killer because she'd had the audacity to break up with the guy who had once been considered their high school's star running back. "So what's your sister doing?"

Hallie wanted to scream when she heard the DJ announce the bride-and-groom dance, because it meant there would be no mad rush for drinks; people loved watching that sappy shit. Allison could loiter and make uncomfortable small-talk for as long as she wanted, and that made Hallie daydream about chandeliers accidentally falling from the ceiling and crushing annoying ex-friends.

"Um, Lillie actually just got engaged to Riley Harper. Do you remember him from—"

"Oh, my God—she's engaged to Riley Harper? He was our homecoming king, right? He's, like, a doctor now?"

Hallie nodded.

"Wow, good for her." Allison looked impressed. "Does she work?"

"Yeah, um, she's an engineer. She just got a job at Fyra."

"You have got to be kidding!" She gave her chic bobbed head a little shake. "You guys are like *Freaky Friday* chicks now."

"What?"

"You know. You were always the responsible, together one, and Lillie was the hot mess shitshow. Now she's an engineer with a doctor fiancé, and you're single and waiting tables and getting into bar fights." She smiled like it was hilarious. "Crazy."

Allison finally ordered a drink and stopped torturing Hallie, but as soon as she walked away, her words played on a continuous loop in Hallie's mind. *Hot mess shitshow. Hot mess shitshow.*

God, *had* they *Freaky Friday*ed?

Hallie spent the next half hour freaking out in her head while she continued slinging drinks on autopilot. *Hot mess shitshow.* It wasn't until "Single Ladies" came on that she embraced her inner Beyoncé and remembered that everything was going to be okay.

Because she wasn't a hot mess shitshow at all. Rather, it was just her "winter."

After she and Kyle split up, Hallie had decided to treat it as "the winter of her twenties." A few dormant, cold months that would lead to a bountiful spring. She'd moved out of Kyle's place and got a cheap apartment—with a roommate. She'd taken two part-time jobs, in addition to her career, to pay down her student loans in half the time.

The way she saw it, she was going to take advantage of her man-free time.

They were dark days, her winter season, but soon they would all pay off.

"YOU."

Hallie looked up and the guy—Jack—was charging straight toward the bar. He looked intense—serious face, tie hanging untied around his neck—and his eyes were fixed on her. He reminded her of the Darkling in that show on Netflix.

Smoking hot and all powerful.

"Me?" She looked behind her.

"Yes." He stopped when he reached the bar and said, "I need you."

"I beg your pardon?" Hallie tilted her head and said, "And what happened to that sweetheart of a girlfriend of yours? Van, was it?"

"We need a bartender in the back." Jack ignored her remark, looking at Julio and saying, "Do you think you can spare her for a bit?"

Julio glanced at Hallie, trying to gauge her reaction before saying, "Yes, but I believe the bride scheduled—"

"She's the one who sent me over. I'm her brother."

"Listen, I don't strip or give lap dances," Hallie said. "So if 'the back' is code for something creepy, count me out."

That made the guy smirk down at her. "Somehow I would've guessed that about you."

"Oh." Hallie pushed back the stray hairs that'd fallen out of her ponytail. "Well, good."

"Follow me?"

"Why not?" Hallie came around the bar and followed Jack as he walked through the throngs of wedding revelers—most of whom smiled at him like he was their favorite cousin even though he appeared oblivious—and when they got to the kitchen door, he pushed it open and held it for her.

"Thanks." She walked through the door, only to see that the kitchen was absolutely deserted. "Um . . . ?"

She turned around, and Jack had dropped his jacket on top

of a box of bananas and he was rolling up his shirtsleeves. He raised an eyebrow and waited for her to speak.

"I thought you said you needed a bartender."

"I do." He casually hopped up onto the stainless steel prep counter and sat so that his long legs were dangling in front of him. "You got me dumped, so now it's your job to get me drunk."

Seriously, dude?

"Yeah, um, you aren't the king," Hallie said, disappointed in his power douche move, "and I'm not interested in being your personal serving wench. But thank you."

"Dear God, I don't want you to serve me." He pointed to the spot beside him on the counter. "I just thought since we both had drinks thrown in our faces by Vanessa Robbins tonight, it might be nice to drown our troubles and share a bottle."

Hallie tilted her head and looked at the bottle of Crown Royal behind him.

Why did that sound so damn appealing?

JACK COULD SEE it in her face the minute she decided. It was like her entire posture relaxed.

And then she smiled.

Not that it mattered, but she was cute. A short little redhead with a big smartass mouth. He actually *had* remembered her from the jewelry store, not because of how she looked but because she'd been funny as hell as she'd shown him a slew of engagement rings.

She came over and hopped up on the counter, crisscrossing

her legs and reaching for the bottle. "First of all, please tell me *you* dumped *her* and not the other way around."

"Obviously," he said.

"Thank God." She rolled in her lips and said, "Second of all, I had nothing to do with the implosion of your relationship."

"Well, if you hadn't said anything . . ."

"Then you'd be engaged to a jealous psycho." She narrowed her green eyes and said, "I think you actually owe me a ginormous thank-you."

"Is that right?"

"For sure," she said, and then she raised the bottle to her mouth and took a big drink. After she finished, she wiped her lips with the back of her hand. "Are you intentionally forgoing mixers? Because I'm okay with that, but since I'm only five feet tall, I'm gonna get there a *lot* quicker without Coke."

He actually felt like smiling when he said, "Fine by me."

"And are you paying for the Uber that I will surely need when we're finished?"

Jack took the bottle as she held it out to him, and his fingers looked gigantic next to hers. He said, "If it comes to that, then yes."

"Oh, it will definitely come to that." She gave him another sarcastic grin and turned her body so she was facing him. "I plan on getting floor-licking drunk tonight, buddy. Like, can't-remember-your-own-mother, vomiting-in-the-elevator-phone-box, is-she-okay-or-should-we-call-someone hammered. Care to join me on the thrill ride?"

Jack tipped the bottle into his mouth and let the liquor burn through him, warming a path all the way down to his belly. She watched him the whole time, and he wasn't sure if it was the buzz or not, but she was starting to look a little hot to him. He finished the drink and smiled as he handed it back to her.

She wrapped her slim fingers around the neck of the bottle and said, "So . . . ? You in, Best Man?"

"I'm all yours, tiny bartender."